Praise for
ADI ALSAID

'Captivating, mysterious, fun, and deep…
for readers of John Green.'
—*Fresh Fiction*

'If you're looking for the perfect summer read, this is it.'
— Hannah Harrington, author of
Speechless and *Saving June*

'Five love stories, beautifully woven together
by a special girl […] A do-not-miss.'
—*Justine* magazine

'A captivating cross-country journey, where four strangers'
adventures collide into one riveting tale of finding yourself'
—*YABooksCentral.com*

'Mesmerising. A story of love, loss, ambition and
finding the true meaning of life'
—*Glitter* magazine

LET'S GET LOST

ADI ALSAID

MIRA Ink is a registered trademark of Harlequin Enterprises Limited, used under licence.

Published in Great Britain 2014
by MIRA Ink, an imprint of Harlequin (UK) Limited,
Eton House, 18-24 Paradise Road,
Richmond, Surrey, TW9 1SR

© 2014 Alloy Entertainment

ISBN 978-1-848-45335-7

47-0814

Harlequin (UK) Limited's policy is to use papers that are natural, renewable and recyclable products and made from wood grown in sustainable forests. The logging and manufacturing processes conform to the legal environmental regulations of the country of origin.

Printed and bound by
CPI Group (UK) Ltd, Croydon, CR0 4YY

Adi Alsaid was born and raised in Mexico City. He attended college at the University of Nevada, Las Vegas. After graduating, he packed up his car and escaped to the California coastline to become a writer. He's now back in his home town where he writes, coaches high-school and elementary basketball and makes every dish he eats as spicy as possible. In addition to Mexico, he's lived in Tel Aviv, Las Vegas and Monterey, California. Visit Adi online at www.somewhereoverthesun. com, or follow him on Twitter: @AdiAlsaid.

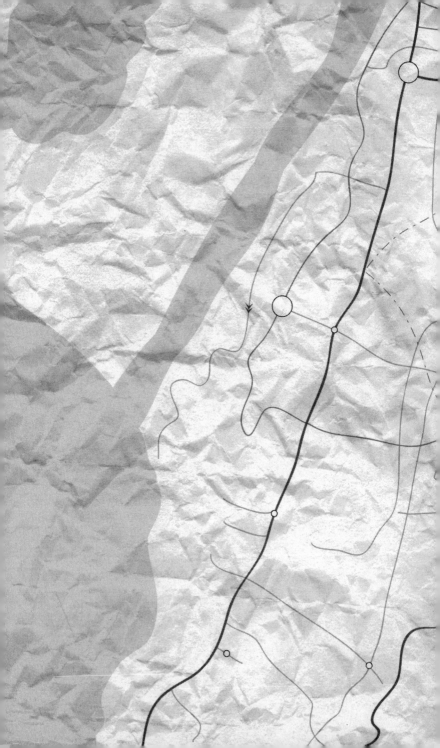

1

HUDSON COULD HEAR the car's engine from blocks away. He stepped outside the garage and closed his eyes, listening, picking apart the sounds so that he would know exactly what he'd have to fix before he even popped the hood.

Standing there against the garage, listening to the still-far-off car, Hudson could forget about everything else. About school and girls and his future and whether his friends were actually jackasses or just acting like them. With his eyes closed, Hudson could reduce the world to a single engine and nothing more; a world where he could not only name every little part but knew what it was for, how it worked, how to fix it.

He opened his eyes when he heard the car's brakes chirp as it slowed to turn into the garage. It was an old Plymouth Acclaim, the kind of car you either happily sent off to die or loved with your entire heart and refused to let go of. It had seen better days, its red paint job chipped and faded, its muffler not doing much muffling. He waved the driver forward to where he was standing. He was still identifying the car's problems when the girl killed the engine and climbed out.

He only allowed himself a quick glance at her, knowing as soon as he saw her that she was the kind of girl who could make you think your life was not complete unless she was in it. She was a jumble of contradictions: short but with long legs, fierce green eyes but a kind expression, baby-faced but wise. She was wearing a snug, plain red T-shirt that matched her car. Her hair was down, the black locks reaching just past her chin.

"Afternoon," she said, offering a polite smile.

He replied in kind, trying to adopt the professional tone he used with most customers. He asked her to pop the hood and then walked to the front of the car to release the latch. He meant to bury himself in work right away, but against instinct he stole another glance. How long would the memory of her face haunt him? Days? Weeks? "You having trouble with anything specific?"

"Well, not really," she said, slipping her hands into the back pockets of her shorts, which made her posture change in a way Hudson couldn't help but notice. The quiet world outside the garage noticed the change in her posture, the damp Mississippi air noticed, even the various grease stains spread out on the garage floor noticed. "I just got started on a road trip, and it's making a lot of noise, so I wanted to be sure it's in shape."

Hudson grabbed a clean rag off a nearby shelf and checked the oil and the transmission fluid. He liked working in relative silence, nothing but the subtle sound of the cooling engine, his hands and tools on the machine. Something about this girl, though, made him chatty. "Where you goin'?"

"North," she said. "All the way north."

"You from around here?" He suddenly felt self-conscious about his drawl, the hitch in his vowels, the overall lackluster quality of his presence.

"Nope. You?"

He chuckled as he ran his hands around the engine, checking for cracks in belts. "Born and raised." He nodded to himself as he made a mental checklist of what he'd need to fix. "Mind if I ask where you're from, then?"

"I don't," she said. He thought he heard her smile, but when he looked up, she was ambling around the garage, curiously examining the shelves and their bric-a-brac. "I was born in Texas. A little town not unlike this one."

"So, if you're from Texas, and you're going north, what brings you to Vicksburg? Not exactly on your way."

"I needed my car fixed, and I heard you were the best around," she said. He looked up again, and she grinned. *Weeks*, he thought to himself. *I'll be thinking about that face for weeks.* She walked around the car and joined him in front of the hood. "So, what do you think? Will she make the trip?"

"When I'm through with her, yeah. I'll flush out all the fluids, make sure your spark plugs are in shape. This belt might need replacing, but I think we've got the parts. I'll check your brakes, too, 'cause they didn't sound great on the way in. But nothing to worry about."

For a moment, Hudson forgot about the girl, thinking instead about getting his hands dirty, splotched by grease that he'd smear across his work pants, adding another battle scar to proudly display.

"You like this, don't you?"

Hudson glanced up to find her standing so close that he could smell her scent fighting through the oil fumes in the garage. "Like what?"

"My face," she said, then smacked him playfully on the arm. "This, silly. Fixing cars. I can tell."

He shrugged, the kind of gesture one makes when there's no choice but to love something. "If you want, you can come inside while I write up an estimate."

"No need," she said. "Do whatever needs to be done. I trust you."

"Um, this could take a few hours," he said. "We've got coffee and a TV inside. Some magazines, too. There's also a pretty good burger joint down the road . . ." He trailed off, realizing that he didn't want her to leave. Usually, no matter what distractions there were around, he could shut everything out and delve into his work. It was the same with studying at the library; friends could come by to tease him, cute girls from his class could take a seat and try to engage in conversation, but Hudson never let himself be swayed.

But there was something about this girl that made him want to hear her opinions on everything, hear about her day, tell her about his own.

"Or, you could stay here and keep me company," Hudson said.

She stepped away from Hudson, but instead of leaving the garage, she grabbed a folding chair that was leaning against a wall and propped it open. "If you don't mind," she said.

Hudson breathed a sigh of relief. How quickly his luck had turned. He'd come home from school to a long, empty afternoon of worrying about tomorrow's interview with the dean of admissions, with nothing but the occasional oil change to distract him. But now he had a full workload ahead of him and the company of a beautiful girl. He wiped his hands on the rag he'd grabbed earlier, and he got to work, racking his mind for something to say.

He could see her out of the corner of his eye, sitting quietly, moving just enough to look around the garage. Her gaze occasionally landed on Hudson, and his heart flitted in response. "Did you know that certain mechanic schools have operating rooms with viewing areas, like you'd have in med school? Just like surgeons in training, there's only so much you can learn in a classroom. The only difference is that you don't have to get sterilized." Hudson peeked around the hood to catch her expression.

The girl turned to him, an eyebrow arched, containing a smile by biting her bottom lip.

"I hear some students even faint the first time they see a car getting worked on. They just can't handle the gore," he quipped.

"Well, sure. All that oil—who can blame them?" She smiled and shook her head at him. "Dork."

He smiled back, then pulled her car up onto the lift so he could change the oil and the transmission fluid. What had driven him to make such a silly comment, he couldn't say, nor could he explain why it had felt good when she called him a dork.

"Have you ever been to Mississippi before?" he asked, once the car was up.

"Can't say that I have."

"How long are you planning on staying?"

"I'm not sure, actually. I don't really have an itinerary I'm sticking to. I might just be passing through."

Hudson set up the funnel under the oil pan's drain plug, listening for the familiar *glug* of the heavy liquid pouring down to the disposal bins beside the lift. He searched for something else to say, feeling an urge to confide. "Well, if you want my opinion, you shouldn't leave until you've really seen the state. There's a lot of treasures around."

"Treasures? Of the buried variety?"

"Sure," Hudson said. "Just, metaphorically buried." He glanced at her, ready to catch her rolling her eyes or in some other way dismissing the comment. He'd never actually spoken the thought aloud to anyone, mostly because he expected people to think he was crazy to find Vicksburg special. This girl looked curious, though, waiting for him to go on.

"Not necessarily buried, just hidden behind everyday life. Behind all the fast-food chains and boredom. People who like Vicksburg usually just like what Vicksburg isn't instead of all the things it is." Hudson plugged the oil drain and started flushing out the old transmission fluid, hoping he wasn't babbling.

"Meaning?"

"It's not a big city, it's not polluted, it's not dangerous, it's not unfamiliar." *God*, he could feel himself starting to talk faster. "All of which are true, and good, sure. But it's not what Vicksburg really is, you know? That's the same thing as saying, 'I like you because you're not a murderer.' That's a very good quality for a person to have, but it doesn't really tell you much about them."

Well done, Hudson thought to himself. *Keep on talking about murderers; that's the perfect way to make a good impression*. While the transmission fluid cleared out, he examined the tread on the tires, which seemed to be in decent shape, and tried to steer his little speech away from felonies.

"I'm sorry, I usually don't go on like this. I guess you're just easy to talk to," Hudson said.

By some miracle, the girl was smiling at him. "Don't be sorry. That was a solid rant."

He grabbed a rag from his pocket and wiped his hands on it. "Thanks. Most people aren't so interested in this stuff."

"Well, lucky for you, I can appreciate a good rant."

She gave him a smile and then turned to look out the garage, her eyes narrowed by the glare of the sun. Hudson wondered if he'd ever been so captivated by watching someone stare out into the distance. Even with the pretty girls he'd halfheartedly pursued, Kate and Suzanne and Ella, Hudson couldn't remember being so unable to look away.

"So, what are some of these hidden treasures?" she asked.

He walked around the car as if he was checking on something.

"Um," he said, impressed that she was taking the conversation in stride. "I'm drawing a blank. But you know what I mean, don't you? How sometimes you feel like you're the only person in the world who is seeing something?"

The girl laughed, rich and warm. "I'll tell you one: It's quiet here," she said. She wiped at the thin film of sweat that had gathered on her forehead, using the moisture to comb back a couple of loose strands of hair. He could hear his dad around the back, testing the engine on the semi that had come in a few hours earlier. Hudson returned his attention to the car, tomorrow's interview being pushed to the back of his mind.

"It reminds me of where I grew up," the girl said. Hudson heard her chair scrape on the floor as she scooted it back and walked in his direction. He expected her to stand next to him, but she settled in somewhere behind him, out of sight. "At the elementary school that I went to, there was this soccer field. It seems like nothing but an unkempt field of grass if you drive by it." Hudson had to stop himself from turning around to watch her lips move as she spoke. "But every kid in Fredericksburg knows about the anthills. There's two of them, one at each end of the field. One's full of black ants and the other red. Every summer the soccer field gets overrun by this ant-on-ant war. I'm not sure if they're territorial or they just happen to feed off each other, but it's an incredible sight. All these little black and red things attacking each other, like watching thousands of checkers games being played from very far away. And it's this little Fredericksburg treasure, just for us."

Hudson caught himself smiling at the engine instead of replacing the spark plugs. "That's great," he said, the words feeling too flat. The girl hadn't just let him ramble on; she'd known exactly what he meant. No one, not even Hudson's dad, had ever understood him so perfectly.

There was a pause that Hudson didn't know how to fill. He thought about asking her why the car was registered to an address in Louisiana instead of Texas, but it didn't seem like the right time. He was thankful when the engine of the semi his dad had been working on started, and the truck began to maneuver its way out of the garage in a cacophonous series of back-up beeping and gear shifts.

When the truck had rumbled away down the street, Hudson turned around to look at the girl, but, feeling self-conscious under her gaze, he pretended to search for something on the shelves beside her. "When I'm done with your car, want to go on a treasure hunt?"

Hudson wasn't sure where the question had come from, but he was glad he hadn't paused to think about it, hadn't given himself time to shy away from saying it out loud.

The question seemed to catch the girl off guard. "You want to show me around?" She glanced down at her feet, bare except for the red outline of her flip-flops.

"If you're not busy, I mean."

She seemed wary, which felt like an entirely reasonable thing for her to be. Hudson couldn't believe he'd asked a stranger to go on a treasure hunt with him.

"Okay, sure," she managed to say right before Hudson heard his dad enter the garage and call his name.

"Excuse me just one second," he said to the girl, raising an apologetic hand as he sidestepped her. He resisted the urge to put a hand on her as he slid by so close, just a light touch on her lower back, on her shoulder, and joined his dad at the garage door.

"Hey, Pop," Hudson said, putting his hands on his hips, mimicking his dad's stance.

"Good day at school?"

"Yup. Nothing special. I did another mock interview with the counselor during lunch. Did pretty well, I think. That's about it."

His dad nodded a few times, then motioned toward the car. "What are you working on here?"

"General tune-up," Hudson replied. "Filters, fluids, spark plugs. A new V-belt."

"I can finish up for you. You should get some rest for tomorrow."

"I'm almost done," Hudson said, already sensing the discomfort he felt any time he had to ask his dad about something Hudson knew his dad wouldn't approve of. "There's just . . ." He looked back to see whether the girl was within earshot. "Well, this girl, she wants me to show her around town." He waited to see if his dad would run a hand through his graying hair, his telltale sign of disapproval. "I promise I'll be back for dinner," Hudson added.

His dad glanced at his old Timex. "One hour," he said, adding a reminder about how early Hudson would have to get up tomorrow to drive the fifty miles to the University of Mississippi campus in Jackson. "We don't want you to be too tired."

"I won't be, I promise," he said, tiny fantasies of the next hour with the girl already flooding his head. The back of their hands grazing against each other—not entirely by accident—as they walked; her leg resting against his as they sat somewhere together, getting to know each other. Already racking his mind for places where he could take her, Hudson thanked his dad with a quick hug and then went back to the front of the car. The girl had a hand resting on the hood, staring vaguely at the engine block. "I just have a couple more things to do, and then we can get going," he said.

"Great." Her lips spread into a warm, genuine smile, and she held out her hand. "By the way, I'm Leila."

He wiped his hand off on his work pants and said his name as he shook her hand. *Months*, he thought to himself, his fingers practically buzzing at the touch of her skin. *I'll be thinking about her for months.*

2

AFTER HE WAS done fixing Leila's car, Hudson went to the back of the shop to change out of his work clothes while Leila settled the bill with his dad. When he came out, he saw her sitting in the front passenger seat of her idling car.

"I'm driving?" he asked as he opened the driver-side door.

"You're the tour guide," she said, making a sweeping gesture with her arm as if to indicate that the world beyond the windshield was vast and unexplored. "Guide me."

She smiled at him, and he thought to himself that she was exceptionally good at smiling. He shifted the car into drive and pulled out onto the street, wondering where to take her, how to get her to smile more often. The obvious treasure was the oxbow, but it was too far away. Everything that was nearby held fond memories—the Coca-Cola museum he'd gone to on every birthday until he was twelve, the ice cream shop that invited its customers to suggest new, strange flavors and had once taken up Hudson's request for Bacon Chocolate—but the only way to transplant memories onto places and make them feel like treasures to her was to talk. He usually didn't have trouble talking to girls, even beautiful ones, but while he didn't quite feel tongue-tied around her, he didn't know how to begin. "It's very red in here," he said at last.

"I know. It's pretty much why I bought it. It was love at first sight."

"So I'm going to go out on a limb and assume red is your favorite color."

"I like red—don't get me wrong. But I have a deep appreciation for anything that is willing to be totally and utterly itself. If you're going to be red, well, then, be red, goddamnit. From your steering wheel to your hubcaps, be red."

Hudson could only nod to himself. He'd never met anyone who talked this way, the way he thought. The brakes chirped loudly as he slowed for a stop sign, and he assured Leila that they worked fine. They just liked to sing. He turned left on Maryland so that the sun wouldn't blind him while he thought of something to show Leila. "What about you?" he asked after completing the turn. "What are you?"

"Me?" she said, feigning innocence. She kicked off her flip-flops and put her feet up on the dashboard. Hudson imagined what it would be like to be her boyfriend, which was the first time he'd ever had such a thought without immediately dismissing it. To go on long drives with her as she sang along shyly to music, to lie on the grass somewhere and confess things to each other, find ways to cuddle around movie-theater cup-holders. "I am a treasure-tourist. And my tour guide has yet to show me a single treasure. Where are we going?"

Hudson took her toward downtown. They passed a couple of motel chains off the highway, a spattering of restaurant and fast-food places, everything flat and that shade of beige that felt duller than gray. Nothing felt like enough of a treasure to show Leila.

Afraid that she'd grow bored, though, Hudson turned the car into the parking lot of the bowling alley as soon as he saw it. Through the large windowpane he could see that the place was full, fluorescent balls rolling down the eighteen lanes in varying speeds, ending in silent white explosions of pins.

"When I was a kid, I came to a slumber party here," he said, looking out at the squat, sky-blue building. He was flooded by warm memories of the night and wished there was a way to share them with Leila, to show her just how special it had actually been. "We bowled until two in the morning and then set up our sleeping bags on the lanes. Any time I drive by here, I wonder how many other kids have had the chance to sleep in a bowling alley before."

Hudson stared out the windshield, admiring how the bowling alley's façade matched the cloudless sky, the tacky and faded window art that had been there since his childhood. He noticed Leila glancing around and realized he'd been quiet for a while. "C'mon, I'll show you around."

○   ○   ○

The place was loud with the usual sounds: balls rolling down the lanes, crashing into pins. A little boy tried to prevent a gutter ball by shrieking at it, and groups cheered a strike. The interior was painted the same baby blue as the outside. A "wall of fame" was on display by the shoe counter. The tiny snack bar practically dripped with pizza grease.

"This turns into a salsa club on Tuesday nights," Hudson said. "The lanes make for a great dance floor."

Leila smiled and gave him a light shove, letting him know that she wasn't falling for it. But she looked around the room as if searching for clues that it might be true. As she swiveled her head, Hudson caught a glimpse of a scar poking out from her hairline behind her ear, just the tiniest sliver of damaged flesh. Then she turned back to him, combing a tress of hair over her ear and hiding the scar. "There's no way that's true."

"Please don't argue with your tour guide," Hudson said, leading them to the shoe counter. Unlike other bowling alleys that invested in cubbyholes, Riverside Lanes had a much different storage system for their shoes.

"This is ridiculous," Leila said, staring at the massive pile of shoes, more than a few of which had fallen off the counter. A group of junior high girls came by, chatting excitedly about weekend plans, each of them tossing a pair of shoes haphazardly onto the pile. It shifted, and Hudson saw Leila brace for the pile of footwear to come tumbling at them.

"No, this is awesome," Hudson corrected. "Whenever the pile falls, an employee yells out, 'Avalanche!' and then everyone in the house gets a free game."

"Wouldn't people just knock it over, then?"

Hudson shook his head, as if no one had ever considered that before. "Where's the fun in that?" He crossed his arms over his chest, admiring the sight of all those separated pairs of shoes, the laces sticking out everywhere, like arms seeking salvation from a pile of rubble.

Hudson glanced at Leila, trying to get a sense of whether she was enjoying herself. Then a couple in their twenties came up to the pile and began to rummage. "The tour will continue this way," Hudson said, touching Leila briefly on the shoulder as he led her through the bowling alley. He walked backward, like an actual tour guide. "On your left you will spot the snack bar, which still advertises freshly made pretzels despite being sold out for the last twelve years. On your right in lane six you can see the local bowling legend known as The Beaver, who's bowled three perfect games and has never smiled at anyone but fallen pins. Please, no flash photography," Hudson cracked, pointing out a hefty man in his sixties whose gut drooped over his belt.

"Our next stop is the men's bathroom," Hudson said, thinking of the chalkboard over the urinals. It was always adorned with a mix of inane vulgarities, doodles, and the occasional heartfelt message, scrawled in sloppy handwriting that indicated its author was either drunk or his focus was split with another task at hand. "You can really see some lovely things there."

There was a pause before Hudson realized what he'd just said. He turned to Leila, who raised an eyebrow at him. "That didn't come out right. I meant that some people really show parts of themselves that usually stay hidden." He tensed a fist closed, stopping himself. "Nope, that didn't clear anything up. What I meant was—" Hudson said, but he was interrupted by Leila bursting into laughter.

Hudson smiled nervously. "There's a chalkboard in there," he started to explain, but he was too enraptured by the sound of her laughter to keep going. It emptied his thoughts, that laugh.

"Don't worry. I assume it wasn't what it sounded like," she said, catching her breath.

Hudson shook his head at himself and turned to the bathroom and pushed the door open. "Tour group coming through!" he announced.

When no one responded, he held the door open for Leila and made a sweeping motion of welcome. "After you, ma'am."

"This is the strangest tour I've ever been on," Leila said, entering the bathroom and giving him an inquisitive look with just a hint of a smile to it.

"Keep your arms and legs inside the ride at all times," he said as she passed by.

Two urinals, a stall, and a sink was all there was to the bathroom. An automated hand-drier that barely whirred hung from one wall. Leila looked up at the chalkboard over the urinals. Hudson followed her gaze, trying to guess which bit of scrawled handwriting she was reading.

Someone had doodled an impressive dragon. *Joan slept with The Beaver!* was scrawled in block letters across the top of the board. And below that, in tiny script, as if the author had meant it as a whisper, *You have been relentlessly on my mind.* Lyrics to a Johnny Cash song, a Bible verse, and a drawing of a penis were scattered across the wall. Hudson couldn't help but smile at the collection of escaped thoughts captured in chalk. He looked back at Leila and saw that she was smiling, too, her hands behind her as if she were appraising a piece of art.

"You see the treasures?" he asked.

She nodded, her lips spreading into a smile, her gaze passing over the smudges of white and blue chalk. "That's my favorite Vonnegut quote," she said, pointing at the line *I urge you to please notice when you are happy.*

Hudson felt himself blush, wondering whether to confess that he'd been the one to write it on the chalkboard a week ago. "This is fantastic," she said. Then she reached for one of the inch-long pieces of chalk sitting on the metallic ledge of the board. Taking only a brief moment to gather her thoughts, Leila stood on tiptoe to reach a blank spot, her neat handwriting standing out against the rest of the words on the board. *People of Vicksburg, you live in a special place.*

Silly, how rewarding just that one comment from her was, how it made Hudson want to keep on babbling, to take her to every single place that he'd enjoyed for even a millisecond.

Hudson led them back to the car, eager to show her anything else at all. They went to the church that had burned down and been rebuilt by the town, the Capture the Flag field at the park by his house, the closed-up candy shop where a dead body had once been found, making the lone remaining bag of root-beer–flavored candy Hudson had in his house feel very much like a treasure.

"You know what? Why don't I take you to go see it?"

"Your house?"

"Yeah," he said, surprised by his own boldness but thankful for it. "You know, for the root-beer candy."

Leila considered him. He held up an understanding hand. "I'm acting purely as a treasure guide here. It might not be the most interesting place to everyone, but it's a place that I know well enough to know where all the hidden details are. Don't you want to see the room that Hudson the famed mechanic has been sleeping in for seventeen years?"

She tilted her head back and squinted as if she were examining him. He worried he'd messed things up until he realized she was mock-scrutinizing him, saw the hint of a smile tugging at her lips. "Do you have one of those race-car–shaped beds?" she asked.

"I do not," he said, pretending to be offended as he switched his foot to the gas pedal. "I got too big for it last year."

Leila burst out laughing again. For fear that he would giggle with pride as soon as he opened his mouth, Hudson kept quiet on the short drive to his house.

o o o

Hudson parked Leila's car in front of his house and handed her the keys as they walked up his lawn onto the narrow porch. His dad's car wasn't in the driveway yet—probably out shopping for groceries for dinner.

"This is the porch," he said, gesturing redundantly with one arm as he jiggled the keys out of his pocket. "We don't use it much."

"How come?" Leila asked.

"Our next-door neighbor is quite the talker," Hudson said, looking around the block at the cars and pickup trucks parked in open garages, the American flags drooping like undrawn curtains in the still air, the bicycles lying on the driveways in after-school abandon. "My dad and I actually missed a movie once because she insisted on filling us in on neighborhood gossip. Someone's cousin had adopted an Asian baby, and that seemed to require a thirty-minute, slightly racist speech." He turned to the door, having finally fished the keys out. "The true treasure of Vicksburg lies in its people."

He turned over his shoulder to smile at her and then led them inside. They went fairly quickly around the house, living room to bathroom to kitchen. He showed her the backyard, the modest plastic patio furniture set up around the barbecue grill. The lawn was big and green, stretching out between the neighbors' fences until it hit a line of trees. After a few moments, when the sun had all but dipped beneath the branches, Hudson led her back inside to show her the rest of the house.

The staircase was just wide enough to allow them to climb side by side. Hudson asked, "So, what are you going up north for?" He honestly didn't really have a strong desire to know, since it would affirm that fact that she *was* going, possibly very soon.

"Haven't I mentioned it? I'm going to see the Northern Lights."

"Oh, nice," he said, his heart dropping a little. "How far north do you have to go to see them?"

"Well, it kind of changes. I'm going up as far north as I can to give myself the best chance."

"Wow. I'm jealous."

"Yeah, I'm pretty excited," she said, but her voice didn't quite convey that excitement. "I'm just hoping that . . ." She trailed off.

"That what?"

"No, nothing," she said, as they reached the landing at the top of the stairs. She held her arm out across his chest. "Wait." She looked at the four closed doors that made up the second floor. "Let me guess." She pointed at the door closest to them. "Master bedroom, bathroom, your room," she said, pointing at each door from left to right. "And, I don't think that's another room, because you've got an only-child air about you, so I'm gonna say that's the linen closet."

"Unbelievable."

"It's a special gift."

"That's special, all right," he said, wondering what she'd stopped herself from saying on the stairs. "How'd you know I'm an only child?"

"We can smell our own," she said with a wink.

Once inside his room, Leila went straight to his bookshelf, where his car magazines and the novels he'd read for school and liked enough to buy a copy were neatly stacked. Her back was to him, her figure silhouetted against the fading light so that she seemed a little less real, a little less like a beautiful girl who understood him standing in his room and more like an apparition that could dissipate at any second. He flicked the light switch on but said nothing, giving her space to explore. He didn't want her to seem like an apparition, wanted to keep her real for as long as possible.

"What's this?" she asked, grabbing a seashell he kept on his windowsill.

He walked closer to her. "That is a souvenir from the first time I went to the ocean. I was bodysurfing, you know, just enjoying getting the crap kicked out of me by the waves. And this one wave just grabs me and beats me down against the shore. I felt my forehead catch on something hard, harder than the sand. So I grabbed at it, and it was this seashell. I think you can still see the scar." He pulled at his hair and tilted his head down so she could see.

She lifted her hand and ran a finger along the scar on his forehead. He could hear her breathing, could smell something sweet on her breath.

"Why'd you keep the seashell?"

"I don't know," Hudson said. "I guess I just liked the idea of having a reminder from such a great day. I didn't want the scar to be the only thing I got to keep."

Leila smiled, her finger no longer at the scar but dropping down, tracing his jawline. Her lips were parted just enough for him to see a thin, glimmering line of teeth set against the pink of her tongue.

Then the garage door rumbled beneath their feet, and Hudson heard his dad's Camaro pull into the driveway. Leila's hand dropped away, and Hudson took an instinctive step back, immediately regretting it. He wanted to grab Leila's hand and place it back on his cheek. Instead, he stood and listened to his dad making his way from the garage to the kitchen, feeling the moment slip away.

3

DOWNSTAIRS IN THE kitchen, Hudson's dad was kneeling in front of the fridge, moving things around to make way for a case of soda.

"Hey, Pop," Hudson said.

"Hey, son." Hudson's dad finished up in the fridge before standing and turning around. His glance went to Leila. "Sorry, I didn't realize you had company." He offered a smile, then stepped around them to leave the kitchen. "Do you mind getting the grill started? I'm gonna hop in the shower." He took a step toward the stairs, then stopped and looked back at Leila. "You're welcome to stay for dinner, if you'd like."

"I'd love to," Leila said.

"Burgers okay?"

"Always," she said. "Thank you, Mr. . . .?"

"Call me Walter," he said, offering his hand with a smile. Then he turned to Hudson. "You're gonna get some rest after dinner?"

"Of course. I was planning to sleepwalk all the way to Jackson so I could be as well-rested as possible before the interview."

"You think you're clever, don't you? Just because you're going to be a doctor?"

"You think I'm clever, too, Dad. Ever since I taught you how to connect to wireless internet, you've considered me a genius."

"Don't give this one any compliments," Walter said to Leila, putting a hand on his son's shoulder. "He'll never forget them." He was tall, still taller than Hudson but thinner, with wiry muscles. The rest of their features they shared: the same strong jaw and big brown eyes. Hudson thought of his dad as young, or at least not yet old, so it was a shock every time he noticed just how gray his hair had turned. "All right, I'll see you guys outside, then."

When he was about halfway up the stairs, Leila called out, "You have a lovely home!"

"Thank you," he called back, his voice fading as he climbed the stairs and closed his bedroom door.

"He's so sweet," Leila said.

"Yeah," Hudson said, picking at a splinter on a kitchen cabinet.

"What interview do you have to be well-rested for?"

"I have this interview with the dean of admissions at Ole Miss. It's to see if they're going to offer me a full scholarship."

"Wow. That's impressive."

Hudson shrugged. "I guess. My dad knows the guy, so he helped set up the interview, and that's why he's a little paranoid about it." Not wanting to think about tomorrow, when Leila might no longer be around, Hudson moved toward the back door. "Let's get the grill going."

Leila nodded and helped him grab a few things from the kitchen; then they went out to the backyard to light the charcoal. The air had cooled pleasantly with the oncoming dusk, only a few streaks of orange light breaking through gaps in the trees where cicadas buzzed. It was a large yard, the grass bright green and healthy. A toolshed stood in the middle, not far off from the fire pit that Walter had dug and lined with bricks. There were a few tree stumps and camping chairs gathered around the pit in a circle, a crushed beer can forgotten in the weeds from the last time his dad's friends had come over. Hudson wished that he had some ability to stop time, to hold the Earth's rotation, so that he could just stand near Leila for a little while longer.

"So, a doctor, huh?"

"Yeah, but it's not a big deal," Hudson said. "Nothing like that seeing-through-doors trick."

"Superpower, not a trick," Leila corrected, grabbing a match and tossing it onto the pile of charcoal. "And I'm sure you have some powers of your own."

"Not really." At that moment, the only superpower he felt he had was that he could spend time with someone like Leila and have her want to stay around for dinner.

"Bullshit," she said, giving him a friendly hip check. "Ranting," she pointed out. "I could listen to you rant about treasures all day."

Hudson tried and failed to keep the size of his smile under control, especially when he noticed that she was smiling back at him. "I'm also pretty damn good at setting a table," he said, trying to draw attention away from his blushing. "I can do it with one hand. And I don't even have to look up online which side the knife is supposed to be on."

"I knew you were holding out on me."

"I'll show you," he said, and he went about setting the table with an exaggerated care that he hoped was funny. Leila took a seat and watched him, a smile on her face. When he was done, he sat next to her as they waited for the coals to heat.

This was Hudson's favorite time of the year, favorite time of day, favorite spot of his house. It was the first time in a while that he was sitting there without a book in front of him. He'd almost forgotten how enjoyable his backyard was when he could simply sit and look around without having to study. Leila leaned back in her patio chair and put her legs up, resting her heels on Hudson's lap. She did it so casually that Hudson couldn't tell just what she meant by it; if she meant anything at all or if she just needed a place to rest her feet and made no distinction between him and any other surface. Or maybe, just maybe, she was as happy to be spending time with him as he was with her.

Hudson barely moved, focusing on the weight of her feet on his lap. By the time his dad joined them outside, Hudson's legs were falling asleep. "We were waiting for the coals to get hot," Hudson said.

"Well, looks like they're just about ready to go," Walter said, even though Hudson knew very well that they'd been ready for a while. Walter grabbed the tray of patties and put three down on the grill, smiling at the satisfying sizzle of the meat beginning to cook.

"Want some help, Pop?"

"I've got it, thanks."

Other fathers might have turned around and winked at their son, or smiled. But Hudson liked his dad's reserved way of showing affection, the silent acceptance of cooking duties.

"So, Leila," Walter asked when the burgers were ready, bringing them to the table, "Hudson tells me you're not from Vicksburg. What brings you over here?"

"I'm zigzagging my way up the country to go see the Northern Lights," she said.

Walter picked at the label on his beer, peeling until the corner curled away from the glass. "That's one hell of a road trip. You're doing it by yourself?"

"Yup." Leila nodded.

"Well, everyone needs at least one long road trip in their lives," Walter said. "I was probably about your age when I did mine."

"Where'd you go?"

"California to New York. Sea to shining sea." He kept peeling the label off, lost in thought. His dad always got that look on his face when he talked about that road trip. Hudson had asked him about it more times than he could remember, but no matter how much Walter told him, Hudson could never really get a feel for what his dad had been like back then. It was strange to think that there was a part of his dad he'd never know, two whole decades' worth of memories that did not include Hudson.

"This kid hasn't taken one yet," he said, snapping out of it and motioning toward Hudson.

"What are you talking about? I've been with you on tons of road trips."

"Doesn't count," Walter said, sipping from his beer. "On your own is what I meant. You get yourself a part-time job in college, something that won't get in the way of your studies, and maybe you'll save up enough to travel during the summers. And, if you really impress me with your grades"—Walter paused for effect—"I might give you a free oil change for your first trip."

"Now I see where Hudson gets his wit," Leila said, kicking Hudson playfully under the table.

He kicked back lightly, wishing that he was barefoot and then feeling a bit creepy for it. "Why the Northern Lights anyway?"

Leila shrugged. "It's just something I know I have to do."

"Life to-do list sort of thing?"

"Something like that," Leila said.

"Is this your first road trip?" Walter asked.

Leila took another bite of her burger. God, she was attractive even when she was chewing. It made Hudson want to cook for her. She gave a slight nod.

When she was done chewing, she took a sip of her soda and wiped at the corner of her mouth with a paper napkin. "I'm on a little break from school right now and thought it was a good time for some traveling."

Hudson nodded, then realized he had no idea what that meant. "Like, college? Did you take a year off after high school?" It was hard to tell how old she was. Between sixteen and ... twenty? Maybe?

"Nope." She took the last bite of her burger, and for a second it seemed as if she'd done that so she wouldn't have to say anything else. Then she swallowed and said, "I've been stuck in kindergarten for years. This trip around the country is so I can finally learn the alphabet."

As his dad chuckled, Leila smirked at Hudson, and he could feel her face etching itself into his memory.

"I'm kidding, Hudson. You haven't been hanging around with a kindergartner all day."

"No? I could have sworn I was. Only kindergartners ever laugh at my jokes."

"I could see that," Leila said. "And kudos for not taking the opportunity to make fun of my height. I set it up perfectly."

Hudson shrugged. "I like how short you are," he said, immediately grabbing a chip from the open bag in the middle of the table and munching on it as a way to keep himself from apologizing for the comment.

The sky had darkened to night, and now the only light came from the pinprick stars and the neighbors' kitchens. But he could see Leila smiling to herself, biting her bottom lip. Then she leaned back in her chair and put her feet on his lap again.

"What are you planning to see along the way?" Walter asked, grabbing a second burger, dressing it with his usual half dozen squirts of hot sauce.

"I haven't really planned much out. I'm just going to play it by ear, see where I end up."

"You've already seen Vicksburg," Hudson said. "It's all downhill from here."

Leila chuckled in a way he hadn't heard before, a laugh that was soft and throaty and that shocked Hudson into goose bumps. "I'm sure the rest of the country will have trouble living up," she said.

After a few minutes, Walter got up to clear the table, and when he was inside, Leila pulled her feet off Hudson.

"I guess I should let you get some rest, then," Leila said. "You've got that interview." She slipped her feet back into the flip-flops and stood up.

The joy he'd felt since meeting her was slipping away, but Hudson didn't know what to say to stop her from leaving. He followed her as she walked to the sliding glass door that led back into the house. She didn't open the door, though, just stood there looking at her feet as if mulling over some thought.

The lights from the kitchen turned on as his dad started cleaning up inside. Hudson could see Leila clearly again, her hands in her back pockets, a half-inch strip of skin visible between her shirt and the waistline of her shorts. Then she stepped forward and pulled him in for a hug. It was surprisingly strong, coming from someone her size, from someone he'd just met a few hours before. It felt achingly good to be pressed against her.

"It was very nice to meet you," she said. "Good luck with everything."

Then she planted a kiss on his cheek and walked inside. It was almost paralyzing, the kiss, the feel of her lips on his skin, the already increasing distance between them. Paralyzing enough that by the time he went into the house, Leila had already said good-bye to his dad and was at the front door. Not just at the front door but halfway out of it already. She noticed him and paused; then she waved good-bye and closed the door behind her.

He stood in the hallway between the kitchen and the living room, trying to get over the shock of seeing her leave so suddenly. When he became aware of the sound of rushing water, he noticed his dad standing at the sink doing the dishes. "Pop, need any help?"

His dad turned, the bottom of his shirt stained dark with water. "No, thanks."

"Okay," he said. "I'll be upstairs. Night." But he didn't move for a while, just stood there staring at the front door.

"G'night," his dad called back. "I'll be by your room at six to make sure you're up. Tomorrow's a big day."

"Right," Hudson said. When he broke out of his daze, he climbed the stairs with measured effort and went into his room, plopping down onto his bed and pulling out the stack of papers he'd printed off the internet full of possible questions he might be asked during an admissions interview. He leafed through some pages, more aware of the sound they made as his fingertips pushed them aside than of the words on the paper. He eyed the outfit he and his dad had picked out for the interview—his blue pinstriped suit, white shirt, jade-green tie. It was hanging on the closet's door handle, the dry-cleaning wrapper keeping the suit from wrinkling.

A couple of minutes later, Hudson heard his dad coming up the stairs, and the lights in the hallway turned off. Hudson realized he hadn't read a single word, so he rose from his bed and walked over to the windowsill. He sighed deeply, as if thoughts of Leila rested in his lungs and all he needed was to breathe her out. As his breath rattled the venetian blinds, he noticed that Leila's car was still parked outside. He stepped to the window and looked through the slats. He could see her sitting inside, one elbow resting against the window, the other hand on the wheel. She pulled her elbow away and looked up at him, her eyes brilliant even from that distance. He thought about the oxbow, about wandering its entire perimeter with Leila by his side, the Mississippi River providing a roar of background noise to their conversation.

Not tonight, he told himself as he poked his head out his bedroom door to make sure the lights in his dad's room were off. *I'm not going to stay home tonight, not when I have the chance to spend time with her.* He went back into his room, pulled the cords that drew the blinds up, and slid his window open. He climbed slowly onto the roof of the porch, then eased himself onto the grass of the front lawn, looking back to make sure his dad's lights were still off.

Then he jogged over to the car. Leila had rolled the window down and watched him approach without saying anything. He leaned toward her open window. "Scooch over," he said in a near-whisper. "I'm driving."

"What about getting some rest?" She raised an eyebrow.

He shrugged and said, "I promised to show you a treasure."

4

IT WAS PITCH-black on the drive, nothing on the country lane but their headlights illuminating the occasional reflectors at the edge of the road. They glowed yellow and then faded back into darkness.

Hudson kept stealing glances at Leila's profile, trying to figure out what made her so attractive, but the only intelligible thought he came away with after each stolen glance was: *I like her face. I really like her face.*

"So, how'd you find this treasure?"

"It's a local tradition. There's always a group of kids that lays claim to it. Then, when they move on—school, babies, getting old, whatever— some new group moves in. One of my friends' older brothers used to hang out there, and when his friends all got jobs in Jackson and Biloxi, my friends took over."

Only after he said this did Hudson realize he and Leila might not have the oxbow to themselves. Friday night in Vicksburg, what else was there to do? He hoped his friends had gone to the bowling alley instead.

"What do you do over there? Dumb guy stuff?"

"Pretty much." He signaled and turned the car onto another indistinguishable country lane. "Toss a football around, light bonfires.

Have some drinks. I'm not a big drinker, so I'm usually the designated driver."

"Hmm, too bad we don't have anything to drink. It'd be fun to get drunk with you."

Hudson let the comment hang in the air and pretended to focus on the road as he turned off onto an unpaved street. The car rumbled over the uneven surface, kicking up pebbles that struck the undercarriage and chimed like a children's toy.

"How far away is this place?"

"We're almost there," Hudson said, pointing lamely at a patch of darkness beyond the reach of the headlights.

When he parked the car, Leila was quick to open the door and get out, letting in a vibrant sound. It wasn't the river itself, the current mostly calm, but everything surrounding it: the nocturnal wildlife, the insects, the flora moving in the breeze, almost like lungs expanding and contracting. Impossible to prove, but Hudson felt that the whole length of the river was contributing to the sound, the casino boats a few miles down, the current crashing into the Gulf of Mexico in New Orleans like a jazz cymbal. It all came together to create this wall of noise that felt somehow tangible.

"This way," Hudson said, starting to head around the trees and into the ravine.

She stepped to him, and before he could realize what his fingers were doing, he took hold of her hand. "Okay," she said, squeezing his fingers back without much fanfare, "lead the way."

Thankful for the darkness hiding his uncontainable smile, he took them around the trees. A couple of times he almost lost his footing, too distracted by Leila's touch to pay much attention to the terrain. They reached the river's edge and started walking downstream. He was hoping that the boat was there. If the rowboat was there, then it meant he and Leila would have the oxbow to themselves and his friends were off doing something else.

"I like this scenic route," she said. "It feels like an actual treasure hunt."

"You'll love this place," he said, spotting the low-hanging branches where they kept the small rowboat hidden. It was there. He let go of her hand to kneel down and pull the boat out of its hiding spot. It was little more than a worn-out canoe, its wood knotty and cracked, its white paint darkened to green by the river.

"Oh, I see it," Leila said, looking out at the river, her hands in her back pockets, that world-changing posture again. "How far is that?"

"Not too far. About sixty, seventy yards, maybe." He put one foot in the boat and turned to offer a helping hand.

She looked over at Hudson and then back at the island. A mischievous smile spread across her lips. She stepped toward him, but instead of taking his hand and getting into the boat, she knelt down and stuck her hand into the river.

"It's chilly," she said. "But the current isn't too bad." She stood back up to her full height, which, admittedly, wasn't very much. "Let's swim across."

She kicked off one of her flip-flops and stuck her foot into the river. Hudson gave her a look.

"Haven't you ever done it before?"

"No."

"Yeah, we're definitely doing this, then."

"What about our clothes?"

"They'll get wet, and then some time after that they'll get dry."

"And our phones? The car keys?"

"Leave them in the car." She walked over to him and pulled him out of the boat by his hand. "Hudson, you're swimming across this river with me."

He resisted for a few steps, dragging his feet. But then he remembered that he'd climbed out his bedroom window and left his house because he wanted to immerse himself in fun for once. "It's very hard to say no to you."

"Why would you want to say no to me?"

Leila laughed and gave his hand a squeeze, then walked them back to the car. Hudson checked the time again before leaving his phone in the glove compartment. If he was tired the next day, he could tell his dad he'd had trouble sleeping out of nervousness. They left their shoes, wallets, and keys inside, then walked back to the shore, treading carefully to avoid stepping on stones or twigs with their bare feet.

They stood at the edge, facing the island, the river's waves lapping at their toes as if trying to coax them into the water. "Look at those stars," Hudson said.

"Beautiful," Leila said, looking up at the night sky. Then she turned back to him and smiled. "Are you a good swimmer?"

"I'm all right," he said. "You?"

"We'll see, won't we?" And with that, she dived in.

There was a very brief pause. A delay between Leila's action and his reaction, that split second during which Hudson asked himself just who the hell this girl was and what she was doing in his life. By the time the thought had passed, he was already jumping in after her.

The cool water was a shock. She was a couple of body-lengths in front of him, her strokes fast, frantic, overjoyed, the sound of her laughter ringing out every time she came up for air. When he almost swallowed a lungful of Mississippi, he realized that he, too, was laughing in between strokes, that his heart rate was spiked by adrenaline, that he was completely intoxicated by the river, by the night, by Leila. He swam faster until he nearly caught up with her, her kicks coming down only a few inches from his face. Swimming around her kicks until he was at her side, he felt his muscles start to burn with effort. Funny, how it took a little bit of pain to remember that certain parts of yourself were alive.

They reached the island's shore at about the same time and climbed onto the muddy grass and flopped onto their backs. Leila's arm was resting across his chest. Without giving the move much thought, Hudson brought his right hand up and laid it gently atop Leila's forearm. He'd expected her skin to be somehow warm, but it was cold from the water. He started to rub, wanting to bring her warmth.

"We are very wet," she said, unsticking her shirt from her stomach with the hand not on Hudson's chest.

"Yes, we are," he said, chuckling.

She pulled her arm away to wring out her shirt. "Yeah, that did nothing." Then she stood up, brushing away the grass that had stuck to the exposed parts of her legs.

As he stood, too, for a second, Hudson was dumbstruck. Although in truth it wasn't just a second; it had been the whole day. Since Leila had stepped out of her car, he'd been dumbstruck by her presence, her beauty. He couldn't keep his eyes off her.

"I'll take the staring as a compliment," she said with a laugh.

"Sorry," Hudson said, looking down at the ground. Even when he was embarrassed, he couldn't look completely away. He watched water dripping down her legs, wondering to himself how he'd gotten to be where he was standing.

And now she was stepping toward him and bringing her arms around his neck, pulling her body against his. "You're shivering," she said.

"I think I might stop shivering soon if you keep doing this thing that you're doing."

She laughed and pulled herself a little closer, so that he could really feel her body heat. Hudson brought up his hand to brush away a wet strand of hair behind Leila's ear, but, not being great at this part of the process, he realized too late that he'd brought both his hands up to her face and suddenly didn't know what to do with them.

She noticed and laughed at him, not unkindly. "I'll just put those right here," he said, placing his hands on her shoulders and trying to laugh off the moment.

She shook her head and then grabbed his right hand and moved it to her neck. "Right here."

He looked down at her, at that fantastic face looking back at him, her lips parted first in a smile and then in preparation for what was to come. Her eyes looking into his, then down at his mouth. Hudson could hardly believe that he was here with her. They began to lean into each other when a sound broke through that insulating buzz of the river.

"Ho-ly shit! Is that Hudson with a girl?"

5

HUDSON'S FRIENDS HAD arrived, carrying a healthy arsenal of cheap beer. They began to clamor and whoop from the rowboat, and Hudson and Leila instinctively stepped away from each other. It was the usual trio—John, Richie, and Scott—each of them wearing a big stupid grin as they reached the island.

"Hudsy! What in the hell is going on here?" John said. He stepped off the boat and toward Hudson and ruffled his hair. "Has there always been a ladies' man hiding behind that smart-kid exterior?"

"Hey, guys," Hudson said. "Um, what are you doing here?"

"What the shit else do we have to do? The better question is, what are you doing here? And why are you wet? And who is this?" John said, looking from Hudson to Leila, then back at Hudson.

"And what the hell is she doing here with you?" Richie chimed in, making no effort to hide the fact that he was staring at Leila, her wet clothes clinging to her body. He ran a hand through his beard, which was red and bushy and had been his trademark since his facial hair started growing in ninth grade.

"I'm Leila," she said simply, offering a wave, making a slight effort to cover herself up.

The three boys exchanged looks. Scott took a step toward Hudson and gave him a strong pat on the back. "Where'd you find her?"

Hudson shrugged, then looked at John and tried to convey with just his eyes that the boys were interrupting at the worst possible time and should immediately get back into the boat and leave him alone with Leila. If his eyes managed to say that, though, John wasn't listening. And if John didn't lead their pals away, there was no way the other two would take the initiative.

"Well, Leila, nice to meet you. Now, who wants to get drunk?" John pulled out a can of beer and opened it with a satisfying snap, immediately putting it to his lips to control the foam. Richie and Scott followed his lead and popped open their own cans.

"We weren't gonna stay long," Hudson said. "I've got that interview tomorrow."

"Oh, shit, that's right," John said. After another long gulp he looked at Leila. "What about you? Do you have an interview tomorrow?"

"Nope."

"Good," he said, grabbing another beer from the pack he'd set at his feet and offering it to her. "You guys in for a game, then?"

Scott and Richie cheered their approval and bashed their cans together in a toast that preceded another long swig. "I can't, man," Hudson said. "We should probably be heading back soon anyway. I just wanted to show her the island."

"She won't have really seen it if she doesn't play Drunkball." John took another quick sip. "One round and then you can go. She can stay."

He looked at Leila and winked, and Hudson felt that sensation that must have been what people meant when they said their hearts sank.

Leila looked over at Hudson, still so close to him that he could pull her in for a kiss, if only he could gather the will to lean all the way in. How he could see the greenness of her irises through the darkness he didn't quite understand. "One game?" she asked.

Hudson took a deep breath, mostly to try to pull his heart back up into its rightful place. Every moment with her in it was a treasure, even if he had to share her. "Okay," he said. "It is kind of pointless to come here and not play Drunkball."

Leila accepted the beer from John, and the five of them started walking toward the thicket of trees. Thankfully the trees were spaced far enough apart that they could maneuver through them unharmed. It was as if the island had known in advance what it would be used for and wanted to offer just enough protection from the outside, adult world for the teenagers who'd someday claim it. Beyond the trees was a large clearing, although it was too dark to make out anything there.

Scott broke off from the group and headed toward the shed, then flicked on the generator, and the lights came on. The lights were about knee high, set up around the perimeter of the field and pointing inward so that the entire area, about the size of a basketball court, was lit up as brightly as a supermarket parking lot. There were random items scattered about everywhere, making the place look like something between a junkyard and a garage sale: twin leather recliners, a glass coffee table, an assortment of patio furniture in various states of disrepair. A large parasol was staked into the ground, a cabinet full of red plastic cups, a huge stuffed version of Rafiki from *The Lion King*. Toward one end of the field was a children's prefab playset, its swings replaced by tires. What must have once been just a pleasant, secluded meadow had since been turned into an elaborate Drunkball playing field.

Richie and Scott, after ogling Leila's body in the new light for a few seconds, raced out to lay claim to the leather recliners, Richie losing a couple of his beer cans on the way. They wrestled for the one recliner that actually reclined. When Scott won the battle, Richie went back to collect his fallen beers, then pulled an MP3 player and some speakers out of the backpack he was carrying and leaned down to plug them into an extension cord that ran from the shed.

"Wow, this is pretty nifty," Leila said, her hands on her hips, a slight shiver to her bottom lip. Hudson felt like pulling her close to keep her warm. "I didn't imagine there'd be lights."

"There didn't use to be," John said. "It was Hudson who got the idea to bring a generator. He set everything up. Even built that shed."

Leila raised her eyebrows at Hudson. "Did he now?"

"Smart guy, this one. It's why we keep him around. Made it a lot easier to play Drunkball. We used to lose a lot of dice and Frisbees."

"Dice and Frisbees? How the hell do you play this game?"

"Come on," John said, leading them toward the middle of the field. "Did you ever read *Calvin and Hobbes*, the comic strip?"

"Sure," Leila said. She was a few steps ahead of Hudson now, closer to John.

"Well, Drunkball is kind of a drunken version of Calvinball," John said as they approached the patio furniture next to the recliners. Hudson pulled a chair out for Leila and took a seat next to her as John continued. "The main rule of the game is that there are no rules. Or at least, no established rules. That way, we never play the same game twice, and we never get bored with it."

"And we all get drunk," Scott offered, already opening another beer.

"Exactly," John said with a smile. "Now, we realized that, as much fun as that idea is, it usually doesn't work that great. We couldn't think of enough fun rules on the spot, and people start losing interest. So we brought in a few different elements to the game to give it some structure. Every round, there has to be a new rule for every element of the game."

Hudson jumped in. "The elements are: Frisbees, dice, cards, and the obstacle course." He pointed at the playset. "The opening round—"

"Wait, so there are no balls involved in Drunkball?"

"Not when it's this group playing," Richie said, barely able to contain his proud laughter.

"You understand that you're incriminating yourself, too, right? If you're saying we as a group have no balls," Hudson said slowly, exaggerating his hand gestures as if he were trying to explain something to a child. "You're a part of this group, and you're admitting to having no balls."

Richie passed a hand through his beard, his brow furrowed as he tried to make sense of what Hudson had said. "All those things you're an expert on, I should have known balls was one of them." Richie high-fived Scott, and they burst into laughter.

"It's impossible to be condescending to these guys," Hudson said to Leila. She laughed and took a sip from her beer, giving his shoulder a squeeze.

John went back to explaining. "Well, there's always the *option* of balls," he said, glancing at Scott and Richie to make sure they wouldn't have another giggling fit, which they did. "There's the option of anything, really. As long as it's a fun rule that everyone agrees on, any player can introduce something new. The elements are just there to give us something to lean on."

"How does someone win?"

"We're seventeen-year-olds with our own island. We're already winners," John said.

Leila laughed again, and Hudson wondered if his friends felt the same way he did at hearing her laugh. If John, at being the one who'd made her laugh, felt the same rush of pride Hudson himself had felt, the same urge to be responsible for her laughter again and again.

"The game usually just kind of dies out when everyone's drunk," Hudson said, watching Leila drink from her beer can. It was true what he'd said about not being much of a drinker, but at that particular moment, having a beer with everyone did not sound like the worst thing in the world. He reached for one from the pack that John had set on the table.

"Whoa, what are you doing there?"

"Grabbing a beer."

John reached across the table and snatched the beer out of his hand. "Of all the nights we play and you never want to drink, you choose the one night before your big interview to join in? Nuh-uh, man. You're not showing up hungover. Leave the stupid decisions to those two." He pointed at Scott and Richie, who, for some unfathomable reason, were thumb-wrestling.

"We heard that," Scott said, not looking away from the battle in front of him.

"You can ref one more time. Tomorrow night, after you've kicked that interview's ass, we can come back here and play another round. We'll all camp out and crash here. But not tonight."

"Fine," Hudson grumbled. "I guess that makes sense."

Drunkball started with an opening round meant to prepare the players for the game ahead. One player would chug a beer while the other players each rolled one die. They'd add up the rolls until the drinker slammed the beer can upside down on the table; then the next person in line would become the chugger, and they'd repeat. Whoever accumulated the lowest score before his beer was finished would get to choose an element first.

Aside from establishing an order of play and matching up a player with the element he/she would be in charge of making up rules for, the opening round also helped to create an establishing buzz. And it loosened muscles to avoid the risk of strains, sprains, or any other injury that might occur during physical challenges.

As ref, Hudson had the privilege of adding any rule at any time, and he had fun with it, making his friends speak in accents or only be allowed to move via cartwheels. He loved the manifestation of Leila's enjoyment—how she reached out her hand and gripped his forearm, once pulling herself into his chest and laughing directly over his heart.

"New rule!" Leila shouted, about forty minutes into the game. They were standing near the playset, catching their breath from a physical challenge that involved juggling dice while going through the obstacle course. Her hair was now dry, although her clothes weren't, her cheeks slightly flushed from the alcohol and the running. "Any time one of you three looks anywhere below my neck, you have to chug the rest of your beer." She paused for dramatic effect, during which Scott lowered his sight to her breasts and drank happily. "And then Hudson gets to slap you."

"Bullshit!" Scott said. "I didn't hear the entire rule."

John looked to Hudson. "Ref, ruling?"

Richie interjected, "Wait, why does he get to check you out?"

"Because, first of all, he hasn't been ogling me as if I'm a thirty-second porn clip on the Internet."

"Are you saying I've been doing that?" Richie asked, trying to sound indignant despite compromising his credibility instantly as he snuck a glance.

"Ah! You did it, too. Chug the beer and get slapped by Hudson!" She laughed, then came over to Hudson and grabbed his arm, pulling him toward Richie and Scott. "Secondly," she added, lining the two of them up and lifting their beers for them so that they'd get to drinking, "I quite like your friend here. In case you hadn't noticed, when you lot showed up, I was getting ready to show him just how much. So, for interrupting us, he gets to slap you."

Leila went back to Hudson and took a sip of her beer, stumbling a little. Then she slipped her fingers in between his. "So, ref, what's your ruling?"

Hudson looked at his friends. Scott and Richie were obediently chugging the rest of the beer in their cans, and John was smiling confidently at Hudson, nodding at him. Leila's fingers interlaced with his, her thumb rubbing lightly against his. "I'll allow it."

Just when he was raising his arm to slap his friends, a noise broke through the trees. They all turned toward it and paused, trying to determine if it had been a figment of their imaginations or maybe just some small animal. Then they heard it again, this time distinct: a voice. John rushed to the shed and shut off the generator. The island fell into darkness again. The five of them held their breath, their eyes adjusting to the dark. Hudson felt Leila step closer to him, her side pressed against his.

Then the beam of a flashlight came shining in through the trees on the far side of the field, opposite from where they'd come in from. No one moved yet. "You think it's cops?" Richie asked in a whisper.

No one said anything. They held still until another flashlight came on, then another.

"To the boat!" Scott said a little too loudly, and they took off running for the trees, laughing with the thrill of a chase.

Hudson and Leila fell behind during the run. They ran hand in hand, trying to lead each other away from rocks on the ground and low-hanging branches. Hudson wanted to call out to his friends that the boat was a bad idea. But they had gained ground, and he didn't want to shout, so he tried to pick up the pace. Leila stifled her laughter behind him as she struggled to keep up. Just when he thought that they'd lost sight of the guys, they ran into John.

"We'll distract them," John said quietly. "It doesn't matter if we get caught, but I'm not letting you risk your scholarship by getting arrested for trespassing. You lay low." Then he ran back through the woods before Hudson could object.

"Shit," Hudson said, looking around, trying to determine in which direction to go. But before he could decide, Leila pulled on his arm, bringing them both tumbling down onto the ground. He worried that she might have gotten hurt, and he called out her name to see if she was okay. Then he felt her press close to him and put a finger to his mouth.

"Shh. We'll be safe here."

6

HUDSON LISTENED FOR noises beyond his own pounding heart. They were lying on the ground, his back pressed against the cool earth. Leila was tight against him, her skin warm and her breathing slow and deep and smelling of an alcoholic sweetness. Her head was resting on his shoulder, her hand still in his.

They'd taken cover where some fallen trees had landed on a little hill, creating a nook that, as it turned out, was just big enough to hide two people. They'd heard the guys get into the boat, the splash of the oars as they rowed away. Some moments later there'd been some unintelligible, muffled shouting. More than three voices, definitely. He and Leila had decided to stay hidden for a while, and that was fifteen minutes earlier. Now Hudson had been lying next to her for long enough to forget the danger and briefly hope that his life could continue simply the way it was. That tomorrow would be a day just like today, with the garage and Leila. Dinner with his dad in their backyard, nothing urgent to say to each other. He wished that could be every day.

Thinking about his dad stirred in Hudson a deep pang of shame and regret that he'd snuck out of the house, been deceptive. Then Leila squeezed his hand, and all his reservations disappeared.

Grass and leaves damp from the humidity clung to his arms. A barn owl screeched somewhere on the island. She looked up at him. "I'm sorry," she said. "I didn't mean to keep you out this late. I think I'm good to swim back across now. Let's get you home."

"No," he said. "There's nowhere else I'd rather be." He put his arm on her back, his fingers coming to rest at the base of her neck, massaging gently.

She smiled and shuffled closer to him, leaning her head against his shoulder. "You're not worried about the interview?"

"No. I'll make it on time. Right now I just want to stay here with you."

Leila curled up against him, her head on his chest, one leg over his lap. When he put his arm around her and they settled into each other, the comfort was so overwhelming that he thought he might fall asleep on the spot. He kept his eyes on the stars until they brought to mind the Northern Lights, at which point he looked down at Leila.

He'd never really done this before, just being close to someone. But this was something people never had to learn, never had to study for. Or, no, that wasn't quite right. This was like fixing an engine. All you needed was to find the right parts and put them together, watch them click into place.

He ran his arm up and down her back, slipping his hand beneath her shirt, exploring her skin with his fingers. It was more as if her skin were leading his fingers around, as if he had no option but to trace the lines of her shoulder blades, to follow the lace of her bra down the strap toward the clasp. His hand lingered there for a second, then, beckoned by her skin, it moved to the open expanse of her lower back, the faint dimples there, the soft curve of her hip. He rested his hand right there, the tip of his fingers at the edge of her shorts.

How long this went on for, Hudson couldn't tell. He pictured his cell phone in Leila's car, imagined his father calling over and over. But having Leila there instantly quelled his anxieties. She'd run her fingers through the hair by his temples, massaging his scalp. Or she'd shift her leg, and he'd feel the warmth of each other's skin go to new, fresh places. As long as she was there and not driving north and away from him, he was happy.

"Tell me a story," she said, the words spoken right into his chest, so he could feel her lips pulling away from and sticking a little to his skin.

"What kind of story?"

"I don't know. Anything. A bedtime story."

He was about to say that he didn't know any stories, but instead he said simply what he was feeling. "This is the greatest night of my life, I think." He paused and let the Mississippi air fill in the background noise as he gathered his thoughts. "Up until now my greatest moment was last year, when this old car my dad and I were restoring finally started. Or the time when I was five, at the park. I don't remember much from the memory except for the fact that I had fallen and was in pain. Then, out of nowhere, my dad came in and picked me up, almost as if I were weightless. I remember how happy and relieved I was.

"But this," he said, emphasizing by pressing Leila closer to him, if such a thing was possible. He could feel her skin filling in the gaps between his ribs, the hollows his hip bones created. "This is the highest peak I've ever reached."

He let some time pass, focusing on nothing but her in his arms. Then he leaned his neck toward her and kissed the top of her head. He kissed her softly, not because he wanted anything, but because he could no longer keep the kiss to himself. Without a word, she turned to him, and before he could think to do anything else, her lips were on his.

They kissed madly, like people who'd been waiting for it much longer than they had. Their bodies seemed to understand each other; their lips parted at the same time, their tongues moved in sync, their hands knew exactly when to grasp on to one another and when to explore elsewhere. Hudson wasn't sure whether it felt better to touch her or be touched by her, and he didn't care to decide.

He was vaguely aware of the night sky, the plentiful stars, the sound of the river and whatever life it contained. They rolled on the earth, and Hudson was aware of the ground only in that it was outside of them, that it was colder than the two of them, conscious of the occasional pebble or scratch of grass. Aside from those minute details, his world was entirely Leila.

○ ○ ○

When they finally stopped kissing, Leila curled herself against him, her head on his chest, one leg stretched across his lap. Hudson was certain that he was grinning like an idiot, but he didn't care anymore.

"Can I ask you a question?" She spoke softly. Not a whisper, exactly, but the kind of tone Hudson had always imagined people used when there was someone in bed with them. Close, intimate, the words not having to work hard to reach the other person.

"Sure."

She hesitated and brought up her hand to his jawbone, running her fingers from his chin to the spot behind his ear. "Why do you want to be a doctor?"

The question surprised him, not just because of the moment but because he couldn't actually remember anyone ever asking him before. "Um, I don't know," he said. "I just do." A mosquito buzzed past his ear, and he halfheartedly swatted at it. "I think I've been working for it long enough to forget the moment I made up my mind."

"Well, if you remember, let me know," she said, moving her hand to his chest and kissing his breastbone, then propping herself up on one elbow and studying his face. After a while she said, "You don't regret coming here with me?"

"Not even a little," he said. "I'm really glad I met you, and there is nowhere else I'd rather be."

She smiled that smile of hers, the smile that he knew he'd be comparing other smiles to for the rest of his life. Then she kissed him, slow and deep, not as hungry as before but just as rich. "Good," she said, and she repositioned herself, her face buried against his neck. Every now and then he'd feel the tickle of a hurried kiss on his skin, and he'd think of it as a kiss she couldn't keep to herself.

"I'm glad I met you, too," she said. "I sort of can't believe I did, this early on my trip. I was expecting something great to happen. Just not this."

"Something like what?"

Leila shifted against him, kissed the back of his hand. "It doesn't matter right now. I've got this."

One of Hudson's hands rested on Leila's waist; the other held her hand. He looked up at the stars in his Mississippi sky, thinking to himself that he never wanted to leave. A sigh escaped his lungs, a deep, gratifying sigh that might as well have been the first breath he ever took. Then, feeling the weight of Leila against him, unable to keep a smile from his lips, Hudson closed his eyes.

7

IT WASN'T THE light of the sun that woke him up, but the heat of the starting day and the sweat dripping down his lower back. Hudson opened his eyes in a panic, immediately noticing the absence of stars, the sky bruising with the oncoming sunrise that, under any other circumstances, might have been breathtakingly beautiful.

"Shit. Oh, shit. Shit, shit, shit." He nudged Leila until she woke up with a sleepy smile. "We have to go. We have to go right now." He lifted her gently by the shoulders until she rolled off him and watched him scurry around looking for the phone he realized he'd left in his car.

"What time is it?"

"Way too late. We have to go."

Hudson started doing math in his head to figure out how fast he'd have to go to make it to the interview on time. Leila was just barely getting off the ground. He looked across to the mainland as if that might help reduce the distance. She stretched, yawning. It was a shame that he couldn't take the time to appreciate her beauty in the morning light.

"Please, Leila, we have to hurry."

This time, he jumped first into the water, going as fast as he could.

When he reached the other side, he tried shaking himself dry as much as possible; then he helped Leila out of the river. Hudson hoped that his clothes would dry in time. He opened the car door for Leila, unable to break that habit even under the circumstances. He rushed around and got into the driver's seat, reached for the glove compartment, and grabbed his cell phone. It was flooded with missed calls and voice mails from his dad. It was 7:15. The interview was in forty-five minutes and about sixty miles away. "Shit," he said, shifting the car into reverse and getting them back on the road.

"Don't worry, we'll make it," she said, placing a hand on his thigh.

He didn't respond, but he brought one hand over to where hers was and gave it a squeeze before pulling it back to the steering wheel. He kept his eyes on the speedometer's rising needle, on the odometer adding on the miles. The car was heavy with silence.

They arrived at the Jackson campus of Ole Miss. It wasn't where Hudson would be attending, since it was just the medical center, but the dean had scheduled the interview there that day to keep Hudson from having to drive the two hundred miles to Oxford. There were a few buildings, and Hudson didn't exactly know which one to park near. He turned into the nearest parking lot and hoped he'd guessed right.

The parking lot was full of cars, mostly older, used models and pickup trucks. A couple of women in nurses' scrubs were sitting on a bench, drinking coffee and catching up on whatever nursing students catch up on.

Hudson pulled the car up to the curb in front of the nurses. He didn't look at the time so that it couldn't confirm his fears.

"Go," Leila said. "I'll park the car here and wait for you to finish. Good luck."

Hudson climbed out of the car, breaking into a sprint toward the nearest building. He knew well before he reached the doors that it was a futile act. He was doing it because his dad was there, watching from someplace inside Hudson's head. Hudson was dressed in clothes he'd not only slept in but had swum across a river in. Twice. His shirt was still a little damp, and his jeans were soaked. Even if this was miraculously the right building and he only had to find the dean's office, he'd be late. A good first impression was not about to happen. His only hope was that the dean would see him anyway, and that Hudson could somehow express himself well enough to wow the dean and make him forget about his tardiness and his presentation. But the chances of that happening in his current condition were unlikely. He'd slept only a few hours, and he could still feel Leila's touch on his skin.

He was just about to try the doors when he noticed a sign pointing to the Admissions Department in the neighboring building. He grumbled a few curse words and changed directions, rushing past the nursing students and hearing just a snippet of their conversation, ". . . it was absolutely awful. I even asked to speak to the manager, and I *never* do that . . ."

Only now, while running through the courtyard, did he realize that his muscles were sore from his night with Leila, wonderfully sore.

Finally, he turned a corner and reached the building entrance. He scanned the directory and rushed up the stairs to the second floor. Hudson felt himself relax a little when he saw the office empty save for a matronly woman sitting at a receptionist's desk. She was large, her hair up in a bun, her eyes rising from her book to look at Hudson. Maybe it was because she looked like an embodied cliché of a teacher, but Hudson thought he recognized her for a second.

"Hi," Hudson said, trying to offer a polite smile and not seem as if he'd just sprinted up the stairs. "My name's Hudson, I have a meeting with Dean Gardner. An interview." He cleared his throat a little and folded his hands in front of his stomach, as if that might hide his clothes.

The woman sighed and put her book down on the desk, turning to her computer screen. She played with the mouse a little bit and then hit the keyboard until the monitor came back to life.

"Hmm," she said after a moment. "You're late."

Hudson nodded, making sure to look ashamed of himself. "I know. I'm terribly sorry. I'll make sure to apologize to the dean. There's no excuse for it."

"Too late," she said with a sigh. "Sorry, hon. The dean waited twenty minutes. Then he had to go to a meeting across campus."

Hudson's immediate reaction was to hang his head. He kept it there for a moment, trying to think, until the receptionist asked if he was okay.

"There must be something I can do," he said. "When's his next open slot? I'll explain as much as I can in however much time he has."

The woman shook her head, angling her eyebrows sadly. She turned to the computer and made a show of scrolling up and down the calendar in front of her. "You were his last meeting here. He's across campus now, then at lunch with the school president, and then he'll be driving back to Oxford straight from there. Nothing I can do."

Despondent, Hudson turned away. He crossed the courtyard slowly, trying to think of how he could possibly explain himself to his dad. The two women were still chatting on the bench, steam rising from their coffee, thick like smoke from a train wreck. Leila had parked on the far side of the lot, her red car pointed away from the campus. She was sitting on the hood, her knees up and legs crossed in front of her, looking out at the road, which was as quiet as you'd expect on a Saturday morning. She looked tired but happy. There was some light bruising where her collarbone met her neck, a hickey Hudson hadn't noticed because of the morning's hectic mood.

Finally she noticed him and slid off the car. "What happened?"

"I didn't make it in time."

She threw her arms around his neck and pulled him in tight. "Shit, I'm so sorry." It was weird how he could recognize the hug's physical comforts yet not be comforted. "Maybe you can reschedule?"

He returned the hug briefly, then pulled away from her. "No, I can't reschedule. I just no-showed the most important interview of my life." He felt like hitting the car.

"Maybe if you—"

"Damnit, Leila, no."

The harshness of his voice surprised them both. He turned so that he was facing the road, Leila's pretty face and whatever expression it was contorted into—sadness, shock, disbelief—just out of sight, where it couldn't weaken the anger he wanted to be feeling.

A loud cackle echoed through the parking lot. Hudson turned around and saw one of the women with her head flung back, laughing. The heavier of the two was talking excitedly, and the laughing one waved her hand, as if begging her to stop.

Hudson caught himself biting on the end of his thumb, a nervous habit he usually tried hard to avoid, since he hated the little bumps of chewed-off skin that were left behind. This time he let himself go on. After a while, Leila walked up to Hudson so that her legs straddled his and he had nowhere to look except at her. She leaned in and kissed him on the cheek. All he could think about was the empty office where he should have been sitting, his back straight, keeping eye contact, projecting confidence and a genuine interest in his education—all those things that FAQs on the Internet had told him to do.

"Let's go," he said after a few moments. "I have to tell my dad."

Leila's eyes narrowed until he could only see green irises and black pupils that matched her hair. He dropped his gaze to the ground, focusing on the line where the paved lot met the grass, thinking about her story of the two different anthills. He walked around to the driver's side, opening the door and getting in behind the wheel before Leila had moved.

He turned the engine on before Leila got in, which she was slow to do. When she did, the air took on, simultaneously, the feel of weight and fragility. They were quiet, the only sound being the car itself, the brakes chirping whenever Hudson slowed for a turn. There was a clear sense that, if either of them spoke, something would break. He adjusted the rearview mirror wide to the right so that he wouldn't have to look in her direction. He drove brusquely, with quick accelerations, sudden braking, and jerky turns. *Angry driving,* his dad's voice said in his head, *is the most dangerous thing on the road.*

When they got back to Hudson's neighborhood, his dad's black Camaro was still in the driveway, sparkling in the morning sun as if it had just been waxed. Hudson parked Leila's car at the curb and let the engine idle for a moment. He gripped the steering wheel, trying to squeeze out the tension from his fingers. His left leg jittered nervously against the door, making something in the car rattle annoyingly.

Who the hell was this beautiful tornado of a girl who had come into Hudson's life and uprooted everything he'd known?

"All I had to do was stay at home," he said, looking out at his house. "Get some sleep, show up there on time. It was so easy. We could have stayed in. We could have . . . I don't know. Why did we have to go to the island yesterday, of all days?"

He could sense her eyes on him. "Your dad's a nice guy. He'll understand."

"It doesn't matter if he understands," Hudson said, his voice rising. "I may have just ruined my future. Don't you get it? This was my one shot at a full scholarship. There's no way they'll give me one now."

She reached out and put a hand over his, but he kept it tight on the steering wheel, his knuckles turning white. "I'm sorry this happened. But wasn't it worth it? It was still the greatest night of your life, right?"

In a few minutes, his dad would walk out, on his way to work. Hudson's stomach turned with guilt at the thought. His dad spent all his time in the garage, wanting only one thing for his son, and now Hudson had thrown it right back in his face, all for some girl. He couldn't help but bow his head, as if his shame could just drop right out of him.

"I don't know," he said, turning toward her. "It's hard to see it that way right now."

Leila's eyes glimmered in the rising sun. What right did she have to be so beautiful at a time like this?

Somewhere in the neighborhood, a car was coming down the road. Hudson could hear its engine, at least a V6, in good shape. Hudson wished they would have just stayed at home, fallen asleep on top of his comforter, woken up on time in merely sleep-wrinkled clothes, avoiding any room for doubt about whether or not it had been the greatest night of his life. But his night with Leila was tainted by this hungover morning.

"I didn't keep you on the island," Leila said, her voice calm, soft. "You did."

"What the hell are you talking about?" Hudson shot back. "The way you stayed parked outside my house last night? How was I not supposed to come running out? And we didn't have to swim across the river—that was your idea. We could have taken the boat, brought our cell phones with us, set an alarm. We didn't have to stay there all night. You knew I had the interview."

"You knew better than I did, Hudson." She brought her feet up to the dashboard, tucking her knees against her chest. "You want to pretend I was in control last night, go ahead. But we both know the truth."

"Yeah, what's that?"

"You chose to stay out there with me. We could have swum back. I even asked you if that was what you wanted." He couldn't take the sight of her eyes anymore and turned away, catching his own reflection in the window. "'No place I'd rather be.' That's what you said."

"I don't remember saying that." Hudson's leg still jittered against the car door, the annoying rattle filling the pauses between words, not letting silence grab hold of the air in the car. "And if I did, it's only because I wasn't thinking clearly." Leila's breath caught, as if it had stumbled on something. He could see her chin quiver ever so slightly.

Outside, Mrs. Roberson was walking her twin Chihuahuas, Bowser and Nacho, their tiny legs scampering to keep pace with her. She waved at Hudson cheerily, dressed in a pink tracksuit, her hair up in a ponytail. He raised his hand in response, feeling the tension in his fingers subside.

"You knew exactly what you were doing, Hudson," Leila said, her gaze following Bowser and Nacho's path down the street. "I think you were looking for an excuse to miss the interview. I think this happened for a reason, and as soon as you're done being scared of admitting what you really want, you'll see that maybe this is for the best."

Hudson snorted derisively. "What are you talking about? Without that scholarship, I can't afford school. Without school, I have no fucking future," he said. He shook his head, amazed that the girl who'd understood him so clearly just yesterday now didn't seem to get him at all.

Leila took her feet off the dashboard, slipping them back into the flip-flops and sitting up straight against the car seat. "Stop lying to yourself. You don't want to go to school, Hudson."

"You don't even know me, Leila. What makes you think you know what I want?"

Leila suddenly opened the car door, swinging around so that her feet were on the asphalt, her back turned toward Hudson. The morning sounds came in through the open door, birds chirping, insects, somewhere a couple of kids laughing.

"I've heard you talk about this town like it's the only thing you love aside from fixing cars. People go entire lives without figuring out exactly what they want from life. You already have it, and the future you and your dad have planned out for you is going to take it away from you." One of her hands went to her face, but Hudson couldn't see what she was doing with it. "You let us fall asleep on the oxbow because this is exactly where you want to be. You weren't just talking about being there with me. You're afraid of leaving Vicksburg, of leaving your dad."

Hudson felt short of breath. He opened his own door and swung his feet out onto the curb, so that he and Leila had their backs to each other, like an old married couple moving to opposite sides of the bed. "You don't know what you're talking about."

He stood up, slamming the door behind him. He meant to storm into his house, but his legs were weak, and he leaned back against Leila's car, his gaze on his front door, the rolled-up newspaper lying on the welcome mat, its pages crumpled from its collision against the side of the house. A few moments passed, Hudson taking deep breaths to steady himself, his legs refusing to move. Then he heard the rubber smacking of Leila's flip-flops stepping toward him.

He couldn't tell exactly what he felt when he saw that she was crying. Whether he wanted to comfort her and wipe her eyes dry or whether he wanted her to keep crying, each tear proof that he was not the only one at fault. There was another part of him that may have even been a bit proud that she cared enough about him to be crying. How could all those things exist inside him at the same time and not tear him into shreds, reduce him to a pile of rubble on the sidewalk?

"Okay, okay. I messed everything up," she said, standing right in front of him. "What can I do to fix this?"

"There's nothing you can do," he said, his voice calmer than he'd expected. It reminded him of his dad's voice. "Maybe you should just go."

A light breeze picked up, sending a waft of fresh-smelling air their way. Hudson realized that the two of them probably smelled of the river, of the ground they'd slept on, of yesterday. For how long would the smell or the sound of the river bring Leila to mind?

Her eyes were red, redder than they should have been, since only a couple of tears had slipped out and dripped wet streaks down her cheeks. Or maybe they were red from straining to keep the tears in. She took a breath, the air rushing into her lungs sounding thin and sharp, on the verge of whistling. "Okay," she said. "I will."

She threw her arms around him, too quickly for him to try to stop her. He could feel her tears dripping onto his neck. The breeze blew again and cooled the wet spots on his neck. It felt as if they might freeze.

Without another word, she kissed his cheek and then moved him aside to get into her car. The engine sounded good when it came to life—healthy, ready for her trip. He watched her struggle with the seat belt, then put the car into drive, glancing back at him and forcing a crooked, broken smile. Then the sun caught the window, and he couldn't see inside anymore, which was just as well, since she was already headed down the road.

The girl responsible for the best night of his life was gone, headed vaguely north—who knew exactly where. He stood out there on the curb for a few minutes, watching his block, the familiar driveways basking in the light of the morning sun. Hudson lingered there, as if waiting for something else to happen. Then he turned to his house, determined to put her out of his mind.

Treasure #2

Taped onto the door of a convenience store in Arkansas was a poster announcing the birth of a goat. "Come meet Darcy!" it said, listing the address and the date of birth (yesterday!). So I went. I don't think I'd ever been to a goat's birthday party before. There was no one else other than the family there, and even though they didn't know me, they served me a glass of sweet iced tea and introduced me to Darcy. Hudson, I've decided that my trip to see the Lights will be a treasure hunt. I'm going to steal your idea to look at the world as if it's always hiding something of value. I hope that's okay.   Take care.   Leila

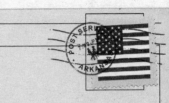

Hudson
I Don'tKnowYourLastName
27 Polar Shrimp Rd.
Vicksburg, MS 39180

BREE

1

THE ONE THING Bree could never deal with was the still time in between adventures. Back in Reno, time had not been valuable, so its waste didn't matter. But now, in her new life, every still moment was a suffocating one, a lost one. And no matter how badly she wanted to move, here she was, walking down the side of the highway in Kansas, kicking tufts of dried grass because there weren't even any pebbles. She waited, bored, for the next car to stick her thumb out at.

The strap on her duffel bag was cutting into her shoulder, so she shifted it over to the other side and examined the little tread marks it had left on her skin. She couldn't tell if the redness was from the strap or from the sun beating down on her all day. The bag wasn't heavy— she never packed much, simply because she had fallen in love with the idea of traveling light—so she assumed that the redness was from the sun. She unzipped the bag and pulled out one of the three shirts she owned, a once-fluorescent-green tank top, and draped it over her head to keep her face from burning.

She sighed loudly and looked up at the sun as if it were to blame for the lack of cars. Here she was, light like dandelion fluff, ready for the wind to whisk her away, and nothing was happening.

Finally, the glimmer of something silver headed her way. She stuck her thumb out and even leaned a little forward, in case cleavage was more easily spotted. She hoped it wasn't a trucker. Truckers were sometimes friendly but too often creepy instead—they were the reason she'd learned to carry a steak knife with her.

The sound of tires rushing against the pavement was as beautiful as any song she'd ever heard. She held her breath as the sedan came into view, but the car showed no signs of slowing, and within seconds the tires had whizzed past her.

Bree cursed at the gust of wind that trailed in the car's wake and had knocked her green tank top to the asphalt. She grumbled as she knelt down to pick up the shirt, so anxious to get going that she almost didn't see the second car coming. She stood back up and stuck her thumb out again, and the car instantly slowed down, the brakes not quite screeching but chirping loudly enough to be heard through the music that was blasting from inside. The car was old and crummy, its red paint job aiming for brilliance but coming closer to dried blood. Even the hubcaps were dark red.

Bree took a couple of steps toward the car and leaned over to look through the rolled-down passenger-side window. It surprised her to see that the driver was a girl more or less her age. She rarely saw other teens on the road, especially not on their own.

"Where you headed?" the driver called out over the music, which she hadn't bothered to turn down.

"Anywhere," Bree called back, exactly as she'd said over and over again, the perfect nomadic answer. She glanced at the interior of the car, taking in the iced coffee in the cup holder, the scattered receipts, the trash bag secured to the gearshift and stuffed to the brim with empty plastic bottles and junk-food wrappers. The inside of the car was red, too, but there it succeeded in its brilliance and looked almost new. The upholstery was red, the steering wheel was red, even the forgotten liquid in the Gatorade bottle on the floor was red.

"Perfect," the girl said, and she motioned with a nod for Bree to come in.

She opened the door and climbed in, hoisting her duffel bag into the empty backseat of the car. She could feel her heart start to beat harder with the familiar sensation of adrenaline and motion. It was as if her heart was not simply pumping blood around her body but pounding the stillness out of her system.

The driver seemed to consider the open road for a second, as if daring it to keep her from gunning her engine. "I'm Leila," she said.

"Bree."

Leila nodded and offered a smile. Then the car rolled forward, and the wind started rushing in through the open window, pulling loose strands free from Bree's ponytail. They flapped stingingly against the back of her sunburned neck and danced wildly across her eyes, thick tresses that had nearly turned to dreads during her nine months of roaming.

After a mile or so, when the song playing through the stereo system ended, Leila turned down the music and rolled up her window halfway. "So, what's your story?"

"I don't have a story," Bree said, still needing to more or less yell over the sound of the highway.

"Everyone has a story," Leila said, combing back her black tresses over her ear, only to have the wind uproot them. It made Bree feel somehow connected to the girl, how their hair danced.

"Well, then, my story is . . ." She motioned to the highway. "You know. Here. Going. The road."

Leila looked over her shoulder, taking her eyes off the road long enough for Bree to get nervous. "Did you run away from home?"

They passed a sign saying that they had fifty miles to go to reach Kansas City, and Bree gave a little nod. She closed her eyes, focusing on the feel of the wind on her skin. She didn't blame Leila for asking, since Bree had wondered the same about others, but she still hated being asked. Mostly because no matter how much she dressed it up with the details of her departure, no matter how much life she'd soaked up since, the basic truth was simple: Yes, she had run away. As they did all too often during quiet moments, thoughts of Bree's sister, Alexis, rushed in. She opened her eyes. "What about you?" She asked. "What's your story?"

"North," Leila said, as if it explained everything.

"That's it? That's not much of a story."

Leila turned to look at Bree, eyes green and full of so much life that Bree almost felt jealous of what they might have seen. "I have to go to Alaska. I've got a rare medical condition where I can't be away from the magnetic poles for too long, or my body starts to decompose."

Bree shifted uncomfortably in her seat, tensing up. She wasn't good at dealing with diseases. She'd dealt with her parents' for long enough. Then Leila cracked a smile. Bree relaxed. "Shut up. I almost believed you."

Leila leaned in toward the steering wheel as her body shook with laughter. "Wow, I did not think that you'd fall for that. I'm not usually a good liar." She controlled her laughter, then said, "No, I'm going to Alaska to see the Northern Lights. I want to take some pictures for my school portfolio."

Bree nodded and looked out her window at the midwestern sky. She sometimes felt as if she might be swallowed up by it. The music coming from the speakers was fast, brimming with energy that resonated with Bree and clashed with the emptiness of the landscape. "That's pretty cool," she said. "Ever seen them before?"

"Just in pictures. Have you?"

Bree turned away from the window. "Yeah, when I was a kid. In Europe." The memory was faint, the sight of the Northern Lights overwhelmed by the presence of her parents. She couldn't even remember if it had been Switzerland or Denmark where she'd seen them, or how her mom had smelled: coffee on her breath or soap on her skin. Bree often wished she'd paid more attention before the smell of sickness started invading everything. "I don't really remember them all that well, though."

"Hmm," Leila said, momentarily lost in thought. She brought a hand up to her mouth and chewed absentmindedly on the skin between her thumb and forefinger.

"How long have you been on the road for?" Bree asked.

"I'm just getting started. The later it is in summer, the better the chance to see the Lights, so I'm going slowly," Leila said, moving both hands to the steering wheel. "You?"

"Um, it's been a few months, I guess. It's hard to keep track of time after a while. Which is kind of how I like it."

"Why's that?"

"When you don't have any reason to think of days as weekdays or weekends, you start to realize that all days are pretty much the same. And that kind of gives you the freedom to do whatever you want. It's a lot easier to seize the day than it is to seize a Tuesday. You have errands on Tuesday. On Tuesday you eat pizza again. Your favorite TV show is on Tuesday, you know? But *the day* ..." she said, adding hand gestures to signify the importance. "*The day* is all just hours you're alive for. They can be filled with anything. Unexpectedness, wildness, maybe a little bit of lawlessness, even." She looked over at Leila to gauge her reaction. "If that makes sense."

Leila glanced away from the road to smile appreciatively at Bree. "Yeah, I think I know what you mean." She turned back to the road. "Seize the Tuesday." A few moments passed. A new song came on, another burst of energy and liveliness. Bree reached back to her bag to grab a granola bar and offered one to Leila, which she accepted with a thank-you.

When she was done with it, Leila stuffed the wrapper into the plastic bag hanging off the gearshift. "You ever find it easier said than done? The whole seizing-the-day thing. *Carpe diem* is a pretty well-known philosophy, but if it were easier to put into practice, we wouldn't have to be reminding each other of it all the time."

Bree laughed. "Yeah, I guess that's true." She uselessly combed her matted hair back behind her ear, only to have the dreadlocks flap in the wind again. "You just have to have something that constantly reminds you to do it. I don't really ever have to tell myself to seize the day. It's just, whenever I'm not, I feel like I'm slowly disintegrating or something. Like my soul is itching, and if I don't actively live my life, it'll never stop."

"Yeah? What is it that reminds you?"

"Dead parents," Bree said. She didn't want to bring the mood down, but it was the one thing she could never lie about.

"Sorry," Leila said. Then, after a beat, she added, "I've got the whole degenerative-disease thing reminding me to seize my days."

"Shut up."

"So, how do you know if you're actively living your life? Is there an exact recipe you could write down for me?"

Bree laughed again, thrilled now that it hadn't been the silver sedan that picked her up. "There's no formula. You're either doing it, or you're not. I just know that sometimes my soul itches, and sometimes it doesn't. This, for example. This conversation. Right now, heading off toward Kansas City or wherever the hell we're going, talking about this stuff. If I were to die right now, I wouldn't be entirely upset."

Leila simply nodded for a while, smiling. The high-pitched sound of the tires carrying them down the highway, the wind pushing against the car in gusts overtook the music for a moment. Outside, the world was exactly three colors: the yellow of the tall grass desiccated by the rainless summer, and the black streak of the road, which seemed to climb straight up into that bright blue sphere of sky.

Without another word, Leila reached for the volume dial and turned it all the way up as she sped the car down the highway. She started smiling wildly, drumming her fingers on the dashboard. When the chorus broke out, she joined in, screaming the words as if the world was meant to hear them. Bree sang right along with her, improvising until she could make sense of the lyrics.

2

WHEN BREE JOLTED awake, they were pulling into a gas station.

"'The Trapeze Swinger' by Iron and Wine," Leila said, unbuckling her seat belt. "If you're even a little bit tired, it's impossible to stay awake for the whole song."

Bree stretched her muscles, trying to find a way to pull every single one of them into wakefulness all at once. "How long have I been out for?"

"Not long—about half an hour." Leila parked the car at one of the pumps. "Sorry if I woke you up. We need gas."

"No, I'm up," Bree said, blinking away the sleep from her eyes. "I hate sleeping anyway. I always feel like I'm missing out on something."

Leila got out of the car, leaning against it as the fuel pumped in. Bree opened her door and joined Leila, squinting at the midday sun. She looked around at the gas station, noticing that it looked just like one in Reno, down to the surrounding trees, the streak on the front window. She and Alexis used to stop there to pick up snacks to sneak into movies, back when Alexis had just started to drive and their dad was sick—well, before Alexis met her fiancé, Matt. Skittles and a bag of chips, always.

"I know what you mean," Leila said. She did that thing where she chewed on the skin between her thumb and forefinger again. "Want anything from inside?"

"I'll come with you," Bree responded. She let Leila start walking and then grabbed her duffel bag from the backseat and swung it over her shoulder. They passed a man in his twenties working the credit-card reader at his automated pump. He noticed them walk by, and Bree could almost sense the stupid and insulting pick-up lines in his eyes. She suppressed the urge to throw something at him and entered the convenience store.

The clerk was tall and sporting a moustache. His build must have once been athletic but was well past its best days. He glanced at them disinterestedly, then went back to watching something on a small TV beside the register.

Leila led the way to the back of the store, which was made up entirely of coolers shelving beverages. Bree joined her and crossed her arms, then looked back to see if the clerk was still distracted. She unzipped her duffel bag and shifted it over to her right side, where Leila was standing. Then she opened the door to the cooler and quickly but casually placed two bottles of water and a tall can of iced tea into her bag. She closed the cooler door gently and stepped away, crossing her arms again.

Leila sidestepped closer to Bree, keeping her eyes on the drinks in front of her. Bree noticed that she was quite a bit taller than Leila, maybe five or six inches. She was also thinner from her months on the road.

Her skin was darker, worn by the sun, and perhaps not at its cleanest. Leila leaned in toward Bree with a slight grin. "What was that?"

"My soul's itchy," Bree said. "Have you ever shoplifted before?"

"No, not really."

"It sounds stupid, but it's kind of a thrill."

Leila didn't look too sure, glancing over at the clerk.

"Seizing the day isn't always about something meaningful," Bree said, slipping another tea into the bag. "Sometimes it's just about indulging in stupid whims that make you feel alive."

Leila made a why-the-hell-not kind of shrug and moved toward the cooler directly in front of Bree. She opened it, keeping her back toward the clerk, and reached in blindly, pulling out the first thing she got her hand on. She slipped it inside Bree's bag, and her eyes widened with excitement.

"You feel it?" Bree asked.

Leila grinned, then whispered a little too loudly, "Let's take more!"

They took a couple of sodas and an energy drink; then Bree grabbed a small bottle of water and kept it in her hand for appearance's sake. The clerk was oblivious or simply too far gone to care. Keeping their faces as stoic as possible, they moved over to the row of candy bars, which proved to be a little too easy. The chocolate bars fit snugly in the palms of their hands, their wrappers too tight to crinkle. They siphoned off a couple of handfuls anyway, and Bree tucked them into one of her shirts inside the bag.

They turned the corner, and Bree nearly bumped into the chips display. Now, this was a challenge. The aisle was closest to the clerk, most of it in plain view if he happened to look up. And there was the way chips bags rustled as soon as they were picked up, as if they were setting off an alarm. And somewhere beneath all of that was the memory of her and Alexis in the movie theater all those years ago, trying to extract chips without making noise, their own version of Operation.

Bree's bag was heavier than it had been in a long time, its strap pulled down by the weight of stolen goods, reviving the sting of her sunburn. Leila kneeled down, pretending to tie her shoes, and shoveled packages of beef jerky and sunflower seeds into the bag. Bree held up a pack of gummy bears and pretended to read the nutrition information. She heard a noise and looked over at the clerk, who had pulled out his cell phone and was scrolling up and down his contact list or his messages, as if begging someone to take him away from his monotony. He looked over at the two of them, his gaze lingering for a while on Leila, whose rear was pointed in his direction as she knelt. Bree adjusted the strap, careful not to move the bag too much.

"I'm gonna head outside for a smoke," he called, his voice gravelly and higher-pitched than Bree had expected. "If you ladies don't mind. Just holler when you're ready to be rung up."

"Sure thing."

He stepped around the counter and then out the door. They could see him through the glass, opening a new pack of cigarettes, tapping it languidly against the flat of his hand.

"He is making this incredibly easy on us," Leila said, a little suspiciously. She looked over at the security cameras behind the register.

"People have a long, stupid history of mistakenly trusting those they find attractive," Bree said, moving over to the coffee section and tossing a couple of glazed doughnuts into a paper bag.

Leila put the doughnuts into Bree's bag and laughed out loud. "Wow, we took a lot." Then she got a mischievous grin that spoke directly to Bree's soul. "Let's see how much we can fit."

What they managed to fit were three frozen burritos, a few packets of ramen noodles, a bottle of hot sauce, and even a perplexing miniature sewing kit on sale for two dollars among the containers of motor oil and antifreeze. They took as much as Bree's bag would allow, and then, just for the hell of it, they grabbed a little more, a packet of Twizzlers, making it impossible to fully zip up Bree's bag, the wrapping showing like the wet nose of a curious pet. Outside, the smoking clerk was staring forlornly out at the highway on-ramp. His cigarette was all the way to the filter, but he lingered a while longer.

Bree got an idea. She walked over to the big cardboard display of a celebrity that was propped up near a stack of soda twelve-packs. She picked it up, careful not to knock anything over.

"What are you doing?" Leila asked her.

Bree handed the cutout to Leila and grabbed a bright yellow packet of gum from the counter. "It's so much more exciting when they can *see* the things you're stealing from them. Just walk out with me and smile."

Leila hesitated, then held the door open for Bree. "Of all the things I'd thought I'd be, I never figured I was an adrenaline junkie. You're corrupting me."

"That's just what boring people call those of us who are open to excitement," Bree said, knowing she was a little full of herself but enjoying the sound of the words anyway, believing them to be true. She stepped outside and immediately addressed the clerk. "I left ten dollars on the counter," she said, holding up her bottle of water and the gum to show what they'd taken. "You can keep the change if you let us take this display."

His vacant gaze went from Bree to Leila holding the cardboard cutout. It was a look she'd seen before, people too far settled into their lives. Then he chuckled and shrugged. "You kids be safe."

They walked slowly but triumphantly to the car, and once inside they burst into laughter, the kind of manic laughter that refuses to die down, grasping on to everything around it and saying, *Look, this is funny, too.* Leila tossed the cardboard display into the backseat and, still laughing, put her forehead on Bree's shoulder. When they could control themselves, Leila started the car, and Bree realized that it had been a while since she had truly shared a laugh with someone. She'd laughed *with* others, sure. But they'd either been drug-addled laughs or laughs directed at a television. Those were isolated laughs, lonelier. This—well, it was sisterly.

3

"I THINK I'VE been here before," Bree said when they reached downtown. She fiddled with the air-conditioning vents, lowered and raised the windows, hoping and failing to find the ideal air flow.

"Kansas City?"

"Yeah," she said, looking around. "My family used to take a lot of road trips. It's hard to tell with downtowns, though. They all have something to distinguish them, sure, but if someone blindfolded you for a few hours and dropped you off right here, it would take you a while to figure out where you were."

"That'd be an interesting social experiment. Blindfold people and drop them in a city they can't immediately recognize."

"I think most people would just curl up on the floor and cry."

"I guess that's what I'm doing on this trip."

Bree raised an eyebrow. "Curling up on the floor and crying?"

Leila laughed. "No. Blindfolding myself and dropping in on strange cities. I guess I know where I'm going before I get there, but I don't think it'd be much different if someone just dropped me off. I'd stumble about, find something to eat, watch people and think about them and the world and, if I'm being honest, mostly myself."

They were at a red light, and Leila was biting the limbs off her gummy bears.

Bree reached for her drink. "This heat's worse than Reno," Bree said. "I should have had to pee twice by now, but I'm sweating out everything I'm drinking."

"Yeah, sorry about the AC. I think the mechanic I took it to didn't fix it on purpose so that I'd have to come back."

"Really? That's messed up."

"No. Not really. It's just an old car." Leila sighed and popped the torso of a gummy bear into her mouth. "So, you're from Reno?"

"Yup. Biggest little shithole in the world."

"When are you going back home?"

Bree shook her head as she chewed down some beef jerky. "I'm not."

"Why not?"

"My sister was making my life hell," Bree said, surprising herself with her candor. She'd only talked about it with one other person, some boy in San Francisco, mostly because he was quiet enough to be a good listener and their skin on each other seemed to pull secrets out of their hiding places. "Our parents died within a year of each other, and she stepped in as my guardian, but she took the position a little too seriously. So I left," Bree said, choosing not to give the whole story.

"Do you keep in touch with her?"

"No," Bree said. She took another bite of beef jerky and watched as a minivan pulled into a parking lot across the street and a young, attractive couple got out. "I didn't leave on the best of terms. We didn't always get along, but after our parents died, all we did was fight. She'd get mad at me for going out and partying—which I was only doing because how the hell else are you supposed to react when you're orphaned at fifteen?—and I'd get mad at her for trying to baby me. Plus she was spending all her time with her boyfriend, Matt."

The minivan let out a beep as its doors locked. Bree watched the couple walk away, the woman pushing a stroller, the man holding a little girl over his shoulder.

"Do you ever miss your old life?" Leila asked.

Bree raised a cold soda can to her forehead as the light turned green. "When I'm in between places, maybe. No matter how much I love the road, logistically it's impossible to keep moving all the time. Sometimes I get the urge to go back. But I can't even imagine facing my sister."

"Why?"

"She never cried at the funerals," Bree said calmly, as if it didn't break her heart just to think of it. It wasn't a lie, but it wasn't exactly the truth, either. "She can say what she will about my actions, but at least I had the decency to feel something."

Leila acknowledged this with a little "Hmm," which Bree preferred over one of those empty responses that most people gave.

After half an hour of aimless driving, the air hadn't cooled at all. The faux-velvet seats had become uncomfortably sticky, so they decided to park and stretch their legs for a bit. Seeking solace from the heat, they chose a spot under the shade of a tree with long, low-hanging branches that reached out over the street like protective arms.

Across the road from them, surrounded by a ten-foot white wall that stretched farther than Bree could see, was the Kansas City Country Club. The landscaping outside was immaculate, everything bright green and evenly trimmed, bushes rounded into perfect spheres. Every now and then a car would drive up to the lone valet attendant. The people getting out of the cars were dressed up, the men in expensive-looking suits, cuff links, and pocket squares, the women decked out in jewelry and brand-name handbags. A big, golden Mercedes came up the driveway. A car like that had never once stopped to pick Bree up when she was hitchhiking.

"I bet that Mercedes has some pretty sweet AC," Bree said.

"I bet," Leila said. She wiped at the sweat on her forehead. "It looks like there's some kind of event going on."

The sun was still high, the sunset a couple of hours away. Bree felt her shirt stick to her lower back. "Yeah . . ." Bree said, her voice trailing off. "You think they'd mind if we borrowed it for a little while?"

Leila turned to Bree, arching one eyebrow. "It would be nice to drive around with some air-conditioning for a bit. Why? Your soul getting itchy again?"

They watched the valet attendant get into the car, drive about fifty feet up the driveway, and turn into the parking lot that was hidden from view. After a few moments he reappeared, trotting back to the entrance, waiting for the next car to show up. He left the keys of the Mercedes on a hook next to about two dozen other sets of luxury-car keys.

"We'll just borrow it for an hour," Bree said. "They won't even notice it's gone."

"I'm not so sure about that. Rich people have a weird sixth sense about their belongings."

"It'll just be a few quick laps on the highway."

"Quick because there'll be someone chasing us?"

"No one will be chasing us."

"I know," Leila said. "I'm stalling because I'm nervous."

"Hey, I'm not gonna deny you the right to be nervous. But once you've dealt with your nerves, I think you know what we have to do."

"What do we say if someone catches us?"

"That we were dying of heat stroke and it was a medical emergency," Bree said.

Leila paused. "Then we'll come right back and leave it exactly where it was before?"

"Same parking spot."

Another car was coming up the street, likely headed for the club. The girls looked at each other, grinning like madmen. Bree could feel her heartbeat speed up.

Bree opened the door. "Come on, we'll grab the keys when the valet's parking this car."

Leila took a few deep breaths, as if she was about to try swimming a long distance underwater. "Seize the Tuesday," she said.

They jogged across the street and hid behind the outer wall of the country club. When they heard the valet start pulling the car around, they left their cover and walked quickly up the driveway. The keys were hanging unprotected, as tempting as pies cooling on windowsills. Bree reached them first, grabbing the set with that recognizable Mercedes symbol glinting silver in the sunlight. It was almost disappointingly easy.

"Just act like you belong here," Bree said as they walked into the parking lot. "The best ID in the world is a smile and a wave."

The weight of the keys in her hand already felt so gratifying, more than her entire duffel bag of stolen goods had. She couldn't wait to get into the car, to start the engine, to drive around and pretend that cold air had been their only motivation.

"Can I help you guys?"

The valet appeared up ahead, a couple of rows over. He wasn't bad-looking, Bree thought to herself. He was goofy in his valet's vest, his white button-down shirt more shoved into his pants than patiently tucked. He had the kind of facial hair that can't quite yet be more than scruff.

"We just need to get something out of the car," Bree said, not slowing down.

The valet squinted at them, noticing the keys in Bree's hand. She closed her fist tightly against them, as if he might try to take them away from her forcefully. She wondered if they could outrun him.

"Oh," he said, starting to walk in their direction. "Are, uh, are you guys club members?"

"My parents just forgot something," Bree said, pointing vaguely in the direction of the golden Mercedes.

Leila followed Bree's lead, but the valet kept walking toward them, as if he meant to cut them off. He'd pulled his cell phone out of his pocket. "Okay," he said, but it was clear that he wasn't going to leave them.

Shit, Bree thought, sensing an impassable obstacle. Then she remembered how easy it had been to just walk away with all they'd stolen at the convenience store, how that guy pumping his gas had looked at them. The Mercedes was only about three cars away now, close enough that the remote would have no trouble unlocking the doors. She met the valet's gaze, searching his rather pretty eyes for something besides suspicion.

"Can I ask you a question?" she said, stepping right up to him.

"Um," he said. They were standing by the Mercedes now. The valet's gaze went from the car, to Leila, to Bree, who was now less than an arm's length away. "Sure."

"When was the last time you felt really alive?"

"What?"

Without another word, Bree put her hand on his waist and pulled herself toward him. She kissed him with abandon. Despite what had happened, Bree still believed in reckless kisses. She pulled back and couldn't help but laugh at the dazed look in the valet's eyes.

"Whoa," he said.

"Listen, I'm going to be honest with you," Bree said, keeping an arm around his waist. "This is not our car. But we're not stealing it."

"No?" He looked at the two girls, and Bree wondered if his worries were already being replaced by fantasies.

"No. But we do plan on borrowing it."

"Uh," he said. "I don't know if I can—"

"Just an hour," Bree said. "We'll bring it back before anyone notices."

"I don't think that's a good idea."

Bree kissed him again. His scruff was ticklish but not in a bad way, more like a finger tenderly grazing the contours of her lips. This time, she brushed her tongue against his before pulling away. A smile tugged at the corner of his mouth.

"You just pretend you never saw us," Bree said, stepping away from him, her heart pounding with adrenaline. "And we'll come back in an hour with the car. Then, when you get off work, we can all hang out together."

He scratched his chin, looked at Leila leaning against the Mercedes, then turned back to Bree, his eyes roaming past the neckline of her shirt. A honk sounded from behind them. "Damnit," he said, turning toward the front of the club. "Okay. Okay. Wait until I pull this car in, and then you can go." He started a halfhearted jog back to his valet stand, looking over his shoulder. "See you guys later," he called back.

When he ran out of sight, Bree turned to Leila and unlocked the doors. "Time for some German air-conditioning."

"You're my new hero," Leila said, climbing into the passenger seat.

Bree smiled to herself and got into the driver's seat. She had expected the interior to smell like leather, or that new-car smell she had once read was actually formaldehyde. But it smelled of stale cigarettes and body odor, of too much cologne and perfume. She wondered if the windows had ever been rolled down.

They started the car and immediately blasted the air-conditioning. It was wonderfully powerful and loud, as if the German engineers who had designed it wanted to create not just air but wind. When the valet drove up in the new car, a silver BMW, Bree waved at him and pulled slowly out of the parking lot and down the driveway. She could feel her heart pounding away the stillness again.

When they reached the street, Bree revved the engine beyond what was necessary, the trees on the side of the road turning into blurs so suddenly that it felt cartoonish.

"Did you hear how he said, 'Whoa,' when you kissed him?"

Bree laughed and pressed the gas pedal down a little harder. It barely offered any resistance. They shot past a yellow traffic light, and a woman walking her dog shook her head in disgust.

They turned the now-cool air-conditioning to its full potential, lowered the windows, and let out a yell that would have made Maurice Sendak's Wild Things quiver with delight. The car roared in unison, the air rushing in and making their hair dance across their eyes. Maybe she was just imagining it, but Bree could feel the adrenaline rushing through her body, microscopic particles crashing around in her veins, little wild things in their own right. She let out another yell, a lung-emptying bellow that the wind grabbed a hold of and swirled together with Leila's laughter.

Bree found the highway and quickly turned the Mercedes onto the on-ramp. She stepped harder on the accelerator, so hard that she could practically feel the fuel burning. Leila drummed on the dashboard as if their getaway was soundtracked by one of those burst-of-energy songs. Bree could see for miles. It was just her, Leila, the Kansas City metropolitan area spread out beneath the big midwestern sky, and the highway disappearing inch by inch into the horizon, beckoning them forward.

4

BREE BARELY NEEDED to nudge the wheel in order for the Mercedes to swiftly maneuver in and out of lanes. This was not the first time Bree had ever driven a car. Alexis had on occasion given her lessons around their neighborhood or in the vast parking lots of shopping malls in Reno. But this was the first time Bree had felt the joy driving could bring, how a car could make its driver feel powerful, like a beast unleashed.

When the flow of traffic started to slow, Bree took the nearest exit. She drove cautiously and inexpertly on the city streets. She took them back downtown, looking for an audience at which to secretly flaunt their stolen car.

"Park here," Leila said, pointing at a small lot. "Let's go find some celebratory ice cream."

"Celebratory ice cream?"

"Nothing's more suitable," Leila said, "not even alcohol. It's the secret every parent instinctively knows: Ice cream makes everything better. I'm surprised hospitals aren't all stocked with every flavor of Ben and Jerry's."

Bree thought back to her parents' stints in the hospital, how she and Alexis actually used to go make ice cream runs, either to fill the time or because their mom couldn't handle eating anything else. "Now you're talking," she said, parking the car. As they got out, Bree thought of something. "How'd you know, by the way? That hospitals don't stock any good ice cream. Who'd you have to visit?"

Leila turned quickly, as if caught doing something wrong. Then she cast her eyes downward and shrugged. "My little sister had tonsillitis."

They found a shop nearby. It was decorated in the vein of an old-fashioned soda fountain; a long counter lined with stools, and, outside, a candy-striped awning over a couple of stainless-steel tables. "This looks so much like a place in San Fran," Bree said, pulling out a chair and turning it to face the street. "They had all these crazy flavors, like roasted pineapple, spicy chocolate, and basil."

Leila licked at her scoop of strawberry and put her feet up on the chair in front of her. "That sounds amazing."

"Yeah. I could rarely afford to go there, which made it so much better when I could."

"How long were you there?"

"Just a couple of weeks, right after I left home," Bree said, watching the traffic go by.

"I've never been. How was it?"

"Bit of a shit show, to be honest." Bree chuckled.

There was a certain amusement in watching how miserable everyone was sweltering, in their cars. Bree liked seeing the little details: ties loosened in a yank or two and then forgotten;

conversations yelled into hidden, hands-free headsets; ponytails coming apart like fabric being unwoven.

"Come on," Leila said, finishing off the last of her waffle cone. "It's been a while since my adrenaline spiked. Let's go find something to do."

o   o   o

Bree and Leila passed a park busy with a number of Little League games. The basketball courts were a blur of bright-colored shorts and shirts. Swarms of bugs surrounded the overhead lights, and Bree parked but kept the engine on for the air-conditioning, then noticed the stale cigar stench and decided to crack the windows. A warm stream of air slipped in through the opening.

Bree thought about the arc of her day in terms of temperature, starting with the sunburn on the side of the road, the sweltering heat in Leila's car, the cold initial blast from the Mercedes, and now the miraculous way that dark could make the air pleasant. "People don't appreciate the Earth's rotation enough," she said, slipping a finger through the cracked window.

Leila laughed. "That was a bit of a stoner comment."

Bree shrugged, relishing the feel of the air on her finger. "Nah, I quit all the stoner stuff when I left San Francisco. The occasional weird comment is all part of seizing the day. The appreciation eventually just comes pouring out of you."

Leila lowered her window and stuck her hand out. "How did you and your sister not get along? You're one of the coolest people I've ever met."

Bree turned to face Leila with a smile. "We just clashed. She was always kind of uptight, and I'm . . . the way that I am. And this is a calmer version, too. A few months ago I was a little more, um, aggressive about having a good time."

"And you said she was being too parental?"

"Yeah. Sometimes it seemed like we were just pretending. She'd get mad and scold me, and I'd throw out these exaggerated teenage clichés, like 'You're ruining my life,'" Bree said in a bratty voice, lowering her window the rest of the way. "I kept expecting Alexis to finally crack a smile, or to cry, or something. But all she wanted to do was discipline me, and that only pissed me off more. I guess on some level I expected that what we'd gone through would bring us closer, you know, bridge the gap between our personalities. Instead, she shacked up with some law student and seemed to hate me more by the day."

Leila didn't respond for a while. They both stared out at the game. "How did your parents die?"

Bree picked at the steering wheel's leather. "My mom had lung cancer. She got sick first. I was fourteen, and Alexis was eighteen." She glanced over at Leila, then ran a finger along the length of the car door, her hands unwilling to keep still. "Within a year, Dad died, too. Sometimes I don't know whether to be thankful or appalled that at sixteen I've already lived so many lives."

Bree sighed, then waved her hand through the warm air. "I'm glad I left," she said, turning to smile at Leila. "I get to seize more days."

"It's been a good day," Leila said.

"Very good day," Bree repeated, glad that Leila wasn't pressing the conversation. "So, what's next?"

"I don't know. I was thinking of covering a bit more ground today. We could go take this car back, pick my car up, and head north for a few more hours."

"Where do you usually sleep?"

"Every now and then I'll get a motel room, but they're so goddamn lonely, I'd much rather sleep in the car." Leila turned down the AC and then lowered her window all the way, leaning her head partly out to sniff the air. "You're more than welcome to tag along, if you don't have any other plans."

"Sweet," Bree said. "No plans. Just how I like it."

"Let the adventure continue, then," Leila said, reading Bree's mind.

A cheer sounded from the soccer field. Bree watched the kids from the scoring team run into a massive hug, the parents applauding wildly, happiness plastered on everyone's face. The kids on the other team looked on at the celebrations as if they wished they'd been invited.

"So," Bree said, as she moved to put her seat belt back on and start the car, "why the Northern Lights?"

"They've been my obsession for a while. My portfolio for school just wouldn't be complete without them," Leila said, just as a cop car behind them let out a quick howl of its siren. The sound was gone almost as soon as it had started, as if it were just clearing its throat to politely interrupt the conversation. Red and blue lights shimmered across the inside of the car. Another squad car pulled into the lot, parking directly behind the Mercedes. It switched on its floodlights, and Bree turned away from the blinding glare in the rearview mirror.

"What are the chances that's not for us?" Leila asked.

Two officers climbed out of each car, hands on the butts of their guns. One of them pointed a flashlight at the Mercedes, which seemed a little redundant with the lights from the cruiser beaming onto them. They approached from either side of the car, taking slow and measured steps. Bree shielded her eyes from the bright lights and wished they'd just get it over with.

The soccer game had slowed to a near halt. All the kids were busy looking at the Mercedes and the police cars, and the adults were halfheartedly trying to get them to keep playing, although they, too, were distracted.

Bree felt somehow bad for the soccer ball rolling slowly out of bounds, temporarily forgotten. Bree imagined that the ball loved nothing more than to be kicked across the field, to feel the blades of grass give way beneath its weight. If not for the very real possibility of getting shot for it, Bree would have sprung out of the car, raced across the field, and kicked the crap out of that ball. It would sail up over the goal, past the edge of the field, across the street, and over the row of houses, rising up higher and higher in the sky like a misfired bullet or a missile seeking destruction.

5

THE HOLDING CELL they were in was about ten by ten feet and surprisingly clean. Bree was lying down on the narrow bench built into the wall, hanging off its edge though she was pressed against the wall. It was made of cold, unforgiving concrete that stiffened her back. Not without a certain amount of satisfaction, she rubbed the sore spots where the handcuffs had pressed against her wrist bones, almost sorry to know that they wouldn't scar.

"Is it just me," Leila said, "or is this cell more comfortable than you'd expect?" She was sitting near Bree's outstretched legs, looking at the floor with her arms hanging low and her fingertips grazing the ground.

Bree ran her finger along the underside of the bench and examined the whorls of her fingerprints for signs of dirt. "Cleaner, too."

Leila sat up quickly, her eyes wide. "Holy shit! This is my first time in a jail cell."

Bree lifted herself up onto her elbows, looking quizzically at Leila. "Mine, too."

"We should be celebrating. This is something to tell the grandkids about."

"That's a good point. How should we celebrate?"

"You think they'll bring us some ice cream if we asked them nicely?"

"If that doesn't work, it's your turn to kiss someone to get what we want."

"Deal," Leila said, rising from the bench and walking over to the bars, which weren't the dirty gray of iron but had been painted a pleasant beige. "Excuse me, officers," she called down the empty hallway. "We haven't received our complimentary scoop of ice cream yet." She paused for a moment. "I know my rights!"

She turned back to Bree and frowned exaggeratedly. "I don't think we're gonna get any ice cream."

"Bastards. We'll have to think of some other way to mark the special occasion."

"Have any ideas?" Leila walked back to the bench and took a seat with her feet tucked under her.

"I'd suggest streaking, because I've never done that, and it might be nice to cross another thing off the list *while* celebrating. But we don't have much running room in here. Plus, maybe it wouldn't be the smartest decision to add to our criminal records so soon."

"Alleged criminal records," Leila corrected. "Are you worried?"

"Nah," Bree said, lying back down as if to flaunt her carelessness. "I'm sure everything will be fine. Plus, they pretty much just wrote my college essay for me. I'll talk about learning from the hardships of my rebellious teenage years, and I'll get accepted anywhere I want." After she said this, Bree realized that there was a tiny inkling of worry in her belly. But it wasn't for herself—she was a minor and at worst might go to juvie for a few months. It was a concern about what might happen to Leila.

A moment passed in which Bree realized how eerily quiet it was. There was just the low hum of a fluorescent lightbulb somewhere down the hall. There was no clue as to what was happening in the outside world.

Leila stood up and walked to the bars. "Anyone? Ice cream?" Her voice broke the silence and echoed down the hallway, eliciting no response. "Jerks!" She plopped down onto the floor, resting her back against the bars, her legs stretched out in front of her. She took off her flip-flops and examined them for a few moments. "Don't you think it's a mistake to let prisoners into a jail cell wearing shoes? They could conceivably be used as weapons. I mean, mine are too light to cause much damage, but I could really slap the hell out of someone."

Bree raised her legs to look at her shoes. They were skater sneakers, once solid black but now faded and tattered, their soles rubbed smooth from Bree's journey. The right one was stained by some unrecognizable, crusty material that she had never noticed before. "Mine are heavy enough to cause some damage. I'm somewhat attached to them, but if it means becoming the first people to break out of jail using only their footwear, I'll gladly sacrifice them."

"Well, we can't just come out guns blazing. We would need a plan."

"Of course," Bree said, sitting up from the bench and joining Leila on the floor. "We should take a hostage. When someone comes to get us, we can use my laces to tie him up. I'll hold a shoe to his head while you slap a clear path ahead."

"What do we do when we make it outside?"

"That's when we start letting the footwear fly. In the confusion of the shootout, we make a break for a squad car. We hot-wire it, take it to a safe location, and paint it red."

"Then we'll live out the rest of our lives as fugitives," Leila said, her voice gleeful. "We'll drive through the whole country, taunting the authorities. Then we'll cross the border and go as far north as the Canadian roads will allow. We'll watch the Northern Lights, then come back to the States and go all the way south to Patagonia to see what the sky does on that side of the world."

Bree was about to voice her approval when they heard the opening and closing of doors, then the heavy footsteps of an officer walking down the hall. "The state requires us to provide you each with a phone call to get in touch with a lawyer or relative," he said as he pulled his keys out.

Bree stayed put, quiet. She could feel Leila and the cop eyeing her expectantly. Leila asked the cop to give them a second and then went over to take a seat next to Bree and waited for Bree to meet her eyes. "I have no one to call," she said softly. "Do you?"

Bree exhaled, maybe exaggerating a little to show that the question was like a punch to the stomach. She shook her head.

"I was hoping maybe you had an aunt or uncle," Leila said.

"Nope. Not anywhere nearby anyway."

Leila brought her hand up to her mouth and bit on the corner of a fingernail. "As surprisingly okay as this stay in jail has been, we're probably going to be in deep shit if we don't call someone. Like, life-ruining deep shit. If there was anything else for us to do, anyone else at all to call, I wouldn't ask you to do this. Unless you can think of something else, we need to call your sister."

"Maybe things aren't that bad," Bree said. "We should wait until someone comes to talk to us and we find out exactly what we're facing." The words didn't even sound convincing to herself, but she was trying to push away the thought of calling Alexis. They hadn't talked in over nine months. Bree had this one recurring nightmare that she was hitchhiking and every car that would stop was driven by Alexis, with Matt in the passenger seat.

"Bree, you and I both know that's not a good idea. We had a hell of a day." She motioned around the jail cell and smiled, still speaking softly. "But I think it's safe to say, this is as far as we go. Now the consequences start to kick in. And if we don't have someone to help us out, they'll be worse than they have to be."

"Leila . . ." she started to say, but she didn't know how to go on.

"I know you didn't leave home under the best of circumstances," Leila said. "But what else can we do?"

"You don't understand," Bree said, surprised at how close to crying she was. "'The best of circumstances' is a hell of an understatement. I can't just call after all this time and ask her to bail me out of jail."

The silence of the cell returned, broken only by Bree's heavy breathing. She brought her knees up to her chest, barely able to fit her feet onto the narrow bench. She picked at the crusty spot on her shoe, which flaked away with a nauseating crackle.

"You can't do a whole lot of life-seizing in here, Bree. I know you don't want to talk to her. But you have to. You're sisters. I'm sure she she'd just be happy to hear your voice."

Bree stopped scraping the thing on her shoe and leaned her head against her knees. "I kissed her fiancé." She took a deep breath, trying to steady her voice, remembering the look on Alexis's face. "I was just being wild, you know? A little rebellion is to be expected when you're being babied. She caught us. As soon as I saw the look on her face, I packed a bag and left."

Bree had thought that the next time she saw Alexis, they'd both be well into adulthood, the wounds they'd inflicted on each other rubbed smooth and painless by time. She'd even had little fantasies of running into her on the street somewhere—New York, maybe—and they'd crack smiles and say, "How's it been?" and go grab a cup of coffee. By then everything would be forgotten or at least irrelevant.

"There's no way I can call her. Not after what I did."

A tress of dreadlocked hair fell across Bree's eyes, and she tried halfheartedly to undo some of its knots.

"Let me talk to her," Leila said after a while.

Bree took a deep breath and shut her eyes. "She won't come."

"We might as well try."

Somewhere, beyond the doors of the holding cell, a phone was ringing. "You don't want to test out the escape plan with the shoes? I think we were really on to something there," Bree attempted.

Leila laughed and squeezed Bree's arm. "Don't worry. I'll take care of everything."

She lingered there for a moment. Bree could hear the cop shifting his weight outside, a slight wheeze to his breathing. Leila gave Bree's arm another squeeze and then called out to the officer that she was ready.

Bree watched Leila and the cop walk down the hall, filling it with the echo of rubber soles hitting the linoleum floors.

◇　◇　◇

Bree couldn't tell how long she and Leila been in the jail. However long it might have been, it was long enough to let the stillness in. That's when she really started to grasp the awfulness of a jail cell. Before, she'd thought that it would be cruel to have clocks hanging around jails, forcing the prisoners to literally watch time go by without them. But now she realized that not having clocks around was the more severe punishment. Just day followed by abstract day, and you, motionless, in the middle of it.

A buzzer interrupted Bree's musings, and the set of doors at the end of the hallway swung open. It'd been so long since Bree had seen a familiar face.

More than anything, she was surprised by the fact that Alexis still looked the same. She was wearing a hooded sweatshirt, pajama pants, and no makeup, so that she looked even younger than she was, closer to Bree's age. Bree had always thought Alexis was prettier than she, and she looked it now. Well-rested, too, as if Bree's absence had been a relief.

A cop was walking beside her, going through a set of keys and clearly not sure which one he needed. Bree didn't stand up, but she watched her sister's slow approach.

Leila lifted herself off the floor and stepped away from the door. She gave Bree an attempt at a comforting smile, although Bree couldn't say she was very comforted. Her stomach was a mess of nerves. She thought she might actually throw up in front of everyone.

Alexis's face was actually quite serene, almost expressionless, only a little different than how she'd looked months ago. Bree remembered the tightening jaw muscles that would preface all those lectures.

Bree kept waiting for something big to happen. For Alexis to yell at her or, for some reason, hug her. But she couldn't gauge what Alexis was thinking at all.

The cop led Leila and Bree down the hall in silence. They went through a few bureaucratic procedures, signed a few forms. One of the officers talked for a while and said, "Do you understand?" when he was finished, but Bree hadn't been listening, so she just nodded. Of all things, Bree was wondering if there were direct flights from Reno to Kansas City or if Alexis had needed a layover. How long had they been in the cell?

A young cop behind a counter gave Leila her keys and told her where her car had been towed. He handed Bree back her duffel bag. As the officer had Alexis sign a couple more forms, Bree felt the pang of anxiety growing, constricting her chest as if it actually had the power to yank at the muscles of her heart. When they were led outside, Bree took a step away from Leila, as if to keep her safe from the altercation sure to ensue.

Here it comes, Bree thought. *A lecture, the big explosion of Alexis's unique brand of sisterly love.* But Alexis just kept walking straight ahead toward the parking lot. There weren't many cars parked, and they all looked the same whitewashed color under the glow of the streetlights. The streets were quiet, the whole suburb past its bedtime.

"That's it?" Bree called out to her sister. "You don't have anything to say?"

Alexis turned around. She looked as if she was about to start yelling but just said softly, "No, Bree. I don't have anything to say to you." She turned back and kept walking to her rental car. It took Bree a second to register that her sister's cheeks were wet, dripping with tears that Bree hadn't noticed at the jail.

"I'm not going back with you, you know," Bree called out, her resolve weakened by the fact that she couldn't remember her sister ever crying before.

"Wonderful. Thanks for making that clear."

Bree stopped walking after her. A white car about twenty feet away flashed its headlights as Alexis unlocked its doors remotely.

"Yeah, I thought so. You're glad to be rid of me."

Leila took a step toward Bree, as if meaning to reassure her but not knowing how.

"Glad to see you haven't changed. Keep it up. Your immaturity is really one of your best traits," Alexis said, now standing by the driver's side of the car. She swung open the door but stayed outside the car, staring at her keys and her feet, a fresh onslaught of tears streaming down her cheeks. They came out so effortlessly, barely a contorted muscle in their wake. Bree had the notion that her sister wasn't actually crying, that maybe Alexis had picked up some sort of disease, and tears were just a symptom.

"Like you were glad to be rid of them," Bree said.

And for once, Alexis's face contorted into a look of flat-out anguish. Bree almost felt relief at the sight of it, at its undeniable honesty.

A few interminable seconds went by. Alexis sobbed openly. Bree wanted to ask where the hell the tears had been months ago but wasn't able to form the words. Leila shifted her weight from one foot to the other. When she managed to control herself for a second, Alexis met Bree's eyes. "I show up in Kansas City to bail you out of jail after I haven't heard from you in nine months, and you don't even apologize for what you did?"

Alexis stopped and harshly rubbed her eyes with the palm of one hand. "Forget about Matt. I thought you were dead, Bree. I called every hospital within a hundred miles. I paid for online newspaper subscriptions in every major city just to check the obituaries, to read about missing people found dead, hoping no one matched your description. You were a brat for months after Mom and Dad died, never once remembering that I lost my parents, too. And all you could do was act out like I was somehow responsible. After everything we went through, you left me alone to worry about you. You didn't give a shit about how it would feel for me.

"Then, nine months later, the worst nine months of a life that's included many, many bad months, I get a phone call from a jail on the other side of the country, and it's not even your voice on the other end. It's a stranger's. You didn't even have the decency to pick up the phone yourself? How can you be so selfish and thoughtless?"

Leila crossed her arms in front of her chest as if to protect herself. Her eyes were fixed on Bree, her gaze steadfast if not for the little dents of worry between her eyebrows. It was quiet outside the police station, but Bree imagined she could hear the sound of things tearing apart.

"Do you really have nothing to say to me?" Alexis said, the car keys in her hand clicking against the window as she leaned on the open door. "Is that how far gone you are?"

The muscles in Bree's chest tightened further. She could still feel Leila's eyes fixed on her, so she craned her neck up and looked for the darkest spot in the night sky. "What the hell are you talking about? You should be the one apologizing. For months after Mom and Dad died, all I heard out of you was complaining. You didn't once say you missed them; you didn't once act like it hurt you that they were gone. All you cared about was spending time with Matt. As if you didn't have any family left at all. This is the first time I've even seen you cry."

Alexis exhaled out her mouth and shook her head. "I cried every night, Bree. As soon as I got to bed, I'd turn on the TV to hide the noise and bury my face in the pillow and weep. It's a wonder Matt and

I stayed together as long as we did, considering how much of our time together I spent in tears."

The memory came back to Bree, how she'd hear the television through the wall and curse her sister for being able to move on so quickly. "If that's true, how come you never told me?"

"I was trying to be strong in front of you. I was miserable. I'm still miserable," she sighed, or gasped, or maybe some mix of the two. "My parents died, and then my kid sister started showing up drunk, hanging out with junkies, and always looking for a fight. How could I have possibly felt any other way?"

She sniffed and, judging by the sound of it, pulled something out of her bag to blow her nose into, though Bree couldn't bring herself to look.

"So you know, to get you out of this mess, I had to call Matt," Alexis added, saying his name as if she were throwing it at Bree. "The last person I wanted to talk to, thanks to you. He called the guy whose car you stole and managed to convince him to drop the charges." She'd said the last bit slowly, as if waiting for Bree to interrupt her. "So you're free to do whatever you want again."

Before Bree could say anything else, Alexis's car door was closing shut. The engine shuddered to life, and the interior light of the car flicked on as Alexis checked herself in the mirror, wiping at her eyes. Then the car started, and Alexis was headed down the road.

Bree waited until Alexis's car was no longer visible before she turned to Leila. She felt herself starting to tremble with oncoming tears, as if Alexis's crying was contagious. "That went well."

She grabbed her duffel bag off the ground and lifted the strap over her shoulder. It scraped against her sunburned neck and sent a sting of pain down her back. Whenever she was faced with a situation she'd never been in before, Bree liked to take note of her surroundings, committed, as she was, to not let life pass by unnoticed. But she barely paid attention to the pleasantness of the Kansas air, or to the officers chatting with their hands on their utility belts in the parking lot; they were forgotten almost as soon as they were noticed, driven out of focus by Alexis's words. Bree felt as if there wasn't even anything around but her and the mess happening inside her stomach. She needed to sit down, but she was afraid that then the tears would come, and she wouldn't be able to stand back up for hours.

"You know," Bree said, taking the stairs so slowly it looked as if she was limping, "I think I'm gonna keep going on my own."

Leila stopped following her. "Why?" She sounded hurt.

"I just need to be on my own for a little while," Bree said. Speaking took an unreasonable amount of effort. She felt out of breath, dizzy, picturing Alexis weeping into a pillow, calling up hospitals, worried sick while Bree herself hitchhiked and shoplifted and blocked out whatever thoughts clashed with her professed love of life.

Leila bit her lip and furrowed her brow. "I don't understand."

"Thanks for a good day," Bree muttered, nearly breathless. "Sorry I got you arrested." She adjusted the duffel bag strap one more time and then turned away from Leila, heading down the road without glancing back, the entire world fading away and leaving her alone with her thoughts.

6

NOT A LOT of people in Mission Hills, Kansas, Bree soon learned, needed to use the highway after midnight on a weekday. After leaving the police station, she'd walked for about half an hour to calm herself. And though she still couldn't think clearly, the ingrained habits of the road took over, and she found herself searching for rides. She'd been standing at the stoplight before the on-ramp for at least an hour now, and the driver of the only car that had passed hadn't even seen her.

She dropped her duffel bag and changed into the fluorescent-green tank top she'd used as a sun shade earlier in the day. Crumbs fell away like snow when she pulled it out. A pair of headlights started her way but turned left a few blocks before the highway. Bree usually found nighttime streets so beautiful, everything lit up in orange and acutely peaceful, the branches and streetlights and asphalt calm, as if sleeping. Now everything just looked lonely.

She spotted a scattering of rocks by the side of the road and picked up a handful of them. Feeling the urge to throw them at something, she decided on the post of the stoplight on the opposite side of the street. She was waiting for that clang of rock hitting metal but kept missing. With each pebble that flew past the post noiselessly, Bree grew angrier.

At the pebbles, at the post, at herself. More than anything, though, she grew angrier at her inner monologue, at how her brain would not stop repeating the same words over and over again in Alexis's voice: *selfish and thoughtless.*

Finally, a pebble caught the stainless steel of the post, and the sound reverberated through the night. Bree raised her hands in the air and let out a triumphant scream. A car on the overhead highway pass sped by unseen. Then the night fell into silence again, and Alexis's voice returned.

Bree sat down on the curb, forearms on her legs, head buried in her lap, like someone too drunk to walk, or someone bracing for a plane crash.

Selfish and thoughtless. Bree wanted to shove the words back into her sister's face. Who'd been selfish first? Long before Bree had left, Alexis had started spending the night at Matt's place, had started canceling lunch plans, acting like an authority figure, when all Bree wanted was an ally. And for who? A dull, barely attractive law student? A guy with aspirations to read through contracts the rest of his life?

Bree stared at the tiny pebbles on the asphalt, at a shimmering glass shard left behind from some long-since cleaned-up accident. She tried not to think about how many nights in the last nine months Alexis had spent alone in an empty house, tissues bunched up and torn all around her like fallen debris. Bree tried to tell herself that it was not because of her. She tried to convince herself that Alexis's insisting on being strong rather than compassionate was the root of the problem, but no matter how hard she tried, the argument didn't stick, pushed away again and again by Alexis's voice: *selfish and thoughtless.*

Then she noticed that the glass shard was shimmering from headlights cutting through the dark. Bree stood up and stuck her thumb out in that classic hitchhiking pose, that cliché without a substitute. Her first thought was to grab some more pebbles and throw them at the car, to hear the rocks bounce off the exterior. But she suppressed the urge.

The car was the kind that Mission Hills residents seemed to prefer, large and luxurious, a black SUV with chrome trimmings. It almost drove by, but then the driver slammed on the brakes, swerving to a stop. The window rolled down, and Bree peered inside but kept one foot on the curb.

The driver had bags under his eyes that Bree at first thought were just shadows. His bald head nearly reached the ceiling, and the seat could barely hold him. The top two buttons on his shirt were undone, revealing an army of curly hairs slick with sweat. He didn't say anything at first, just stared in a way that made Bree unzip her duffel bag and feel around inside for the steak knife.

"I need to get to the bus station," Bree said, trying to make out the object in the SUV's cup holder.

"How's it going?" he said, putting his arm up and resting a hand on the passenger seat's headrest. She got the impression that he could open the door on the other side of the car without having to move much.

Bree caught the sickly sweet smell of whiskey. "The nearest bus station," Bree repeated, still groping through her clothes and leftover junk food for the blade. "Can you take me?"

"Oh, sure, I can do that for you." Not bothering to hide the fact that he was trying to get a look down her tank top, he leaned toward her, knocking over the fifth of whiskey that had been resting in the cup holder. He didn't seem to notice.

Bree looked down the road, hoping maybe another car might come by. The road was empty, though, just the asphalt lit up by streetlights, the silhouettes of trees on the side of the road, not even a house or closed business in sight. She pulled her hand out of her bag and checked the side pockets. "How far away is it?"

"Close," he said. "Very close. We should go get a drink first, though." As he said this, he seemed to remember the whiskey bottle. "Ah, shit," he said, and he leaned over to search the floor for it.

Any other night, any other place, Bree would have walked away. She would have walked all night until she stumbled onto a bus station, if she had to. But she knew that Alexis's voice would be right alongside her. She just wanted movement again.

She sighed and grabbed the door handle but didn't open it yet. "Just the bus station would be fine."

He pulled himself back up, muttering, the bottle in his hand. He unscrewed the cap and took a couple of swigs. "One drink," he said, wiping his mouth with the back of his hand. "Come on, get in."

Bree felt that with the knife in her hand, getting into the car might not end up being the stupidest thing she'd ever done. It wouldn't be smart, she admitted, but maybe this would just be one of those stories she told later in life about the recklessness of youth. She unzipped the bag all the way and looked as she moved aside the chips, the miniature sewing kit, and a pack of gum. But the knife wasn't there. The cops must have taken it.

And yet she found herself starting to pull the door handle. She caught a glimpse of herself in the SUV's door. She looked tired, worn, the orange glow from the streetlight up ahead surrounding her reflection like some ill-deserved halo.

The driver raised his eyebrows and smiled as Bree swung the door open. "That's what I'm talking about," he said.

Just as she was about to climb in, Bree heard a familiar chirping and turned to see a car pulling up behind the SUV. The headlights shining in her face made it hard for Bree to make anything out.

Over the sound of the two engines idling, Bree could hear music coming from the car's speakers. The singer's voice was whinier than Bree usually liked, but she was already feeling the urge to turn up the volume. The music got a little louder as Leila opened her door and left her car, coming to Bree's side. She peered into the SUV, and the driver smiled. "Two of you? That's fine. Plenty of me to go around."

Leila put a hand on Bree's shoulder. "I've been driving around in circles for an hour trying to find you," Leila said quietly. "I figured you just needed some time to cool off."

For a moment, Alexis's voice in her head quieted. Bree had never been happier to see someone before. "Good timing," she said, slamming shut the SUV's door, prompting unintelligible yelling from the driver. "You saved me from the worst decision of my life."

When Bree got into Leila's car, she saw the cardboard cutout in the backseat and wanted to laugh but couldn't find it within her and just exhaled through her nose, as if her body had lost the ability to laugh outright. She buckled her seat belt and turned up the volume, then closed her eyes and let the music drown out her thoughts. Leila pressed on the gas, and they turned onto the highway.

Selfish and thoughtless, her brain whispered one more time. Bree thought about what might have happened if she'd gotten into the SUV, pictured how the crash might have occurred. She pictured Alexis getting another unexpected phone call, imagined that her sister might feel—somewhere beneath her sorrow—relief.

The sobs came all at once. They were in her throat before she could stop them, had her gasping for breath before the tears had even reached her cheeks. They dripped down onto the red upholstery of Leila's car, shimmering under passing streetlights for just a second before soaking into the fabric in dark, blood-colored circles.

Leila didn't say anything for a while, but she turned down the music and handed Bree some napkins from the bag of doughnuts that was still in the car. "I know you love your life on the road, Bree," she said, reaching over and grabbing Bree's hand. "But maybe you love the *idea* of loving it more than you love the life itself."

Bree wiped at her eyes, smearing some of the wetness across her eyelashes. A car passed them on the other side of the divider. Its headlights turned into radiant suns by the drops clinging to Bree's lashes. She blew her nose into one of the napkins Leila had given her. For a long time, she said nothing, just felt the tears refuse to stop coming, the knot in her stomach unwilling to come undone until Bree admitted what she knew was true. More cars passed by, lighting up Leila's car with their headlights for just a moment before disappearing down the road, oblivious and indifferent to what Bree was feeling. "She was right," she said finally, gripping a used napkin so tightly that it kept the shape of her closed fist even after she dropped it into the plastic bag hanging from the gearshift. "I am selfish and thoughtless. I thought I was living the way you're supposed to, not taking things for granted. But I was mostly being an asshole, wasn't I?"

"I wouldn't say that." Leila chuckled.

"No, I was an asshole. I kissed her fiancé and then disappeared. I let my sister think I was dead. And I never apologized to her. She was just trying to take care of me." Bree's voice trailed off, the realization of what she'd done suffocating her words.

"People hurt each other," Leila said without much inflection in her voice. "It happens to everyone. Intentionally, unintentionally, regretfully or not. It's a part of what we do as people. The beauty is that we have the ability to heal and forgive."

Bree let Leila's words hang in the air. Throughout her trip, she'd looked at the night she'd kissed Matt as if it had been a clear example of a day seized. Kissing someone you wanted to kiss, heeding that spontaneous little voice inside of yourself and not looking back felt as if it should always be a victory.

But now it felt like nothing more than a selfish impulse. The tears started to come again. She felt them roll out on their own accord, unaccompanied by any sobbing this time, just like the way Alexis had cried at the jail.

Bree sat up, tugging at the seat belt that was pressing too tightly against her. "I'm such a screwup," she said, grabbing another napkin and wiping her nose. "I don't know what I can say to make it okay, but I need to tell her I'm sorry. We need to find her."

"Okay, we will."

"How?" Bree said. "I don't know where she is. I don't remember her cell phone number. Do you have it?"

Leila shook her head. "They looked up your home phone number for me at the police station."

"So, she's gone." The surge of tears blurred Bree's vision, and she let them drip.

"I think I know where to go," Leila said.

As the car picked up speed, Bree held on to Leila's comforting hand and allowed herself to cry.

7

IT WAS 4:00 A.M., and Bree had lost count of how many hotels they'd gone to looking for Alexis. They'd been circling the airport, stopping in at every place they spotted. It might have been easier to keep track if hotels didn't all use the same color palette: the same light yellow walls, dark green carpet, and vermilion furniture.

Leila had been certain that Alexis would be staying at one of the hotels near the airport, waiting for a flight in the morning. But they hadn't found her, just a succession of desk clerks shaking their heads at their computer monitors and saying, "I'm sorry." The lobbies were always empty, the parking lots outside still, as if the Rapture had come and left only hotel employees behind.

"Haven't we been in this one already?" Bree asked as Leila pulled into a parking spot near the entrance of yet another airport hotel. "I don't see the point anymore, Leila. We're not going to find her."

"Come on," Leila said, unbuckling her seat belt. "I have a good feeling about this one." She gave Bree a couple of encouraging taps on the thigh and then got out of the car. Bree sighed and followed her, feeling for once like going to sleep.

The lobby walls were the color of honey mustard, the carpets patterned with jade and maroon. There were two women standing behind the front desk. The older woman was scowling at some papers in front of her. Her wispy blond hair was up in a loose bun, and she had wrinkles that seemed too deep for her age. Her name tag was pinned straight on her shirt, shiny but chipped in one corner, so that the *e* at the end of *Marjorie* was half-gone.

The younger woman looked tired but cheerful. Her red hair was styled just like Marjorie's, but every strand was tightly in place. Her name tag simply read *Trainee*. When they noticed Bree and Leila walking toward them, Marjorie whispered something into the younger woman's ear and took a step back. *Trainee* softened her face into a courteous expression, although it couldn't quite be called a smile.

"Good morning, ladies," the trainee said. "How can I help you?"

"Hi," Leila said, starting the same explanation she'd been giving all the hotel clerks. "We have to get in touch with one of your guests." She gave Alexis's name.

"What's the room number?" the woman asked, turning to her computer and placing her French-manicured fingertips on the keyboard.

"We don't have the room number, actually. Just the name."

Trainee typed something into her computer but offered no reaction about what came up on the screen. The woman hesitated, then looked over her shoulder at Marjorie, who shook her head tersely. "I'm afraid I'm not allowed to give out any guest information." The trainee folded her hands on the desk. "I'm sorry."

"So, she *is* a guest here?" Bree said, feeling her pulse start to quicken.

"Um, well—" the trainee started to say, before she was interrupted by Marjorie.

"Ma'am, we're not allowed to give out any information." She stepped forward, moving the younger woman aside. Bree couldn't help noticing the adhesive bandages covering two of the fingernails on Marjorie's left hand.

"It's a family emergency," Leila said. "You don't have to give us any information. If you could just call her room, that'd be very helpful."

"I can't have the guests be disturbed at this hour," Marjorie said.

Bree fought the urge to be combative. "Please help us out. I really need to talk to my sister. Can you at least tell us if she's at this hotel?"

"I'm sorry, ma'am, but there's nothing I can do. It's against company policy." Marjorie stood up straight, moving her hands behind her back like those of a soldier at-ease. The trainee gave Bree a compassionate look and mouthed an apology.

"What's against company policy?" Bree said, raising her voice. "Getting two family members in touch with each other in an emergency?"

Leila put a hand on Bree's shoulder and eased her out of the way so that Leila was standing directly in front of Marjorie. Bree took a couple of steps toward the faux fireplace to calm herself down before returning.

"Marjorie," Leila said with a smile. "We don't want you to do anything against company policy. We just need to get in touch with my friend's sister right away. What can you do to help us?"

The woman raised her chin defiantly. Bree saw that her default expression was a frown, the corners of her mouth drooping down as if she was constantly expecting disappointment. "I can't give out guest information, and I can't disturb the guests."

"Do you have a manager we could talk to?" Bree said as calmly as she could.

Marjorie tapped the business cards on the desk. *Front Desk Supervisor*.

"Great," Bree said. "A miserable person on a power trip. That's exactly what we need." She grabbed one of the business cards and started ripping it to shreds, shaking her head.

Leila gave Bree a look that she immediately understood. *Let me handle this*. Bree ducked her head in agreement but kept ripping the business card into smaller pieces until Marjorie's name and title were no longer readable.

"Sorry about my friend. She's had a rough night," Leila said. She leaned forward and looked into Marjorie's light blue eyes. "One of my favorite song lyrics from a band called Modest Mouse is this: 'The whole world stinks, so no one's taking showers anymore.'

"Maybe you've had a worse night than my friend here. Your boss yelled at you, or a customer was rude. But the way I see it, there's only two ways to go about things after a bad night. You either stink it up with everyone else, or you take a shower.

"I can guarantee you that I've got a story that will make you thankful your problems are as small as they are. Hell, I'm sure you have a story that will make me feel like my problems are small. But what good is that? Everyone pointing out how awful everything is instead of trying to clean it up a bit?

"All you have to do is tell us the room number. Just this one tiny thing that'll make the world a little better." Leila clasped her hands together, not so much a pleading gesture as a hopeful one.

Bree looked up from the little pile of business card scraps she'd gathered while Leila was talking. The lobby was quiet in the wake of Leila's speech, which felt like a good sign, even though all the other hotel lobbies had been just as quiet. Something in Marjorie's expression had changed, though. Maybe it was kindness; maybe it was just mercy.

Marjorie cleared her throat. "I can't help you." She turned to the trainee. "Always follow company policy." Then she slid a business card across the desk to Leila. "If you find out the guest's room number, please feel free to call back."

Bree shook her head in disbelief. She thought about throwing the business card scraps in Marjorie's face, or running down the halls and waking up everyone in the hotel, but she didn't have the energy. She grabbed Leila's arm and led them away from the desk. "Let's just go," she said.

When they pushed open the doors to the parking lot, Bree was shocked at how much the air had cooled.

"What a bitch," Leila said. She was looking down at the business card Marjorie had given her. "I can't believe how heartless she was."

"Yeah," Bree said. She wasn't in the mood for frustration. She just wanted to shut down for a while.

A quiet moment passed. The airport was right in front of them, and Bree could see taxis headed toward the terminal, dropping off the earliest wave of business travelers. Bree wondered how much consolation she would get from simply returning to her life on the road, trying to love the thought of it even when she didn't love the thing itself.

"Two-one-eight!" Leila shouted, breaking the silence.

"What?"

"Two-one-eight," Leila said again, handing Bree the business card and turning back to the hotel. "Marjorie took a shower." Bree looked down at the card and turned it over, seeing the numbers written in neat, curling digits on the back.

Bree's heart sped up. Alexis was here. Bree had no clue what to say to her, but everything could turn out okay. They jogged to the entrance and went straight to the elevator. Bree's thoughts raced madly on the slow ride up.

The doors opened on the second floor, and they stepped out into the little elevator nook. There were two chairs and an accent table holding a plastic bouquet of brightly colored flowers. A sign on the wall directed guests one way or the other depending on the room number. Bree glanced down the hallway, then turned to Leila. Leila looked as if she'd carried the day's events seamlessly, as if the life could never be drained from her eyes, no matter what was thrown her way.

"Thanks, Leila," she said. "For convincing me to call her. For seeing through my bullshit when even I couldn't."

Leila smiled warmly. "Don't mention it," she said, and she plopped herself down on one of the chairs. "You go ahead. I'll hang back here."

Bree lingered for a second, then nodded and turned down the hallway. At room 218, Bree skipped the dramatics of taking a deep breath and knocked loudly on the door. If her sister wasn't going to forgive her, she wanted to get it over with.

Alexis answered the door wearing the same pajamas and hoodie that she'd shown up in at the jail. In the harsh glow of the hallway, her face looked much older than it had a couple of hours ago. Her eyebrows were slightly raised, as if she expected to be amused. *Get on with it*, her red eyes were saying.

"I never should have left," Bree said. "It was selfish and thoughtless— you're right. I made both our lives harder than they already were."

Bree became aware of how quiet the hallway was. Alexis was leaning against the doorway, her hands tucked into the front pocket of her hoodie. She looked completely unmoved by Bree's words. But Bree couldn't stop.

"I'm sorry I never asked about how you were doing. I assumed I understood what was going through your head, and I shouldn't have. I'm sorry I kissed Matt. That was such a shitty thing to do. I'm sorry I put you through everything I did. I'm sorry I put *us* through that. Life was hard enough without me acting like an idiot." She wiped the back of her hand across her nose. "If it helps at all, I love you. I know we didn't always get along, but these nine months away from you, I've felt you missing from my life. And I want you back in it. I'd understand if you don't want to see me again, but I had to apologize."

Alexis's face remained unchanged. Bree turned to leave. At least she'd tried.

Before she could take a step, though, she felt Alexis grab hold of her arm and pull her into a hug. It was a tight hug, so warm and recognizable. She could smell the strawberry shampoo on Alexis's hair, the same brand they'd both been using for years. Bree pressed her cheek to her sister's, felt their combined tears scurry down her neck. They'd hugged like this so many times throughout their parents' sicknesses.

"I'm sorry," Bree said again, resting her head on Alexis's shoulder.

"I was so worried about you. My little sister, out in the world, all alone." She pressed them closer together. "It's okay. I forgive you. Just never put me through anything like that again." She sniffled and then gave a laugh. "Of course I want to see you again, you goof."

Bree laughed too, felt her nose get all snotty with tears. She unabashedly wiped her nose on Alexis's sweatshirt. The sisters pulled apart and stood in the hallway at Alexis's door, basking in the moment of happiness.

o   o   o

It was hard for Bree to leave Alexis's side, even if it was just for a few minutes. She gave her another hug before she left the room and joined Leila in front of the elevators.

"How'd it go?" Leila asked.

Bree beamed a smile in response.

"Good," Leila said, returning the smile. Then she stood up from the chair and called the elevator. "Walk me to my car?"

"Of course," Bree said, still smiling.

They crossed the hotel lobby, nodding at Marjorie as they passed her desk. Bree even raised her hand in a shy, thankful wave, but Marjorie didn't look up to acknowledge it.

Bree pushed open the door that led to the parking lot, the early morning air greeting them. The first inklings of sunrise colored the horizon. Bree had learned how to leave with ease, but good-byes were another thing altogether, this one in particular.

Leila was walking slowly, too, elongating the trip to the car.

"Alexis wants me to go back home with her."

"That's great," Leila said, her smile wide and sincere. She gave Bree's forearm a supportive squeeze. "That's what you wanted, right?"

"To be honest, I hadn't even considered what would come after I said I was sorry. She asked me if I wanted to go back home."

"Are you gonna go?"

"I told her I want to go back with her but on my own terms. A road trip from here to Reno, no itinerary, no plans, no rush to get back. Just me and her on a shared adventure."

"Make sure you get a car with air-conditioning."

Bree laughed until they reached Leila's car. More than anything, Bree would miss how easily laughter came in Leila's company. She ran a finger along the hood of the car, leaving a trail in the thin layer of dust.

"People can say whatever they want about you, Leila, but life is not boring when you're around."

"And it's not very legal when you're around."

"I do what I can." Bree shrugged. "You sure you don't want to come in and sleep for a few hours? We can all leave in the morning."

Leila seemed to consider this for a second, toying with the car keys in her hand. "No," she said. "I think I'm gonna get back on the road. The Lights are calling."

Bree nodded, surprised to feel herself fighting off tears. She pulled Leila in for a hug. "Maybe we'll run into each other again somewhere."

"Yeah, maybe," Leila said, hugging back tightly before letting go.

Leila unlocked her doors and handed Bree her duffel bag. Bree slung the strap over her shoulder and looked into the car. "What the hell are you going to do with that cardboard display?"

Leila laughed as if she'd forgotten it was there. She shrugged. "Use it for carpool lanes, the occasional snuggle on cold and lonely nights."

Bree laughed, then gave Leila another quick hug. "Take care, Leila."

"You, too," she said, climbing into her car. She started the engine and rolled down her window. "If you ever need someone to help you break out of prison with footwear, you know who to call."

Then she backed out of the parking spot, shifted into drive, and left with a wave. Bree returned the wave, although she was pretty certain Leila could no longer see her. Then she grabbed her duffel bag and walked back to the hotel to rejoin her sister, already imagining all the places they'd see together.

Hey, Aunt Cathy,

I found these beautiful old postcards in a little shop in Chicago and thought you might enjoy one. There was also a rack of postcards that had already been written on and delivered, some of them more than thirty years old. They didn't necessarily say anything special, just something like "I'm in Hawaii and thinking of you, Love, Simon." But it was great flipping through all of them, reading the thoughts people wanted to share across a great distance. Plus, since postcards are so easy to snoop in on (hi, postal worker!), it only felt natural to be reading strangers'. I hope you guys are doing well. I am. I promise. Thanks again for everything. I'm in Chicago and thinking of you.   Love, Leila

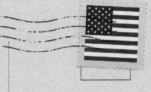

Cathy Harrison
412 Rainbow Blvd.
LaPlace, LA 70068

1

"ELLIOT," MARIBEL SAID, reaching out to lightly touch his forearm. Light forearm touches were exactly how all the great love stories began. He knew he'd remember this moment forever and that, sometime in the future, he'd be able to recount the details for her: how beautiful she'd looked, how she'd reached out to touch him with the arm that wore the corsage he'd made for her, the one that matched the orchid on his lapel. He'd be able to recite word for word her response to his long-awaited admission of love.

He prepared himself to remember, resisting—hopefully, for the last time—his urge to kiss her.

"I really value your friendship. I do. And I don't want to lose what we have." She leaned in and kissed him on the cheek. "So let's not complicate things, okay? Let's keep things the way they are."

This is the wrong movie, Elliot thought to himself immediately. Those weren't her lines. This was prom, and her nearly lifelong best friend had just confessed his love in a big speech. They had a whole summer of romance ahead of them. After the light forearm touch, she was supposed to kiss him. She was supposed to say, "I know." And, "Me, too."

It was not in the script—in any version of the script Elliot had envisioned for tonight— for her to give him one of those smiles that he'd fallen in love with in the first place, and then walk away. But that's exactly what she did.

o   o   o

Everything about the world felt heavy to Elliot. His feet carrying him down the sidewalk, the bottle in his hand, the bourbon on his tongue. The tuxedo weighed down on him as if it wasn't just cloth but a tangible reminder that this night was supposed to be about him getting a weight off his chest, not this brutal opposite.

After procuring a bottle of bourbon and taking a few swigs, Elliot had left the hotel ballroom in Minneapolis and started to walk the eighteen miles back home to Burnsville. After walking about a mile and a half through downtown, avoiding the knowing looks of adults who were clearly more accustomed to walking under the influence, he stopped to recover by leaning against a building. He closed his eyes for a moment, but he could still see the look on Maribel's face: unmoved. A wave of nausea came over him, so he opened his eyes again and took a deep breath. If life were anything like the movies, it'd be raining. But the Minneapolis night was perfect, a few stars even showing through the spaces between buildings. Laughter rang through the night from the crowds of people spilling out of every bar on First Avenue. It felt as if the city itself was laughing at him or, worse, indifferent to his heartbreak. *They never say yes when you want them to*, the music coming from bars was saying. *Why do you think we're all in here drinking?*

Something was tickling his chin, and he grabbed for it, finding the orchid boutonniere that he'd worn to match Maribel's corsage. He yanked the flower from his tuxedo and, before he knew what he was doing, chucked it into oncoming traffic. It flew ungracefully through the air, its white outer petals flapping like broken wings. Managing to avoid the grill of a passing pickup truck, it landed on the asphalt unharmed. Elliot kept his eye on the flower, its bright purple inner petals flecked with crimson, like a bruise. It wasn't long before a car's tire squished the orchid into the road. In the camera in his mind, Elliot zoomed in on the smashed flower and held the shot for a beat, letting the sound of passing cars bleed together with the opening notes of a song. The petals had been torn apart, the flower's bulb mashed into the unforgiving ground. He thought to himself that he knew exactly what that felt like.

Forgetting his nausea, Elliot uncapped the bottle of bourbon and took another swig, spilling some on the lapel of his tux. Then, abandoning his resolution to walk home, he came up with another plan. He could imagine some deleted scene where Lloyd Dobler from *Say Anything ...* laid himself down in the middle of the road, letting the rain wash over him. If only it were raining.

He put the cap back on the bottle and stepped away from the building he'd been leaning on, lurching toward the street. He compared this march across the sidewalk to the approach he'd made at the prom, and he quickly decided that this was the easier one. Its conclusion was more predictable, and there was less suffering involved.

At the edge of the curb, he didn't even hesitate. He stepped into the street without as much as a drunken stumble. Then he took an extra step so that he was right in the middle of the lane.

Elliot could tell nothing about the oncoming car from its headlights, only that it was headed his way. He waited for a montage of his life to flash before his eyes, but all he got was Maribel and how she'd looked when she strode into the hotel ballroom. She'd worn a purple dress that matched exactly the hue of the orchid's inner petals. Her hair was up, pinned in such a way that allowed only a couple of wavy blond tresses to slip down like sunlight through leaves.

Maybe it was that the tuxedo was black, or that everything about Elliot was a little dark: his hair, his vaguely Middle Eastern-hued skin, his brown eyes. Or maybe Elliot was just too skinny to be noticed. The driver seemed unaware that he was standing there and continued toward him at top speed. Out of instinct, or perhaps just a drunken failure of conviction, Elliot jumped back toward the curb. His movement must have registered with the driver, and the brakes screeched out loudly.

As the car skidded past Elliot, a slew of honking horns rang out in its wake, so loud that he almost didn't hear the sound of breaking glass. His heart was pounding, but Elliot wondered only briefly at his own well-being. He looked on, dumbfounded, as the car came to a stop.

It took Elliot a second to realize that the crash had come from the car's side-view mirror clipping the bottle of bourbon he had been holding in his hand, and that he hadn't, after all, escaped unscathed. As soon as he looked down, he felt the warmth of blood flowing through his fingers, even before he felt the sting of the alcohol seeping into the wound. He held his hand up to his face. In the weak light of the streetlamps, it was hard to tell where the blood was coming from, only that there was a lot of it. His hand was shaking, bringing into view little shards of glass that took turns catching the light, making them twinkle like stars in a child's drawing.

He looked away from his hand toward the car that had managed to mostly avoid him. All he could focus on were the bright red brake lights. Then the door opened, and the driver rushed out, one hand covering her mouth in disbelief while the other held up her strapless sundress as she ran toward Elliot. "Holy shit! Are you okay?"

Elliot just nodded, looking down at himself as if to point out that he was mostly whole.

"I almost killed you," the girl stammered, her hand still covering her mouth. "I am so sorry."

Cars passing by honked their horns at the two of them standing in the street, blocking their path. "I'm bleeding a little," he said.

"Oh, my God," the girl cried out. She grabbed Elliot's forearm and inspected his hand. "I didn't even see you."

She ran back to her car and returned with a handful of napkins imprinted with various fast-food logos. She put the stack of napkins in his uninjured hand and started to dab at the bloodied one. As if from a distance, Elliot watched her go about the task with inherent care, like she was an archaeologist exhuming an artifact. "I can't believe I almost ran you over," the girl said, her voice quivering. She didn't ask him what he was doing in the middle of the road.

Elliot couldn't tell if he was light-headed from the booze or the loss of blood. "I think I'm okay," he said. In the passing headlights of another car, he saw the girl's face, her brow furrowed in consternation.

"You're not okay. An idiot just hit you with her car." She tossed a bloody napkin aside and pressed a fresh one to his palm. "There's a lot of blood here."

"Some of it might be bourbon," he said. "It probably looks worse than it is."

The girl looked up at Elliot with worry, then went back to carefully sopping up the blood with the napkins. They were cheap and rough, and if not for her delicate touch and the booze, Elliot would probably have been in a lot more pain. "You need to go to a hospital."

He felt the blood slip beneath his sleeve, and as his shirt sopped it up, a sticky warmth spread all the way to his elbow. The wound started to appear through the blood, a deep gash diagonally across his palm and a few small streaks on his fingers. "I'll be okay," he said. "I'll just clean it up when I get home, and it'll be fine."

A few more cars honked at them. Someone rolled down a window in passing and shouted at them to get out of the road.

"That's sensible advice," the girl shouted back at them. "Very helpful—thank you!"

Elliot laughed, then stopped when he felt a burp coming on.

"Jerks," the girl said. "But they're right. Let me take you to a hospital. They'll know much better what to do with your hand."

He had a quick vision of Maribel visiting him at the hospital, worry all over her face, asking him why he'd been standing in the middle of the road.

"It'll stop bleeding in a bit," he said. He pushed the remaining stack of napkins into the bleeding palm. "I'll just apply some pressure and . . ." He grimaced at the flood of pain pulsing from his hand.

"This is my fault," the girl said. "Let me at least take you home."

"No, that's okay," Elliot said. But the girl was already leading him toward the car. He focused on trying to walk in a straight line. His feet dragged across the pavement, crunching over the bottle's shards of glass. They reached the car, and the girl helped Elliot ease into the passenger seat.

"Just keep pressure on your hand," she said.

"I'll try not to bleed all over everything," he said. Then he looked around, as if to determine what to avoid bleeding on the most. "I'm sorry. I think I already did."

The girl laughed. "No, that's just the upholstery."

"Oh." He gazed up at her, noticing only that her hair was shorter than Maribel's. It took him a moment to remember where she'd come from. "I'm Elliot."

The girl smiled. "Nice to meet you, Elliot. I'm Leila." Elliot nodded and put his head back against the headrest to close his eyes. He heard his door shut, and a few seconds later Leila joined him inside the car. "You can't fall asleep quite yet," Leila said. "Where am I taking you?"

"Burnsville," he said. His head was spinning now, the pain in his hand throbbing. This was definitely not how the night was supposed to go. He breathed slowly, trying to quell his insides.

A few more cars honked behind them. "Okay, okay," Leila called out through her open window. "I'm going."

She shifted into drive, and Elliot immediately felt the strains of motion. He turned his head to the window, feeling for fresh air. His window was only cracked, so he fumbled around with his good hand until he realized that the window didn't have a button but one of those cranks. After some struggling, he lowered it all the way. Bloodied napkins flapped in the wind.

"Elliot? Stay with me, okay?"

"Mmm," he moaned in response. He needed the weightlessness of sleep. He needed to forget about Maribel and prom, needed his body to forget about the bourbon.

Something in his stomach twitched. He tried to signal Leila to pull over, but before he could, the vomit was coming out in a puddle at his feet, debris-like chunks on his lap. A streak went from the dashboard, across the air-conditioning vents, over most of the door panel, and finally over the edge of the lowered window, dripping a trail onto the asphalt.

As soon as he was done retching, Elliot laid his head back. "I'm sorry," he said, meaning the words not just for Leila, but for Maribel, and even for himself. Then he closed his eyes and fell asleep.

THE FIRST THINGS Elliot saw when he woke up were ambulance lights flashing quietly, with no accompanying sirens. He turned his head to see the surrounding boonies of Burnsville, the thick trees that surrounded everything in his hometown. Watching the red lights dancing quietly on the trees, he thought for a second that maybe he'd gone deaf. Then he heard the sound of footsteps, and Leila's face appeared at his window. She'd parked the car and walked around to help him out.

"Come on," she said, opening the door. "Let's get you fixed."

"Where are we?"

"We're at the hospital," Leila said. "You passed out before you could give me an address, and your hand's still bleeding pretty bad."

"I'm sorry about your car."

"That's okay." She reached over to help him unbuckle his seat belt. "You didn't mean to do it." She smelled nice, and Elliot felt embarrassed about what his own breath might smell like.

Leila helped him ease out of the car. Then she put his good hand over her shoulders, put her arm on his waist, and told him to keep his bleeding hand elevated. As they hobbled across the parking lot, Elliot tried hard to not seem so drunk.

The emergency room was empty save for a woman trying to quiet a screaming toddler, and the nurse sitting at the receptionist desk. Leila sat Elliot down on a chair and checked in with the receptionist, returning with some paperwork. As Leila asked Elliot his basic information to fill out the forms, Elliot looked at the crying toddler, hoping that the kid's lack of visible injuries meant that he was okay, just cranky, and that his mother was a little too overprotective.

"Reason for visit?"

Elliot turned to Leila. "Really?" He held up his hand, trying to keep it turned away from the toddler to prevent further freaking out.

"I'll just put down 'drunk.'"

"That works," Elliot said. He slid down the plastic chair so that his neck rested on the back. The less his head spun, the more his hand hurt.

Leila took the forms back to the receptionist, who said they'd be attended to shortly. After a minute or so, the mother and her toddler disappeared behind a set of double doors. The child's wailing faded like, fittingly, that of a departing ambulance.

"So," Leila said. "What's your story?"

Elliot could feel her gaze on him; his alcohol/blood/puke-stained tux, his bloody hand, his lack of a boutonniere. "That's not a story anyone wants to hear," he said, avoiding her gaze.

"Well, if you bleed to death, I want to be able to tell people a little bit about you."

Elliot chuckled, then put more pressure on his cut, yelping out in pain.

"Come on. I took you to a hospital, even though I hate hospitals. You puked all over my car. You owe me a story."

"I thought you said that was okay."

"Yes, it's okay. But I make it a strict policy not to hit people with my car and then not find out who they are."

"You're taking this whole being in the hospital with a drunken stranger awfully lightly."

"I almost killed you. Without a little bit of levity I'd have to deal with the guilt." Leila smacked him lightly on the bad arm, and he squirmed in his seat. "Don't be shy. We've got nothing else to do in this waiting room."

When Elliot didn't respond, she softened her voice. "Was it a girl?"

Elliot turned to her. "How'd you know?"

"You were stumbling around drunk in a tux on the side of the road during prom season. Consider it a lucky guess."

Slumping farther into the hard, plastic chair, Elliot closed his eyes. Something inside him hurt, and it had nothing to do with his hand or the alcohol. "I had it planned so perfectly. Lloyd-Dobler-holding-a-stereo-over-his-head perfect. At least, it should have been perfect."

"Who's Lloyd Dobler?"

"You've never seen *Say Anything…*?"

"Never heard of it."

"*Ferris Bueller's Day Off? The Breakfast Club?*" Leila shrugged. "Oh, man, you're missing out. Eighties movies are the best. When my parents first moved to the States, they were worried that they wouldn't be up-to-date on pop culture. They bought as many movies as they could and watched them over and over so they could pick up on slang. My house is full of VHS tapes, still. I grew up watching them. They aren't like movies these days. You don't need a $200-million budget to show a guy getting the girl."

"But your girl turned you down?"

Elliot opened his eyes again. The receptionist had left the room, and it was just him and Leila, the fluorescent lighting of the waiting room casting an unappealing glow on everything it touched, from the pale green walls and gray plastic chairs to the racks of pamphlets with little diagrams and bulleted lists of symptoms.

"Come on," Leila said. "Your worries don't actually drown in the alcohol. You have to let them out." She offered a smile and nudged him lightly. "Tell me about this girl."

He sat up, careful not to move his hand too much. The nausea was mostly gone now, but he could still feel the alcohol pounding through his veins and clouding his thoughts. "I'm a pretty forgetful guy," he said. "But everything she says, I remember. I remember what color her hair ribbon was when we met on the first day of fifth grade. I remember that she loves orchids because they look delicate but aren't, really. From the single postcard she sent me when traveling with her family two summers ago, I remember what my name looks like in her handwriting."

"What's her name?"

"Maribel," he said. He loved saying her name out loud, loved the feeling of each letter shaping his lips. "I've loved her for a very long time. We're friends; we have been since elementary school. Never more than that, though."

He turned to look at Leila. She was sitting with her legs tucked under her, her fingers absentmindedly tugging at the hem of her sundress. "And you never told her how you feel until tonight?"

Elliot shrugged, looking at his bloody hand. "I could never decide how."

"You never thought of, 'Hello, friend. I love you. Let's make out?' It works every time."

"I actually did think of that one. I've thought of every single way you could possibly admit your love to someone. I couldn't decide if I wanted to just blurt it out while hanging out, or to write her a letter, or make a big gesture, or come up with one of those step-by-step plans that villains in teen movies are always coming up with to get a girl to fall in love with them. You wanna know how much it costs to write someone's name in the sky with one of those planes? Because I looked into it."

"If it's more than the cost of a lobster, it's not worth it. Take her to a restaurant, buy her a lobster, and write her name in butter on the tablecloth. That would totally work on me."

Elliot gave her a sideways glance and laughed.

"I bet you hadn't thought of *that* way to say 'I love you.'"

"Almost. I was gonna go with crab legs."

"That would have been a mistake," Leila said. She tucked her legs farther under her. "So, why tonight?"

Elliot took a deep breath, and the gross aftertaste of vomit made him turn away on the exhale, embarrassed. "I knew I wanted to tell her before high school was over. So I decided to tell her how I felt at the prom, in front of everyone. There's nothing more romantic than someone who's not scared to put themselves out there for the one they love.

"I'd play the scene out in my head, and it always felt romantic, like something out of a movie. I could only imagine it ending well. I could always feel the kiss coming."

Elliot was interrupted by a nurse calling his name. Leila came along as he followed the nurse down a hallway and into a small examination room, where a doctor was washing his hands. He cleaned the wound, pulled out the glass, and stitched it closed, all without a word. He worked gruffly, as if he were fixing a broken toy. Elliot tried to keep his wincing to a minimum, but he must not have been doing a great job, because at one point Leila offered her hand to squeeze. When the doctor was done dressing Elliot's hand, he deftly found a vein in his other arm, plugged in an IV, and told him to keep it in for twenty minutes, then call the nurse. "It'll sober you up," he said, sounding like a judge passing down a sentence.

As soon as he left the room, Leila hopped onto the patient table alongside Elliot, crinkling the paper. "I want to hear your speech, the one you made to what's-her-name."

"Maribel," he said, not wasting an opportunity to let her name pass through his mouth. "I obviously didn't get the girl. There's no happily-ever-after here."

"Give me the speech anyway."

Elliot met her insistent gaze and realized for the first, somewhat clearheaded time that she was pretty. Not Maribel, but pretty. Then he looked down at his feet dangling off the table. "I don't think I'm ready to relive that moment quite yet."

"Fair enough," she said. They fell quiet, but Elliot could feel her gaze still on him. "You're okay, though?"

Elliot held up his bandaged hand. "All patched up."

"That's not what I meant."

"Yeah, I know." He shrugged.

"Listen, I know we just met . . ." Leila started to say, but her voice trailed off before she could finish the thought. There were loud voices coming from down the hallway, and before he could make out what they were saying, Elliot knew exactly who the voices belonged to.

"Uh-oh."

"I knew that one of these days you'd end up in the hospital," his mother said before she'd even entered the room. The door swung open, revealing a middle-aged couple with nearly matching Afros of the Jewish variety. His dad was wearing pajama pants and slippers, a stained T-shirt for which Elliot knew the man would receive grief as soon as Elliot's mother noticed it. Elliot instinctively moved his uninjured hand to cover up the bandages, but he either did it too slowly, or his mother had been preparing to shriek anyway, and nothing was going to stop her. "My baby!"

"Oh, Jesus," Elliot said.

"Don't you start with the 'Oh, Jesus,'" his mom said, rushing over to inspect Elliot's hand, as if she was certain that there was no way the doctor could have done the job thoroughly enough. "What have you done?"

"What is that on the tux?" Elliot's father stepped forward, squinting at the various stains as if trying to read them.

"Will both of you please just take it easy?" Elliot said, looking over at Leila and grimacing in embarrassment.

His parents didn't seem to notice her presence in the room. "Take it easy? My son's bleeding in the middle of the night, and I'm supposed to take it easy?"

"I'm not bleeding, *Ima*. I'm okay."

"I hope when you have children, you never have to learn the grief of getting a phone call from a hospital in the middle of the night. I'm surprised neither one of us had a heart attack and is sitting here next to you plugged into a machine." His mom adjusted the strap of her purse. "All right, *mamzer*. If you're okay, tell me: Why are you in a hospital?"

"Does anyone remember what the rental place's policy on stains was?" Elliot's father was inspecting the cloth of the tuxedo between his fingers, his glasses lowered all the way to the tip of his nose.

"It's nothing," Elliot said. "I'm fine."

"You're fine, sure. You smell like a vagrant. And what's this for?" She pointed to the IV. "Tell me what happened, or I'm calling that doctor back in here to pull the stitches out. And you better hope he's willing to; otherwise, I'll do it myself."

"Sharon, I think he's been drinking," Elliot's dad said, sniffing at the tuxedo jacket.

"Don't talk *shtuyot*," she said, "He doesn't drink." She scowled at her husband, then looked back at Elliot. "You don't drink."

Elliot pulled the cloth away from his dad's fingers. "Dad, please stop smelling me. Mom, just calm down for a second." He looked over at Leila, who was clearly trying to contain her laughter and look serious.

"*Nu?* I'm waiting."

"The thing is . . ." he said, not knowing at all what the thing was or how to express it to his parents.

Thankfully, a nurse came in at that moment. Had she known what was waiting in the room for her, she might have let Elliot have a few more minutes of IV fluid on the house. Elliot's mom instantly assailed her with questions about Elliot's condition and prognosis and at-home treatment. "Is there a pharmacy in the hospital? Is it open? What brand of gauze do you trust the most? How many painkillers is it safe to give him? Look at how much pain he's in; can't he have more?"

The nurse hurriedly directed Elliot's mom to the pharmacy.

"Come on"—Elliot's mom motioned for his dad to follow—"before they close." At no point had the nurse hinted that the pharmacy might be closing.

"You," his mom said, pointing at Elliot from the doorway. "We're not done with you." Then she headed down the hallway, an echo of chattering in her wake.

The nurse shook her head as she removed the needle from Elliot's arm and taped a cotton ball to the speck of blood that appeared.

"Wow," Leila said.

"I know." Elliot held up a hand to show he completely understood every thought she was having related to his parents. "Ugh, it is going to be a long night for all the wrong reasons," Elliot said into his hand, which he then used to rub his face. The fluids had helped sober him up a little, but the outside world seemed intent on keeping him as dazed as possible.

When he looked back up, the nurse was gone, and Leila was standing in the doorway, surveying the hall. She came over to Elliot and pulled him off the patient table. "Let's go," she said.

"What? Where?" The paper cover on the table ripped as he stumbled off. He followed Leila out of the room, past an orderly wheeling an empty gurney and a man whispering into a cell phone.

Leila didn't say anything until they were back in the ER waiting room and headed toward the exit. "We're going to get the girl."

o   o   o

"Slow down," Elliot said, as she pushed the doors and led them to the parking lot. "What do you mean, get the girl?"

"Look, in all romantic comedies, there's always a scene in the movie where we think the boy's lost his chance before he gets the girl." She was still pulling him by his good hand toward her car. "That's this, right now. You think you've lost the girl. But not yet. Not if I have anything to say about it." She opened the passenger door for him as if he were still drunk and bleeding. "I have a feeling that's why we—forgive the choice of words—ran into each other. I'm gonna help you get Maribel."

"That's very nice of you to offer, but I think I should go back in there and deal with my parents."

"No. Your parents will be there to deal with in the morning. It's prom night. What you should do is go after the girl."

"You keep saying that," Elliot said. He was shaking his head, even though he could feel a small part of him flaring with hope. "But life's not like the movies. You try to live your life like the movies, and you end up with a bloody hand and a broken heart."

"That actually sounds like a line from a movie," she said, walking around to the driver's side. She opened her door, then looked at him over the roof of her car. "What would Lloyd Dobler do?"

"I'm not Lloyd Dobler." He felt like screaming, but instead the words sounded sad, defeated. Leila ignored the comment and slipped into the car, forcing Elliot to sit next to her to continue the conversation. "I'm more like Duckie from *Pretty in Pink*, and maybe it's time I accept that. Maribel said no. I should let it go."

Leila leaned across the center divider and reached for Elliot's seat belt, buckling him in with an assertive click. "You don't have to be Duckie, whoever that is. You don't have to give up. Would Lloyd Dobler ever give up?"

Maybe the look Leila was giving him should have come across as crazed instead of enthusiastic. Maybe she should have seemed more delusional than inspiring. But, as she turned the key in the ignition and the engine started, Elliot couldn't help but feel that life could still be like the movies. With this girl's help, he might still have a chance at that orchestra-swelling kiss.

"Let's go get the girl."

3

TOP-FORTY MUSIC filled the dark of the hotel ballroom where prom was still raging on. Candy-colored lights roved the walls manically. A stage had been built in the far side of the room for the band, with a sizable dance floor. All the couples danced close together to make it hard for chaperones to know who was pressed against whom.

Elliot and Leila were in the men's bathroom. Elliot had excused himself to go get cleaned up, but Leila had just followed him in, checking the counter for wet spots before hopping onto the marble surface.

"So, what's the plan?" She had to say it loudly, since the walls practically pulsed from the music from the ballroom. The stained-glass lamps hanging by the mirrors were rattling like snare drums.

Elliot slid out of his jacket and started wetting some paper towels. "Um, I don't know, actually. I guess the declaring-my-love-for-her strategy didn't work so well, so I should probably try something else this time. Something . . ."

He gestured with his hand, as if trying to draw the next word out of the air. "I don't know," he said. "Something more successful, hopefully." He tried not to gag as he brushed chunks from his tuxedo.

"Something bigger," Leila said. Then she reached into a pocket in her dress and pulled out a pack of gum, offering it to Elliot. "Bigger and maybe a little minty. No offense."

He took the pack and popped two pieces into his mouth, grateful and embarrassed. "Sure. Bigger would work." He added a dab of hand soap to the fabric, half hoping it would miraculously make him look spotless. "Something more cinematic."

They were quiet for a second, listening to the music through the walls while Elliot tried his best to make his tuxedo look presentable. Then they heard the crowd cheering as the band stopped playing. "We're gonna take a quick break and then come back for our last set of the night." Another roar ensued.

A few moments later, three of the band members walked into the bathroom, congratulating themselves on how it was going. Elliot knew all three of them from school. Two of them were fellow seniors. The drummer, Kurt, was in his English class. The third guy was a sophomore who was somewhat legendary because of his guitar skills. Rumor had it that the band had gigs booked on the East Coast for the rest of the summer, mostly thanks to the guitarist. They stopped in their tracks when they noticed Leila sitting on the counter.

"You're in the right place," she said, waving them in.

They looked over at Elliot, who shrugged. They hesitated, then returned the shrug and walked toward the urinals. Kurt said hi to Elliot as he passed by. "What the hell happened to you?" He eyed the tux and the bandaged hand.

"That's a long story," Elliot said, now scrubbing at his pants, trying not to use too much water so it wouldn't look like there was also urine on the tux, the one body fluid he'd managed to avoid.

"I hit him with my car, and then he threw up," Leila said.

"Okay, so it's not that long a story." Kurt chuckled. "I thought you were in here the whole time."

"I left for a bit," Elliot said, not wanting to get into the whole thing.

Apparently, Leila didn't mind getting into it. "Maribel turned him down."

Elliot gave her a disbelieving look.

"What? You're not James Bond," Leila said. "There's no reason to keep it a secret. If you love the girl, you let the world know. That simple."

Kurt zipped up and came over to wash his hands. "Everyone kinda knows about that anyway, man. So, what, she friend-zoned you?"

The other two band members, ignoring the conversation, were discussing what to play in their last set. They flushed and approached the sink, and Elliot moved aside to let them use the faucet.

"No," Elliot said. "That's not what happened. 'Friend-zone' takes all the heartbreak out of it. Call it what it is: The girl I love rejected me."

"Prematurely rejected," Leila said. "He's gonna win her over."

Kurt used the automatic hand-drier for a few seconds before patting his hands dry on the back of his pants. "Yeah? How are you planning to do that?"

"We don't have a plan yet," Leila said to Kurt. "We just know it's going to be big."

Elliot laid his jacket down on the counter, giving up on the stains and just placing paper towels over the parts that were still wet. He looked from Kurt to Leila and then to the other band members.

"That leaves us with five minutes to kill," the guitarist was saying when the hand-drier turned off. "We could stretch out the banter a little, or I was thinking it'd be kind of funny if we play that 'Don't You Forget About Me' song. You know, ironically."

"We've never practiced that song," the singer answered, his eyes wandering to where Leila was sitting.

"How about a Weird Al song?"

"Damnit, man, we need something we've practiced before."

"Shit, forgive me for trying to think of ideas. I don't hear you coming up with anything," the guitarist grumbled.

"It's not a matter of thinking of ideas. We need one more song for the set, and we know two that we won't have played yet. We're either playing Ace of Base's 'All That She Wants' or Jay-Z's '99 Problems.' Which is it gonna be?"

Elliot could start to picture it: the camera angles, the shots of the crowd singing along, interspersed with close-ups of Maribel's smiling face, the kind of energy that could leave you breathless.

"I think I have an idea," he said.

o   o   o

There was a moment of excitement and self-confidence before Elliot realized that he was actually going to have to get onstage and sing. And not just any song, but "All That She Wants," about a woman so lonely, she hunts men down, looking to get pregnant. Not ideal, but he happened to know every Ace of Base lyric there was, thanks to his dad's obsession with the band.

The hope was that saying the words "This is for you, Maribel," onstage would make it all enough. If movies had taught him anything, it was that embarrassing yourself in the name of love could only lead to positive things.

They left the bathroom as a group, walking with Leila hidden among them so that the front-door chaperone wouldn't notice her.

"We'll be back onstage in about five minutes. We'll go through the rest of our set to warm up the crowd for you, and then we'll call you up," Kurt said, which was right around the time Elliot's nerves became aware of the situation.

He felt himself starting to sweat, which made his bandaged hand itch. He looked around the crowd, trying to spot Maribel. There weren't quite as many people as when he had left, but the ballroom was still crowded, kids sneaking pulls from flasks by the snack tables, couples making out against the walls, the dateless standing around in groups.

"Where is she?" Leila said. "Point her out to me."

"Leila, I don't think I can do this." His stomach rumbled as if in agreement. He wondered if maybe the hospital should have pumped his stomach, even though he'd kind of done that on his own. "I can't sing. I can't dance. I've never even been to karaoke." He started breathing faster. "Oh, God, what have I done?"

Leila stepped in front of him and put her hands on his shoulders. "Hey, look at me." She stared at him until he met her eyes. "It's going to be okay. It's always a little scary to go after what you want. But she's gonna see what you're willing to do for her, and she's going to love it. You can do this."

"No, seriously. I can't sing. However many vocal cords people have, I think I've got half that. When I try singing in the shower, the water gets cold. Every time, I swear, like it's trying to get me to stop."

"Elliot," Leila said. "What are we here to do?"

"Have a panic attack?"

Leila gave him a shake. "Say it."

Elliot looked around the room. He could see a few of his friends on the far side, looking a little buzzed but mostly bored. A girl from his calculus class was sitting down at a table, alone, angrily texting. Two teachers stood guard by the emergency exit, not exactly chaperoning but trying to make it look like that was what they were doing. Elliot wanted to catch a glimpse of Maribel in her purple dress, but he was also terrified of how much it would hurt to see her again.

"Say it," Leila said again. Elliot managed to mutter something in response, something even he couldn't hear. The crowd let out a few cheers as the band took the stage. "Okay, here's what we're gonna do." Leila grabbed his hand and led him to some nearby chairs. She sat him down and pulled up a chair in front of him. "I want you to close your eyes and picture yourself kissing Maribel. In front of everyone, or somewhere private, or anywhere at all."

Elliot did as he was told. The thought came naturally to him, he'd been doing it for so long. He felt a happy shudder work down his spine the moment he imagined their lips touching. His mind flashed to kissing her in an open field while on a picnic; on her bed, with all its excess pillows; casually, in a movie theater before the lights dimmed, as if he'd been doing it for years.

"If you don't do this, you will probably never get to kiss Maribel," Leila said. "Ever. So it's pretty simple. Go sing. Sing well or badly—it doesn't matter, as long as you sing your fucking heart out," Leila said, raising her voice as the band started up again.

Though his nerves didn't loosen up, Elliot found himself nodding. "I'm not sure what it says about my luck that I managed to get run over by the one person in Minnesota who could deliver a speech like that."

It was hard to tell in the crappy lighting, but it looked as if Leila was blushing a little. "What can I say? I'm a hopeful romantic. Maybe someday you'll return the favor."

The band finished playing their funny cover of a popular rap song, and when the crowd's round of applause was over, Kurt grabbed the microphone attached to his drum set. "Now, ladies and gentlemen, we have a very special treat for you this evening. Please welcome to the stage, in the name of love, the musical stylings of Elliot Pinnik!"

A couple of people clapped, and someone let out a whistle. Elliot practically jumped out of his chair and started making his way toward the back of the ballroom, marching so that he wouldn't have time to change his mind. A drunk girl he didn't know shouted out, "Yeah, Elliot!" He walked past his friends, who looked confused about where he'd been and why the hell he'd be going up onstage.

He staggered up the stairs on the side and avoided looking out at the crowd, walking directly to the singer. When he grabbed the microphone and turned to the audience, he was surprised to find that they were mostly shrouded in darkness. Bright overhead lights pointed at the stage made it hard to see anything but silhouettes, and the nauseated feeling in his stomach quieted down. A few more people cheered.

"Maribel," he said, his voice unfamiliar on the speakers, "this is for you."

Kurt hit his drumsticks together, "One, two, three, four," he shouted out; then the music exploded all around Elliot.

He felt he was swimming in it, as if the music was coming from the air itself. He started tapping his good hand against the side of his leg in time with the music, then bobbing his head. Before he knew it, he was taking hold of the mike stand as he danced, waiting for another measure of music until it was his turn to join in.

When he sang the first line of lyrics, it didn't even feel as if the sound had come from him.

"She leads a lonely life," Elliot shouted into the microphone.

He could hear the sounds of the crowd breaking through the music. It made him think of the scene from *Ferris Bueller's Day Off* at the parade where Matthew Broderick sings along to "Twist and

Shout." Channeling his inner Ferris, Elliot started to jump around on the stage, closing his eyes as he belted out, "All that she wants is another baby." He jumped up onto the raised platform where Kurt's drum set was, then jumped back down and air-guitared next to the sophomore guitarist. He'd always heard people say that one should dance as if no one was watching, but until that moment, he'd never really understood what they meant. Something inside him simply let go, and it felt fantastic.

It was over before he knew it, and when the last of the instruments fell quiet and the noise of the crowd took over, Elliot felt he *was* Ferris Bueller. He felt ready to jump off the stage and kiss Maribel. He imagined that the people on the dance floor would part to make it happen.

So he did. He jumped off the stage, looking for Maribel in the crowd before he'd even landed. Instead of parting, though, the crowd converged on him. Hands patted him on the back and stuck out in the air, seeking high fives. "That was awesome!" one of the soccer players he'd never talked to before shouted into his face.

Maneuvering his way through the crowd, Elliot kept looking for Maribel, even calling out her name a few times, though no one paid much attention to what he was saying; they were all too busy congratulating him.

Eventually, prerecorded background music started playing through the speakers, and the crowd gave him a little room to move. He spotted his friends and, a little out of breath, made his way toward them.

"Shit, man," Mario said. "That was pretty incredible. I can't believe you just did that." Mario had been Elliot's best friend for years, and he was rarely moved to positively comment on anything.

"Thanks," Elliot said, as the other guys in the group offered their congratulations. "Do you guys know where I can find Maribel? I haven't seen her."

"Oh, she left," Mario said.

"What?"

"Yeah. Like, an hour ago."

"More, probably," Damon added.

"Shit," Elliot said.

"Yeah, that'll kill your buzz," Mario said. He pulled a flask from the inside pocket of his jacket, took a swig, and then passed it around. "She went to the after-party at that kid Bobby's house. We were about to head over there. It's too bad. You really put on a show, man. Didn't know you had it in you."

He gave Elliot a light punch on the shoulder, which Elliot barely even felt. As they had been much of the night, his feelings were focused on his stomach, which seemed to be saying, in its grumbling and gurgling language, "Goddamnit." The adrenaline in Elliot's veins drained away. He pictured Maribel at a party, holding a red plastic cup, talking to her friends, oblivious of his performance.

Leila stepped into the circle, her eyes wide and full of excitement. "Did it work? Where is she?"

"She's gone," Elliot said.

4

LEILA DIDN'T LET Elliot sulk for even a moment. She grabbed his arm and led him straight to the exit. "There's always a house party in those movies," she said. "It feels to me like we're headed toward a movie-like happy ending."

Elliot didn't say anything. He climbed into her car, noticing for the first time the bizarre cardboard cutout resting in the backseat.

"He keeps me from getting too lonely while I'm on the road," Leila explained.

He turned to face her. "What do you mean, on the road?"

"I'm not really from around here. I've just been checking out the Twin Cities for a few days. I was actually on my way out before this crazy drunk kid walked into my car."

"No! What a bastard," Elliot said, offering her a smile. "Where are you headed?"

"Alaska."

"Cool," Elliot said. "Any particular reason why?"

"I'm gonna go see the Northern Lights. He really wanted to go," she said, gesturing toward the backseat. "I can never say no to him."

He laughed, but he could sense there was something underneath

Leila's humor. "Is that really why you're going? Just to see the Northern Lights?"

"That's not a good-enough reason? People go to Buffalo just to see Niagara Falls."

"So, why the Northern Lights and not Niagara Falls?"

"I think a celestial miracle in the midst of the natural beauties of Alaska is a little more interesting than a bunch of water in Buffalo. Plus," she said, starting the engine, "I promised my grandma that I'd see the Northern Lights in person, since she never got to."

Elliot considered Leila. Her fingers, small and bare of rings or nail polish, held the steering wheel loosely. Her expression was blank as she looked out at the street.

"Which way am I going?"

Elliot pointed to the right, his eyes still fixed on Leila's profile. After a few more directions, Leila glanced at him, briefly, as if checking one of her mirrors. "What's the plan this time around? Still going big and cinematic?"

"I don't know if I have another performance like that in me." Elliot fiddled with the window crank. "I'm gonna try the declaration of love again. The first time around, if I'm being entirely honest, I wasn't very smooth. I mostly stammered, and she cut me off before I could finish. And not in the *Jerry Maguire*, 'You had me at hello,' kind of way. She stopped me and fled."

"Well, she can run, but she can't hide."

Elliot laughed, despite the lingering sense of shame he felt about his first attempt with Maribel. He could almost feel it on his skin, like something that needed to be scrubbed away. "That was the creepiest thing you could possibly say under the circumstances."

"It wasn't appropriate? It sounds like something they say in the movies."

"It is. But usually the bad guys say it to the good guys, or the good guys to the bad guys. It's more of an action-film cliché. Not the stuff of rom-com."

"Oh," Leila said. "Well, forget I said it." A moment went by. "Damnit, I should have stopped talking after that speech. It would have established an aura of mystery and wisdom."

"Leila, you hit me with your car in the middle of the night, and despite us knowing practically nothing about each other, you're intent on fixing my love life," Elliot said. "Trust me, the aura's there."

When they arrived at the party, Elliot was expecting to find the mayhem and chaos of graduation parties depicted in the movies: drunk people throwing up in the bushes, couples making out everywhere, someone in a wacky costume running down the street. What they found was a fairly quiet street without a lot of available curb space to park at and one large house with the lights on. There was a faint thumping of music in the air, and people's far-off voices.

Elliot and Leila made their way up the stepping stones that cut through the front yard and led to the door. A fountain of an angel trickled water serenely into its wide basin. A sign on the door read, NO POINT IN RINGING THE DOORBELL—IT'S REALLY LOUD IN HERE.

Don't worry. We bribed the neighbors. No one's calling the cops on us. Come in, have a drink. Keg's in the back.

They pushed the door open, releasing the sounds of the party. There were possibly two different songs playing, although that might have been Elliot's unfamiliarity with electronic music. Or maybe it was the roar of people shouting and whooping that sounded like an added bass line. A smattering of kids hung around near the door, leaning against walls and taking timid sips from red plastic cups, checking the time.

Leila and Elliot moved past the front entrance into the hallway that led to the kitchen. Signs had been taped up on the walls all over the house, pointing the way to the bathrooms or the booze or, in true high-school-movie fashion, the sex dungeon. "God, I hope she's not in the sex dungeon," Elliot said.

"What's she wearing?" Leila asked, standing on tiptoe to try to see over people but failing at it. Most of the people around were in tuxedos and prom dresses, making Leila's yellow sundress stick out.

"A purple dress, with a matching orchid corsage." They squeezed through the hallway and into the kitchen. "I was afraid she'd have a date for the prom, and he'd be the one giving her a corsage," Elliot said. He had to speak almost directly into her ear so she could hear him over the music. "But she and some friends said they didn't need to be hanging off some guy's arm to have a special night. So, I got to give Maribel the corsage I made her."

"You made her a corsage?"

Elliot felt himself blush. "I had to look up online how to do it."

"That's sweet," Leila said with a smile. "And she wore it?"

"Yeah." He shrugged. "Most people don't get it, but we're actually really good friends."

They stood by the stockade of alcohol in the kitchen for a few minutes, waiting for Maribel or one of her friends to show up to get a drink. A guy in a Vikings jersey that Elliot recognized from his freshman-year art class stood next to them as if waiting for a bartender to come by.

"Hey, Victor!" Elliot said, after finally remembering his name. "Remember me?"

"No," Victor called back resolutely, still waiting for someone to pour him a drink.

"Oh." Elliot frowned, then realized he wasn't all that offended. "Have you seen Maribel around? Maribel Palacios?"

"She's standing right next to you, bro," Victor said, clearly pointing at Leila.

"Right," Elliot said. "Thanks."

"He was helpful," Leila said, turning to a group of girls on the other side of the bar and asking after Maribel.

Maribel wasn't exactly one of the popular kids, but she was on the student council and acted in a lot of the school plays, so Elliot figured asking random people would eventually lead to something. But only a couple of those they asked knew who she was, and only one guy had seen her. "Somewhere around here," he said uselessly, reaching for a bottle of vodka.

After a couple of minutes, they decided to move on toward the living room. The lights were off, and bright green lasers shot across smoke that Elliot hoped came from a smoke machine and not an actual fire. The room was packed with people dancing, a DJ playing music from his computer. Elliot had a hard time imagining Maribel among the throng of sweaty bodies, so they headed outside.

The backyard was a huge expanse of lawn surrounded by trees, adorned with statues and a shimmering pool. One couple had laid claim to some patio furniture in a distant corner, but the rest of the lounge chairs were taken up by stoners looking up at the stars. The smoke looked like a conglomeration of factories letting out steam.

Elliot and Leila stationed themselves by the keg and looked around for Maribel.

Two guys Elliot knew stood in line for their beers. Peter Jones, who Elliot heard was headed to MIT on a scholarship, turned to his buddy. "You know what I've never understood about life?"

"We've reached that point of the night already? It's epiphany o'clock?"

"World population is weighted to females, right?" Peter went on, ignoring his friend. "Fifty-two percent of the planet—something like that. Everywhere in the world, there's more women than men. It's a mathematical fact."

"Yeah, so?"

"Why have I never been to a party that reflects that ratio? Seriously, look around. It's easily a three-to-one lead for the penises. And that makes this a pretty successful party. Usually it's at least five-to-one.

Why are parties exempt from mathematical probabilities? What kind of laws are they being governed by? I don't get it."

"You need a girlfriend, man."

"I definitely need a girlfriend."

Finally, Elliot spotted one of Maribel's friends, Stephanie, coming outside. Aside from the fact that she was a junior on the yearbook staff, Elliot knew very little about her. They caught up to her as she was lighting a cigarette. She looked embarrassed by Elliot's presence, avoiding eye contact with him. Maribel had obviously told her what had happened.

"Hey, Steph. Is Maribel here?"

Stephanie exhaled a puff of smoke and eyed Leila curiously. "Yeah. Why?"

"I just need to talk to her."

She flicked her cigarette with her arm extended way out to avoid getting ash on her dress. "You know that the only time you've ever talked to me is when you're looking for her, right? Any time I see you heading my way, I have to think: Okay, where is Maribel?" She glanced at Leila, as if trying to place her, then finally met Elliot's eyes. "Next time you're in love with a girl, it might be a good idea to try talking to her friends."

Elliot didn't know what to say to that. He stammered a couple of times, then looked at Leila as if she was his interpreter.

"What?" Leila said. "She's right."

Steph sighed, bringing the cigarette back up to her lips. "I saw her inside," she said. "She was going upstairs."

"Thanks," Elliot said. He felt like he should say something else, but Leila repeated the thanks and then started to pull Elliot back across the yard toward the house.

They slowly pushed their way through the crowd, Leila looking around and pointing things out, as if Elliot had never been to a high school party and seen people doing keg stands and double-dipping chips in the guac.

"There are eighteen people on their phones in this room alone," Leila said from behind him as they tried to slink their way through the kitchen and past the dance floor. "Who are they texting if everyone they know is here?"

"Are you serious?" Elliot said, raising an eyebrow.

"That guy almost put his phone in the onion dip!" Leila shrieked with delight. "And that girl looks like she's about to—yup. She just threw up. And there is no commotion about it. Elliot, why is there no commotion?"

"Do people not throw up at the parties you go to?"

Leila ignored the question, swiveling her head around to take in more of the sights.

Elliot made his way deeper into the party, and Leila trailed behind. Elliot had assumed the upstairs area would be off-limits, but the staircase wasn't cordoned off, and the paper signs invitingly pointed the way toward MORE BATHROOMS, COATROOM, AND OTHER PLACES TO GET WALKED IN ON WHILE MAKING OUT OR WORSE.

"Better this than the sex dungeon, right?" Leila said. Elliot groaned involuntarily. "Kidding," she said, and she gave him an encouraging pat on the back. "Wait, no. I'm not kidding. This *is* better than the sex dungeon. I'm just sorry I mentioned it."

"Leila?"

"Yeah?"

"That aura of mystery and wisdom we talked about? Wanna get back to it?"

"That's the nicest way anyone's ever told me to shut up," she said, leading the way up the stairs.

They tiptoed around a girl who had passed out in the middle of the stairway. Leila glanced, expressionless, at the family photos on the wall. At the top of the stairs was another living area with a couch and a big-screen TV. People drunkenly played video games as they passed around a hookah hose, failing to blow smoke rings in the air. A couple cuddled on the far end of the L-shaped couch. The girl's dress was bright purple, and for a second Elliot's stomach dropped, as if he were free-falling. But then the girl turned to look over her shoulder at Elliot and Leila, and he saw that the girl was a redhead with a nose ring and that the dress wasn't even the right shade of purple.

They moved on, knocking on doors and stepping inside. Every time Leila pushed a door open, Elliot held his breath, hoping Maribel wasn't in there with someone else. In one room, people sat on the floor listening to Pink Floyd with their pupils dilated. The bathroom smelled faintly of vomit. The master bedroom was the only one that was locked.

At the end of the upstairs hallway, they reached the only door they hadn't checked. It was cracked open, and they could see that the room was dark. Another paper sign had been taped onto the door, warning people to enter at their own risk. Leila put her hand on the door.

"Wait," Elliot said, reaching out for her shoulder, "what if she's in there with someone?"

"The lights are off."

"Not exactly a source of comfort there, Leila."

"Maybe she's alone in there and napping or something? I don't hear any sounds coming from inside."

Leila pushed the door open with one shove.

"Anyone in here?"

She took a step forward, and Elliot followed to get a better look. There were indistinguishable noises coming from somewhere in the room, and he got that ineffable feeling that someone else was there.

"Hello?" Elliot tried. "Maribel?"

The noises continued, whoever was making them paying them no mind. Elliot grasped at the wall, searching for the light switch. He could barely make out Leila moving forward with her arms outstretched. She cried out as her foot or shin bumped into something.

As soon as Elliot found and flipped the lights on, the door slammed behind them. Elliot didn't know what to react to first: the surprise of being shut in, the couple on the bed aggressively making out (not Maribel, at least), or the fact that the walls were completely covered in shelf after shelf of Cabbage Patch dolls. Hundreds of creepy plastic faces stared out at them like something out of a B horror movie. Some of them were old enough that they'd lost all their hair, or a limb, or their facial features had been eroded away, leaving them faceless except for the bump of a nose, a blue smudge where an eye used to be.

The couple on the bed—thankfully, still clothed—finally noticed that the lights had come on and stopped making out. The girl sat up, glared at Leila and Elliot, then slapped her boyfriend across the face. "Tacos for dinner, forties at the prom, and you texted your friends to walk in on us again? I'm so done with you."

"Babe, I don't know these people," Carl cried, holding a hand to his quickly reddening cheek.

As Leila let out a laugh, Elliot felt himself start to hyperventilate. He could feel the Cabbage Patch dolls' eyes on him. The slight smiles etched onto their plastic faces looked as if they were purposefully mocking him. Even Carl could get the girl, even if he was about to lose her now. He rushed to the door and pulled frantically on the handle. It was locked from the outside. He rattled the knob a few times and called out for help but was answered only by the sounds of the party raging on.

"Very funny," he called out. "You locked us in the room. Now stop being dicks, and let us out."

A little girl's voice called out from the other side. "Can't you people read? That's my room, and you need my permission to go inside. So now, you need my permission to come back out."

"Is that a child?" Leila asked. "What is a child doing at this party?"

"Kid! We were just looking for someone. Please let us out!"

"Nope," the little voice answered, already fading away.

Elliot pounded on the door, but even he could barely hear his own knocking above the beat of electronic music. He let his forehead drop against the wood.

"You promised tonight would be special!" Carl's girlfriend was yelling in between sobs.

Elliot banged his head against the door. This was not how his night was supposed to go. He felt Leila's hand on his shoulder. "Hey, we'll get out of here. Don't worry."

"Look at what you did," Carl said, pointing at his girlfriend sobbing into the pillows.

"Sorry," Leila said, "we were just looking for someone."

"Yeah, well, they're not here. Now will you please get the hell out?"

Leila made a show of jiggling the door. "Did you miss that whole part about us being locked in here?"

"Whatever," he mumbled, turning his attention back to his girlfriend, whose whole body was shaking. Carl tried to put a hand on her back, but she smacked it away. "C'mon, babe. I love you, okay? Don't be so dramatic."

Elliot stared in awe as the girl lifted herself from the bed and smiled. "You do?" Within seconds they were back to making out, the noise of smacking lips like food being chewed with an open mouth.

Elliot put his back to the wall and slid down to the floor, rubbing his face with his good hand. Leila took a seat next to him. "I'm dead, right?" he said. "You ran me over with your car, and I'm now in hell."

"I must have killed both of us," Leila said, grimacing at the unsightly exchange of saliva taking place on the bed.

"You don't happen to know how to pick a lock, do you?"

Leila shook her head slowly. "If I do, I'm not aware of it. Think you can break the door down?"

"I'd like to say yes, but I'll probably just end up having to go back to the hospital." Elliot looked at his bandaged hand, wondering if the scars would ever be anything other than a painful reminder of that night. "I can't tell which is worse: them, or the dolls. I feel they're going to come to life and try to tickle me." He shuddered at the thought.

Elliot banged his elbow against the door behind him, hoping someone would hear the knocking, or that the little girl would let up.

"I love you so much," Carl said, kissing his girlfriend, though she continued to sob.

She pulled away, her eyes blinking back tears. "You do?"

Leila and Elliot looked on with a mix of awe and repulsion as the couple went back to making out, murmuring not-so-sweet nothings to each other in between sloppy kisses.

"We have to get out of here," Elliot said.

"Immediately," Leila agreed. She stood up, looking around the room as if a second door might appear. She put her hands on her hips as she thought. "Windows!" she cried out. "A house like this wouldn't have an upstairs bedroom without windows." She moved to the back wall of the room and started clearing dolls from their shelves. Sure enough, the Cabbage Patch kids had been covering up a window.

Elliot rose to his feet and rushed to Leila's side. Fortunately, the shelves themselves weren't bolted into the wall but were just fitted into slots on supporting beams on either side of the window. The two of them started pulling the shelves out, laying them down on the floor next to the dolls, which were just as creepy looking up at them from below.

When Elliot removed the last of the shelves, Leila reached for the window. "Maribel, here we come," she said, and pulled up. The window didn't budge. Before Elliot could feel too dejected, though, Leila reached and flipped the latch that was locking it into place. She tried again, and this time the window opened easily, letting in the warm summer air. Elliot poked his head out the window. There was a ledge right below them, and they were no more than ten feet above the lush front yard. Even without the desperation of being stuck in that room, it didn't seem like a long way down.

Leila hoisted herself up and through the window. Elliot, operating mostly with just one hand, followed her carefully. They climbed down onto the ledge, hands flat against the side of the house to steady themselves. Leila turned to Elliot with a smile. "We're not giving up on this, even if it takes us all night. You'll have your big movie moment."

And then they jumped.

5

ELLIOT LANDED ON the grass with a thud. There was a shooting pain coming from his hand, but he was so happy to be out of that room that he ignored it. When he looked up at the house, the lights in the Cabbage Patch room turned off. "Where to now?"

"I don't know," Elliot said. "She could be at another party, or at someone's house."

"Why don't we just call her?"

"She accidentally put her phone in the washing machine the other day. Hasn't gotten a new one yet."

"That's inconvenient. What about one of her friends?"

"We don't have a whole lot of mutual friends," Elliot said. "My social circle has a diameter of, maybe, four people." Leila didn't laugh. "Not that I need much more than that. Three good friends and someone to be hopelessly in love with—that's about all I can handle." He chuckled to himself, but she was still quiet.

Leila looked up and down the street, chewing on her bottom lip. "Where else could she be?"

"The record store," Elliot realized aloud. "Sometimes she likes to go think on the roof of the record store where she works."

"Last day of high school, and my best friend just professed his love for me," Leila said. "If it were me, I'd be probably feeling pensive. Let's go check it out."

They returned to Leila's car. Leila put on some music and started the car, and Elliot closed his eyes and thought of Maribel, imagining that the toe prints on the windshield belonged to her. After only a few minutes, though, the car started groaning, slowing down, and then advancing in small bursts that snapped Elliot from his reverie.

"Shit," Leila said. She reached to turn on the hazard lights just as the car slowed to a stop.

"What? What happened?"

"We may have run out of gas." She turned off the engine and tried starting it again, but it wouldn't take. "Damn. It can usually go a solid twenty miles after the light turns on."

"Why didn't you stop to get some?"

"I got caught up in this whole Maribel thing." Leila smacked the steering wheel and leaned back in her seat.

Elliot's stomach grumbled another *goddamnit*. "Do you have Triple-A or something? Although at this time of night it's gonna take them forever to get here." He looked at the windshield to find the toe prints, but the car was between streetlights, and the marks had disappeared in the dark.

"No," Leila said, giving the engine another try.

Elliot picked at a still-crusty spot on the tux, feeling deflated. "I guess that's a sign, then. This probably isn't going to happen tonight."

He examined the stuff that came off under his fingernail, grimaced, then wiped it back onto the tux.

"Hey, none of those guys in the movies ever have it easy, right? Getting the girl of your dreams is supposed to be an obstacle-filled journey."

"Great, we have the tagline for my night. And how, pray tell, are we gonna get around this particular obstacle?"

"You get up and push from the back. I'll steer and push from up here," Leila said, opening her door.

"What?"

"We'll push the car to the nearest gas station."

"You're joking. It's, like, two miles away. I can barely even walk two miles with a backpack on. You want me to push a car that distance when I only have one functional hand?"

"If you're fishing for another rousing speech, you're not getting one. Now get out, and help me push."

Elliot shook his head, then got out of the car, walking around to the back and trying to figure out a way to get enough leverage to push without hurting his already-injured hand. After a few clumsy, painful attempts, he finally found a comfortable position and started pushing the car. Leila was directly in front of him, one hand on the steering wheel to keep the car straight, leaning over as she helped him push. He kept his eyes on the ground. "We're going straight two blocks and then turning right," he said. "If I haven't passed out by then."

There were no other cars on the road, and the night was still.

Elliot could hear their slow footsteps as they pushed the car forward, the tires passing over the gravel sounding like bugs being squashed. In the distance, the brilliant skyline of the Twin Cities illuminated the horizon, little trails of light cutting through the darkness that separated the golden sight from Burnsville.

"You okay back there?" Leila called out.

Elliot was breathing heavily, his body exhausted by the long night and the alcohol and the blood loss. "I'll be okay. I'll just buy a Gatorade at the gas station. And maybe have a lung transplant." He stopped pushing for a second to catch his breath. "I think the last time my heart rate was this high was in fifth grade." Another deep intake of breath, the air painful in his throat but soothing when it reached his lungs. "We played tag during recess one time." He went on that way for a few more blocks, wheezing until he'd caught his breath and then telling Leila, a few words at a time, how Maribel had come running at him and how his heart had been torn between wanting to run fast to impress her and standing still so she'd plow into him.

"Such a romantic," Leila said. "If she could hear you talk like this, I'm sure she'd already be yours."

Elliot felt himself flush. His friends had always been supportive, but no one other than his own fantasies had ever made it seem like being with Maribel could actually happen. He kept pushing the car.

"Which did you end up going with? Did you run or stay still?"

"I took three steps and then tripped. She helped me up before tagging me. Happiest day of my life."

Leila laughed out. It was a wonderful sound that echoed down the empty street and made Elliot wish that Leila had been in his corner a long time ago.

When they finally reached the gas station, they took a moment to catch their breath. It had taken less time than Elliot had thought it would. He hadn't realized earlier, but the gas station was on the same block as the record store. His first good-luck stroke of the night.

"Good," Elliot said, sniffing at his tux. "The one smell this jacket needed: sweat." He looked across the street at the record store. There was a sign on top of the building, making it impossible to see if anyone was on the roof, which, coupled with the view of the Performing Arts Center and the Minneapolis skyline, was why Maribel loved going up there.

"Come on," Leila said, moving toward the convenience store. "I'll buy you a Gatorade."

They picked up some drinks and a travel-sized deodorant spray for Elliot, but when the cashier tried to ring them up, Leila's credit card was declined. "Shit," Leila said. "It must be all the traveling. The bank gets confused that I'm in different cities every day. I know I said it was on me, but I don't have any cash. Do you mind?"

"I don't have any, either," Elliot said. "I gave all my money to some guys at prom for that bottle of bourbon."

They looked pleadingly at the cashier, who shrugged and picked up the magazine she'd been reading. They dragged their feet back out the door. "You know what? Don't worry about the gas," Leila said. "We're on a mission, right? You go check the record store. I'll stay back here and check my car for any cash I might have lying around."

"What should I say? If she's even there."

"It doesn't matter. Just talk to her the way you talk *about* her, and you'll be fine."

He looked over at the record store. The lights were all out except for the ones illuminating the billboard-size sign on top of the building. He could just make out the window art announcing new arrivals and special sales, most of it in Maribel's neat handwriting.

"Leila?"

"Yeah?"

"If you ever need help chasing after the boy of your dreams, you can count on me to help."

"Thanks. I might have to take you up on that."

Elliot crossed the street in a half jog, checking for traffic. He went around the back of the record store, unlocking the gate the way Maribel had showed him. He climbed onto the dumpster to reach the stepladder that led to the roof. His heart was beating so loudly that he could feel his pulse in his empty stomach. He took a few deep breaths and then started climbing. Throbbing pain shot through his hand with every rung, but Elliot pictured Maribel sitting up there in her prom dress, her back bare to the warm summer air, her big brown eyes narrowed in thought, and he climbed faster.

He reached the last rung and hauled himself onto the roof. It was a completely open space, nothing between the ladder and the street-facing sign but a few pipes. Elliot stepped toward the middle of the roof, even though he was clearly alone up there. It wasn't just the visual evidence; Elliot could feel Maribel's absence. He felt for a second as if he would never see her again, that the emptiness of the rooftop signified not just another obstacle but that she'd been removed completely from his life. He didn't know how many more of these false hopes he could take.

He walked toward the sign, then peeked around it to look across the street at the gas station. Leila was inside the convenience store, leaning against the counter and talking to the cashier. What kind of teenager traveled on her own to Alaska to go see the Northern Lights? What kind of girl was willing to help a total stranger out the way she was doing?

Elliot climbed back down the ladder and crossed the street to the gas station. Leila saw him coming and walked out of the convenience store to meet him. For some reason, Elliot waved at her, as if he hadn't seen her in a long time.

"No luck?" she started saying, before focusing on his raised hand. "Whoa, you're bleeding."

"Huh?" He turned his bandaged hand. A small circle of blood had appeared over his palm, and it was spreading slowly. "Crap."

"I'd offer to take you back to the hospital, but . . . you know." She gave one of her tires a kick.

"There's a twenty-four-hour CVS a couple of blocks from here. Some fresh gauze is all I need."

"That's what I like to hear," Leila said

○ ○ ○

At the CVS, they tried Leila's credit card again with the same results. Then they tried convincing the manager to let Elliot take the gauze now and come back with the money the next day.

"It's an emergency," Leila said, pointing to the blood coming through the bandage.

"I'd recommend going to a hospital, then."

"Please, sir. If I don't bring you the money tomorrow, you can call the cops on me. Worse, you can call my parents. I've been ignoring them all night and they'll probably give you a reward just for telling them I'm alive. My name's Elliot Pinnik. I live on—"

"It's $7.49." The manager said. He put his hands on his hips and furrowed his brow, the classic adult stance signifying that the conversation was over.

Elliot and Leila left the CVS and stood out in front. "I kind of hope I bleed to death, just so he'll have to deal with the guilt." He sighed and picked some dirt off the bandage. "So, tireless cheerleader, now what?"

Leila bit her bottom lip, then kicked at a pebble on the ground. Elliot followed the pebble's path across the parking lot until a car pulled in and blinded him with its headlights. By the time his eyes had recovered, the car was parked, and a guy wearing sweatpants and a stained T-shirt was walking toward the entrance of the CVS. He looked like he hadn't slept in weeks.

"Excuse me, sir," Leila said as he approached. "I know how this is going to sound, but we're in—"

"Sorry, no change," the man replied, barely looking at them as he entered the store.

Leila watched as the automatic doors slid shut behind him; then she turned to Elliot. "Huh. So that's what that feels like."

"Should we try to steal the gauze?"

"No!" Leila yelled, strangely forcefully. "No shoplifting." She calmed herself down a little. "Hopefully someone shows up who has a good heart and will be willing to lend us some money. If they're willing to give us some gas money, too, we'll go to Maribel's house and wait for her to show up. Take a seat, and look like you're in pain. But don't show the bloody side of your hand; we don't want to freak people out."

Elliot did as he was told, taking a seat on the curb of the parking lot. There was no movement for a while. The tired guy left the store with a jumbo pack of diapers and drove off. A middle-aged woman who'd been smoking in her car tossed the cigarette butt onto the ground without bothering to stamp it out and completely ignored them as she marched past them. A couple of guys in their twenties actually stopped and listened to Leila but eyed Elliot suspiciously and then shook their heads. Elliot's foot started falling asleep, and he thought back to seventh grade, when Maribel had hosted a movie night at her house. He had sat on the couch, and she took the spot on the floor by his feet, at one point even resting her head against his knee. Afraid that he would break whatever spell she had come under, he hadn't moved for the remainder of the movie, even when his foot had been asleep so long it hurt.

A van pulled into the lot. Elliot tried to look innocuously glum and let Leila do the talking. He kept his eyes on the ground. He heard the door of the van open, followed by a familiar voice.

"If it isn't the man of the night!"

Elliot looked up, confused. It was Kurt. "What the hell are you guys doing here?" Kurt asked. He nodded at Leila, who gave him a wave back. "How'd it go with your girl? After the show you put on, I thought you'd be somewhere romantic and with a mattress."

"She wasn't at the prom anymore. She didn't see it."

"That sucks. Did you check that kid Bobby's party?"

"Yeah, she wasn't there, either. We've been looking for her all night."

"Why would she be at the CVS?"

"We just had to take a quick detour to get myself patched up." He raised his hand so Kurt could see the blood.

"Gnarly," Kurt said, nodding at the sight.

"But it turns out we don't have any money," Leila chimed in.

"How much do you need?"

"Seven-fifty," Elliot said, rising to his feet.

"Plus some gas money. If that's okay," Leila added.

"Your performance tonight is worth at least that much," Kurt said. He motioned for them to follow him inside and paid for Elliot's gauze, then gave Leila a twenty for gas. Elliot gave the manager what he hoped was a smug look.

When they were back outside, Elliot recalled what he could from health class to apply the fresh gauze. Despite the blood, the wound didn't look too bad. Only one of the stitches had come undone, and most of the blood had coagulated already. "Thank you so much," Elliot said.

"Don't mention it," Kurt replied, pulling out his keys from his pocket. "By the way, have you guys checked Ruby's Diner? There's a bunch of people over there sobering up with coffee and graveyard specials. I just drove past, and it looks like half the school is inside. I wouldn't be surprised if you find Maribel there." Kurt shook Elliot's hand, then waved good-bye to Leila. "Good luck, man. Everyone's rooting for you."

As they watched Kurt's van pull out of the lot, Elliot wondered if he'd misheard. Was it possible that everyone actually cared what happened between him and Maribel?

"What do you say?" Leila interrupted his thoughts. "Ruby's Diner?"

"At this point, I'm half expecting Ruby's Diner to be full of zombies or something."

Leila smacked him across the chest. "I said, 'Ruby's Diner?'"

"I've been in love with this girl for as long as I can remember. Of course I'm going to Ruby's Diner," Elliot said. "But I'm allowed the occasional smart-ass comment, aren't I?"

"You have a very conservative definition of the word 'occasional.'"

Elliot shrugged. "Whatever. At this point, I'd happily fight zombies to get to her."

6

LIKE PRETTY MUCH everything else in Burnsville, Ruby's was just a short drive away. Elliot barely had time to sort out what he was feeling: the hope and the hopelessness combined, the night's exhaustion and lingering adrenaline, Maribel's absence and how strong his desire was to just be near her again, to tell her in ways he'd failed to before how much he loved her.

Leila parked her car in front of the restaurant. Elliot could recognize some of the cars in the parking lot, and he could see through the large windows that the diner was packed—no small feat for 4:00 a.m. A few kids stood outside smoking, their shirts untucked and their bow ties undone. The girls' hairdos had started to sag and uncurl, hair spray finally losing the battle against gravity. Everyone looked tired but proud of their tiredness, as if the night's exhaustion stood for all four years of high school, and they wanted to show the world that they'd survived.

"Want me to wait out here?" Leila asked.

"No. Without you I wouldn't have made it this far." He tried to spot Maribel inside, but there were people everywhere. A waitress carrying a tray loaded with pancakes and sausage hip-checked someone out of her way. "Plus, in the movies there's always someone who starts the slow clap. I'm entrusting you with that role."

They got out of the car. Elliot brushed his good hand down his tux. He wished he hadn't thrown the boutonniere into the street; it would help make him look a little more presentable.

"How do I look?"

Leila stepped in front of him, straightened his jacket by the lapels, brushed imaginary dirt (or maybe not that imaginary) off his shoulder. "You look like you've been through hell. But that's what you're supposed to do. Go through hell to get the girl." She looked up at him and smiled, her eyes lighting up, showing no trace of the distance he'd occasionally seen in them. "You look great."

Inside the restaurant, it was even busier than Elliot had been able to tell from looking through the windows. So many tables had been pushed together that the diner resembled a German beer hall. Kids were packed into booths like clowns in a car. They had broken off into the usual cliques and shouted at each other from across the room. Some were sipping on coffee, some were wolfing down greasy breakfast food, and some had fallen asleep with their foreheads against the table. Strays—either drunkenly lost or drunkenly social—roamed the corridors between tables. The servers, mostly women in their fifties, looked focused and angry but mostly confused that their usually slow graveyard shift had been hijacked by rowdy teenagers. The only adult customers, two men in tank tops and trucker hats, were seated at the counter, clearly trying to shovel their scrambled eggs down and pay their bill as quickly as possible.

Before Elliot could start to move forward, someone came up from behind and put an arm around his shoulders.

"Elliot! You are my freakin' hero, man," said the unknown voice. Elliot swiveled to get a look at the guy, who turned out to be a football player that Elliot had only had a couple of classes with throughout high school. The guy smelled like whiskey, and Elliot felt a flush of shame at the realization that he had smelled the same way earlier in the night. "What you did at prom?" The football player put a hand to the side of Elliot's head and made an exploding sound, complete with a spray of spit. "So cool." He pulled his arm away and gave Elliot a light slap on the cheek. "So freakin' cool." Then he walked away, stealing the toast off someone else's plate as he passed by.

As soon as that guy was gone, Elliot saw Anthony from his math class walking steadfastly toward him. He was pointing at Elliot with one hand, his other raised up for a high five. Elliot obliged, careful to remember to use his uninjured hand. The sound of their palms smacking against each other rang out through the diner. Anthony walked away without another word, but the high five had alerted others to Elliot's presence, and he was soon surrounded by a chorus of clamoring voices.

"Epic!" someone yelled out.

"I can't believe you did that," a girl named Diana said, smacking him on the shoulder. "That made prom, like, memorable, you know?"

Several others approached for high fives, and among other things, Elliot's performance was referred to as "legit," "pro," "badass," and, in a strange twist of anachronistic slang, "neat." He had never known that people liked to express their congratulations in such a variety of unwelcome physical contact, either. Elliot hid his bandaged hand in his jacket pocket to keep it from getting hurt.

"You might not need me. Looks like there are plenty of people who want to start the slow clap for you," Leila whispered into his ear.

He grinned at Leila and then realized that what she'd said was true. Never before had he felt so many eyes staring at him with approval. The hands kept coming at him for high fives, and each one he returned with growing enthusiasm, the smack of palms meeting sounding each time more satisfying, like deconstructed applause.

This was it, the turning point of his night. Any moment now, the crowd of smiling faces would part slowly for him, one by one stepping aside until they finally revealed Maribel looking on at him. She'd smile and say something sweet and charming and instantly classic, something quotable. This was how his night was supposed to go, and now it was happening. She was at the diner. Elliot could feel it in the air.

He stepped forward, scanning the booths on his left, the tables on his right. The white noise of so many chattering voices felt like silence to him, like the precursor to a pop song that would erupt only after he and Maribel finally kissed.

As he passed the table where all the drama geeks were sitting, someone grabbed Elliot's wrist and pulled him in. "Here you go," the guy said, putting three pieces of bacon into Elliot's hand. "You deserve this."

Confused but thankful, Elliot nodded and took the bacon. He felt a tap on his shoulder, and his heart quickened, thinking it was Maribel.

"I'm actually pretty hungry," Leila said once he'd turned to face her. "Do you mind?"

He handed over the bacon, wiped the grease off against his pant leg, and continued down the aisle. The basketball players were all eating voraciously; the artsy kids were holding their empty coffee mugs up in the air, gesturing for a refill. Peter Jones, the MIT student-to-be, was looking around the diner forlornly, counting. "I just don't get it," Elliot heard him say.

Then, like the sun breaking through on a cloudy day, a flash of purple shone from the far side of the crowd.

All he could definitively see of the girl was her dress hanging out the side of the booth, that unmistakable shade of purple. She was in the corner booth, her back turned toward Elliot. When a waitress passed by and moved someone out of the way, Elliot could see Maribel's hand resting on the table, the orchid corsage prominently displayed on her wrist.

Elliot spoke over his shoulder to Leila, not willing to lose sight of Maribel. "That's her."

Without waiting for Leila's encouragement, he strode through the diner, sidestepping everyone who was obliviously standing in the middle of the aisle, the drunks sprawled with their legs poking out from the booths. He lost awareness of how hard his heart was beating, how many knots his stomach had twisted itself into, whether his hand still hurt. All he had in mind was Maribel.

Her name was on the tip of his tongue before he reached her; he felt so ready to speak it out loud, to tell her exactly how much she meant to him. But she wasn't alone.

In the booth with her was a guy. Some guy Elliot had never seen before, someone who, as far as Elliot knew, didn't even go to their school. He was in a tux, immaculate. Maribel was laughing at something the guy had said. They didn't even notice that Elliot was there.

Unable to avert his eyes, his feet seemingly unwilling to carry him away, Elliot could only look on as the girl he'd loved for the better part of a decade leaned forward and kissed the unknown guy.

Throughout their friendship, Maribel had on occasion given Elliot a peck on the cheek. Once, the peck had slipped from his cheek to a place that could almost be considered beneath the earlobe. This, however, was no peck. Maribel's hand, the one with the corsage on the wrist, went up to the guy's face and pulled him in closer.

Elliot's heart broke all over again before the act had even finished. Everything he'd gone through that night, only to find her like this. He wanted to disappear. He felt as if he *was* disappearing, like his body had finally had enough of tonight's shit and was hitting the self-destruct button. As if, any minute now, he would simply explode.

He'd thought that unrequited love was torture. He thought he'd understood what the orchid had felt like being run into the ground like that. But he'd only been lying there all night, still whole, and now Maribel was the tire smashing him into the asphalt.

Finally, mercifully, the stranger sensed Elliot's presence and pulled away from Maribel. When she noticed his attention was elsewhere, she turned around. Her eyes instantly met Elliot's.

How unfair that the person breaking your heart could still be resoundingly beautiful, that her face was still the one you loved the most in the world. In those eyes of hers, Elliot spotted a look that must have been pity. He wondered if it had always been there and he'd just missed it all these years. Suddenly aware that he would rather be absolutely anywhere else on the planet, Elliot turned back the way he'd come. By the time he passed Leila, he was nearly in a sprint, wishing he could forget about the whole night.

7

ELLIOT WAS QUIET on the drive to his house. He didn't want to talk about Maribel, didn't want Leila to feel sorry for him, didn't want to give in to that building pressure of tears behind his eyes. The sky over the horizon was starting to brighten into lighter shades of purple, the clouds that had been there all night starting to reveal themselves.

Leila parked the car. There was nothing Elliot wanted more than to shed the dirty tuxedo, crawl into his bed, and pray for sleep. However, the lights were on throughout his house, meaning his mom had stayed up waiting for him, her panicky imagination no doubt making her worry more than necessary, especially since he'd been avoiding her calls all night. So, instead, he and Leila walked around the corner to the small playground at the park. They seated themselves on the swing set, looking out at the clouds slowly turning pink and orange. The chains creaked under the strain of Elliot's weight.

He could feel Leila's gaze on him. "Please don't ask me if I'm okay."

"I wasn't going to. I know you're not."

Elliot leaned his head against the swing's chain. A tear rolled out of the corner of his eye, and he brushed it quickly away.

Fuck Molly Ringwald and her happy endings. Fuck Lloyd Dobler, who, if he had existed in real life, probably *would* have lain down in the middle of the road, and he wouldn't have waited for a rainy day to do it. They were the reasons that Elliot's chest felt like it had collapsed in on itself. It was because of them that he'd allowed himself to love Maribel for so long; it was their fault that he had deluded himself into thinking that a sweeping romantic gesture could convince someone to love you when they didn't.

"Life's not like those movies. It was stupid of me to think it ever could be." He kicked at the ground, mud sticking to the tip of his shoe. "I should just stop watching them; they're messing with my head."

Elliot wiped at his eyes again, trying to will away his tears. The chains of the swing creaked with the movement. He'd often sat with Maribel at the park, on those very swings, killing time on empty afternoons. It had felt as if they were living in a world made just for the two of them.

The first rays of the sun appeared, clearly delineated through the clouds like something out of a painting. The clouds were golden, the baby-blue sky tinted with bright orange hues. "Goddamnit, sky," Elliot said. "Now's not the time to look so picturesque. I'm trying to make a point about life being crappy."

Leila chuckled beside him. She was gently rocking herself on the swing, her feet pushing against the ground but never leaving it. Her sundress swished quietly with the movement. They looked on at the inappropriately majestic sky. "You know what would happen next in the movie, right?"

Elliot sighed, hoping she wouldn't try to keep his hope alive. He turned to look at her, surprised at the realization that he'd only known her a handful of hours. It felt much longer than that. She planted her feet firmly to stop her swaying and met his eyes. He was taken aback by how striking they were, as if it was the first time he'd really seen them. Then she leaned in and kissed him.

It took him a moment to register what was happening. Her mouth was on his, soft and warm and exhilarating. His eyes were still open, and he could swear he saw the world starting to change. The light around them turned golden, soft, as if filtered through a lens. He closed his eyes, hearing music in his head that easily could have been coming from everywhere all at once.

He was wrong; life could be like the movies. He kissed back, his heart swelling.

Then Leila pulled away from him, placing one hand flat against his chest. The sun was starting to show over the horizon, orange and blinding, making her eyes shine. "Don't get the wrong idea," she said. "That was just to show you that it can happen to you. That you can get a happy ending, if you find the right person." She removed her hand from his chest but kept her eyes on his. "I know you were hoping that person was Maribel. But just because things turned out differently with her, that doesn't mean you'll never get to experience movie love."

Elliot unconsciously ran his tongue over his lips, the taste and feel of Leila's mouth lingering in his.

"It will happen to you," Leila said, turning back to face the sunrise.

"You're a great guy, and you're willing to fight for those you love. Someday, someone will see that. And she'll love you for it. One day, Elliot, you *will* get the girl." Leila looked down at the ground and started rocking herself again until the chains squeaked. "Just not today."

Elliot didn't know quite what to say. He joined Leila in staring at the sunrise and slowly rocking the swing. Birds chirped to greet the day. A cardinal perched on a nearby tree was looking in their direction, whistling a song in Morse code, one long note followed by three short ones. Then it took off, a red streak disappearing into the trees.

"This isn't going to be the last time you're in love," Leila continued, "and it's probably not going to be the last time you're heartbroken. You can't go walking into traffic every time it happens."

Taken aback, Elliot turned to Leila. "I was just a little . . ." he started to say, but Leila gave him a knowing look that kept him from trying to make up an excuse.

"You're too special a guy to do something as stupid as you almost did tonight."

"Okay." Elliot nodded, looking down at his feet.

"I want you to promise me that nothing like that will ever happen again."

"I promise," he said quickly. Squinting against the sun, he reached his hand out to her, pinky outstretched.

Leila looked at him, a little confused.

"You've never done a pinky promise?"

She shook her head.

"Put your pinky out like this." When she did, he wrapped his pinky around hers. Anytime he'd made a pinky promise with Maribel, he'd thought of it as one-fifth of holding hands. "Pinky promises are even more serious than regular ones. So, I'm pinky-promising you that it'll never happen again."

Squinting through the strengthening sun at their hands, Leila said, "Good. I know we just met, but if I find out you break this promise, I will hunt you down."

"I believe you," he said. They pumped their arms a couple of times like a handshake, and then Elliot let Leila's pinky go. "Where the hell are you from that you don't know about pinky promises?"

Leila shrugged and threw her legs out in front of her to get the swing going. "Wisconsin," she said.

Elliot leaned against the chain, watching her. The wind rippled her dress and her hair; a smile spread her lips. Taking note of his exhaustion, Elliot realized how differently his night might have ended up if it hadn't been Leila's car that he'd stepped in front of.

After a couple of minutes, Leila stopped swinging. "I guess I should let you get to bed, huh? You've had a long night."

"Ugh. I still have to deal with my mom," Elliot said, getting up from the swing. "But I might as well face the music now while I can still get some sympathy points for my hand."

Leila gave him a smile. "She'll get over it."

"In three or four years, maybe." He offered her his good hand to help her get up from the swing, and they started walking back to his house. "Thanks for helping tonight. Or at least trying to."

"My pleasure. Don't feel shitty for too long. You tried your best."

"Thanks to you."

She smiled again. It was such a warm smile, it made Elliot jealous of her regular friends, whoever they were. "No thanks necessary. Just remember our pinky promise."

"I will." Yawning, he stretched his arms out over his head, feeling his back crack slightly. They'd reached his house and were standing behind the tree in his front yard in case his mom was peeking out. "Are you leaving now, hitting the road?"

Leila crossed her arms over her chest, then covered her mouth as his yawn spread to her. "Yup. The Northern Lights are calling."

Elliot nodded as if he understood why she was going, as if he understood anything about her. "Is it okay if we hug? It just seems like a lesser good-bye won't do."

Leila laughed and stepped to him, wrapping her arms around him uninhibitedly. She was a great hugger, firm and affectionate. She gave an extra squeeze at the end, which he took as one last act of cheerleading on her behalf. *You're going to be okay*, her hug seemed to say.

When they pulled apart, Leila gave him another smile, then raised her hand in a gentle wave. "Bye, Elliot."

"Bye," he replied. She turned to walk back to her car, so he headed across the yard to his front door. He forced out a sigh, hoping it would somehow help him prepare for his mom.

That's when he saw the note taped to his front door. It was a plain piece of notebook paper folded in half. His name was neatly written on the front, the handwriting instantly familiar. Elliot plucked the note from the door and opened it.

I'll be at the record store until nine. Please come. I need to see you again. Love, Maribel.

Elliot's heart started beating, a smile already forming on his lips even before he'd seen the last line she'd written at the bottom of the page.

I should have been kissing you.

Elliot turned around and saw Leila in her car, getting ready to go. He sprinted to her, clutching the note in his hand. Speechless, he handed her the note through her open window.

Leila read the note and gave it back to him, smiling as widely as he was. "I guess your movie's not over yet."

He read the note again, running his finger over the fold, the ink that Maribel's pen had left behind. Then he slipped it into his pocket and looked at Leila. "Mind dropping me off somewhere?"

Bree,

Some days, I get in my car and the tank is full and I'm not expected anywhere and there's thousands of miles' worth of roads waiting to be driven on. The world is my oyster, as they say (Why do they say that? How does oyster=possibilities?). But I'll sit there, frozen, not sure where to go. And sometimes, already driving, I'll feel like taking the next exit and seeing where it'll lead, but for some reason momentum won't let me. I sped through all of South Dakota and Montana this way. Did that ever happen to you? Or does it have less to do with traveling and more to do with me? How are you and Alexis getting along? I keep expecting to bump into you two on the road, but maybe the universe isn't yet ready to handle you and me side by side again.   Seize the Tuesday. Leila

Bree Marling
128 Seven Hills Dr.
Reno, NV 89511

★ U S A ★

SONIA

1

THE NOISE IN the restaurant had built to a dull roar. Silverware clinked against plates; laughter reverberated off the brick walls. Every few minutes a busboy carrying a plastic container full of dirty dishes would shove open the kitchen doors and let out a cacophony of ladles scraping against pots, the sizzle of something being sautéed.

Sonia closed her eyes the way Sam had taught her to and listened for the occasional word that could be heard over the chatter. Sometimes, the two of them would make a list of the words they heard and then string them together into nonsensical sentences. Sonia never told Sam that she used to save those sentences in secret. She'd turn them into a line in a poem or dialogue in a short story.

In the months since Sam's death, though, Sonia had only managed to hear Sam's name in the murmuring.

Why Sonia expected things to be different at the rehearsal dinner for Sam's sister, she didn't know. She opened her eyes and noticed Martha and Liz waving her over from across the restaurant. She put on a smile and made her way to them, greeting them with hugs, as though they hadn't seen each other in a long time.

"God," Liz said, holding her wineglass out to a passing server for a top-off, "I cannot get over how great you look in that dress."

"Absolutely beautiful," Martha agreed, making Sonia blush.

"If Sam were around, he wouldn't be able to keep his hands off you," Liz said, nudging Sonia. Martha shot her a look, but Liz just shrugged and said it was true.

Sonia looked down at the flowered dress as if it was embarrassing her, patting its hem down with her fingers. "He would have loved those Thai-chicken thingies."

"I know!" Liz cried out. "When we did the tasting, there were so many delicious hors d'oeuvres to choose from, but I couldn't turn them down. Sam would have killed me if he knew I'd passed up on anything Thai."

The roar of restaurant chatter had come back, and the three of them looked out at the room, their eyes following a waiter's trajectory around the tables, filling up glasses of wine.

Sonia sipped her soda, trying to not look in the direction of the groomsmen. "Thanks again for making me a bridesmaid," she said. "It means so much."

Liz rolled her eyes. "Will you stop thanking me, already? It would have been weird not to have you as a bridesmaid."

"I know, but, still . . ."

"'Still' nothing. You're basically my sister." She took a swig from her wine and waved at someone. "Duty calls," she said with a smile, and she made her way to a group of her friends at a corner table.

"Can you believe she's getting married?" Martha asked. "I feel old."

"The first time I met her, she was coming down the stairs in her pajamas, carrying that stuffed duck. She looked twelve. I thought Sam had been lying to me about having an older sister in college."

"Roger says she still sleeps with it sometimes."

Sonia laughed. "I guess there's no rule about having to get rid of your stuffed animals when you get married."

"Yeah," Martha said, her eyes still fixed on Liz. "I still see her at that age. Twelve, I mean. Carrying notebooks full of boys' names, squirming when I hugged her in public. I still see her when she was two, smushing food into her hair. I see them both at every age they've ever been." She fell quiet, then shook her head and looked at Sonia. "Look at me, getting all nostalgic."

"It's okay," Sonia said. Noises coming from the kitchen now sounded like basketball shoes squeaking against the court. Sonia thought of how Sam used to obsessively wipe his hand against the bottom of his sneakers to clean the soles. His palms would be black by the end of every game, and Sonia would worry about germs.

"I'm so happy you're here. It wouldn't be the same without you." Martha let out a sigh, then put a warm hand on Sonia's bare shoulder. "This is a weekend for celebrating. You should help yourself to some wine."

"I will," Sonia said, even though she had no plans to comfort herself with alcohol. If there was celebrating to be done, it was to be done alone with Jeremiah. Immediately after that thought crossed her mind, Sonia felt a wave of guilt come over her and decided that a glass of wine might be a good idea. "I'll go get one right now."

"Good," Martha said, her hand giving Sonia's a light squeeze. "Make sure you get some of the dessert, too. It's your favorite, key lime pie."

Sonia smiled and then turned to go find a waiter with a tray of wineglasses. As soon as her back was turned to Martha, she felt herself start to tear up. She picked up a napkin from a nearby table and dabbed at her eyes to keep her makeup from running.

◇　◇　◇

Later that night, Sonia slipped out of her hotel room and tiptoed down the hall in her sleeping shirt and some shorts to knock on Jeremiah's door. As she walked, she could feel the buzz of alcohol in her veins from the few drinks she'd had at the hotel bar with the wedding party. Jeremiah answered with his shirt unbuttoned, the shadows emphasizing his subtle ab muscles, which hadn't completely disappeared into the year's worth of college drinking and lazing he'd been doing.

"Hey," he said.

She lingered for a moment, not entirely sure why she'd come. It would be safer, smarter, to be back in her room, writing as she did every night before bed. Then Jeremiah broke into that smile of his and reached for her hand, and she remembered how comforting his presence was.

He pulled her in for a kiss, shutting the door behind her.

"I've been wanting to do that all day," he said, the two of them lip-locked and waddling backward until they fell onto the bed. Sonia could feel the taste of wine on her own mouth, the taste of beer on his. She pulled her shirt off over her head and leaned back down to kiss him.

"Me, too," she said, as he ran his hand through her hair.

She felt his heart beating beneath her, felt her own heart beating back. She tried not to imagine some hidden illness lingering within, something in his brain about to silently pop. Since Sam's death, she'd started seeing disease in everyone around her. Whenever she laid her head against Jeremiah's chest, she had to keep herself from counting heartbeats, from listening for skips that might take him away, too.

"You are the best kisser on the planet," Jeremiah muttered.

"You sure about that?"

"Yup," he said, moving away from her lips to plant those quick kisses he liked to give on the corner of her mouth and her cheeks, as if he couldn't afford to miss even an inch of skin. "I've done plenty of research. Thousands and thousands of women."

She pulled away from him, holding his head in place so he couldn't come after her for more kisses. "You are a terrible pillow talker. Please don't start talking about statistics."

He pulled away from her arms and looked back to where his head had been resting on the bed. "This isn't technically pillow talk. We are at least two standard deviations away from the closest pillow."

"I don't know much about statistics, but I'm pretty sure that that statement didn't make any sense."

"You don't make any sense," he said, bringing her back in for another long kiss.

Sonia had been shocked the first time they'd kissed. It'd been a great kiss, hard to pull away from, lingering on her lips for so long that she'd spent the rest of the night guiltily wondering whether Sam had ever been a good kisser and she simply hadn't known the difference until Jeremiah came along.

As he was wont to do, Jeremiah suddenly stopped kissing her and spun them around so that she was beneath him. He simply looked down at her, his hand combing through her hair in that way that made her want to close her eyes and smile for hours.

"Whatcha doing?" she asked, holding him closer.

"Just looking," he said with a smile. He held her gaze for a second, then kissed her neck. She'd noticed that he couldn't hold eye contact for a long time, and for some reason she adored that little bit of shyness. "You're absolutely beautiful."

Sonia smiled at him, pulling him in for a cuddle, weaving her legs between his. "Your pillow talk has vastly improved in the last thirty seconds."

"Again, not pillow talk," he said, studying her face as if he'd never before seen anything like it.

The room was quiet except for the whirr of the air conditioner and the occasional soft smacking of Jeremiah's kisses. Sonia caught a glimpse of the muted television showing sports highlights, and she was thankful it wasn't basketball season. Outside the room, a couple of people clamored down the hallway, laughing—drunk, from the sound of it—probably other wedding guests. Jeremiah moved his hand from her hair down to her collarbone, running a finger up and down a couple of times before leaning in to retrace the path with kisses.

It was only in these moments that Sam's absence didn't hurt. When this moment ended and she was back in her room alone, Sonia knew she would be so racked with guilt that she wouldn't be able to sleep. But for now, that constant ache she'd been living with for almost a year was nearly forgotten.

"I want to dance with you tomorrow," Jeremiah said. "At the wedding."

Sonia sighed. "With Sam's family there? Yeah, I don't think so."

"Come on," Jeremiah said. "I've been looking up video tutorials online on how to salsa, and I'm almost at the point where I can dance in rhythm."

"I'm impressed. But you'll have to show off your skills with someone else."

"I don't want to dance with someone else."

"That's very sweet," Sonia said, putting a hand on his cheek. "But it's not happening."

"Why not?"

"Because they'll know," she said simply, hoping it would kill the conversation.

Jeremiah sighed, picking at a thread on the comforter near Sonia's head and rolling it between his fingers. He looked at her, his eyes green and beautiful, a hint of sadness in them. "So what?"

Sonia leaned in to kiss that spot where his neck met his jaw. Every now and then while making out, he would stop and point to that spot and say, "Here." It was the look on his face after one of those kisses that had made Sonia realize she loved him, though she had yet to tell him.

"Let's not talk about it," she said.

Jeremiah pulled away. "I think we should."

Sonia groaned and rolled away from beneath him. The dull ache returned to her stomach, that hidden area of her gut that had come alive as soon as Sam was gone. Sonia moved to the desk in a corner of the room. She pulled out the chair a little too brusquely and had to catch the tuxedo jacket that Jeremiah had laid over it.

"Do you not want to be with me?" Jeremiah asked, sitting up, his eyes averted.

"You know that's not it," Sonia said, folding the jacket over her lap and smoothing out the fabric.

"Then what is it?"

Sonia didn't say anything.

"I know you've been through a lot, So. I know that a part of you still loves him and probably always will. I understand that, and I'd never ask you to try to forget him." He rubbed one arm with the other, cracked his knuckles, and looked up at the ceiling. When he spoke again, his voice was shaky, and the pained look on his face made Sonia want to both kiss his neck and yell at him for bringing this all up. "I'm too crazy about you to keep this bottled up."

Sonia crossed her arms in front of her chest, suddenly feeling exposed. She glanced up at him. He met her gaze and didn't look away, and she could feel tears welling behind her eyes. "I just can't dance with you," she said.

"You can. It would just be a dance."

Sonia felt a chill, and she unfolded the tuxedo jacket from her lap and slipped her arms through the sleeves, though it did nothing to calm the goose bumps on her skin.

Jeremiah still hadn't looked away, and she could see an added shimmer in his eyes. "Are you over him? Enough to be with me?"

She tried to stifle the sob in her throat, but it broke through, loud and sharp in the quiet hotel room.

Finally breaking eye contact, Jeremiah looked down at his lap. "I need to be alone for a little while," he said.

As soon as she was out of the room, Sonia felt like she was suffocating. She rushed down the hallway to grab her purse out of her room and then took the stairs, desperate for fresh air. It wasn't until she was outside that she realized she was still in Jeremiah's tuxedo jacket.

Everything about the town of Hope, British Columbia, screamed quaint. The light posts were made to look like old-style gas lamps. The streets were lined with three-story brick buildings, mom-and-pop stores, flowerpots, and so many benches that the whole town could be accommodated for street-side seating at a moment's notice. The pretty streets were perfect for the kind of aimless, hand-in-hand wandering she and Sam used to do whenever his family invited her up here to their cabin. She'd tried several times to capture the charm of the city in writing, but it always evaded her.

Sonia made her way toward a convenience store, hoping it'd still be open so she could get something to calm herself down. Halfway there, she burst back into tears and had to stop to steady herself against a car, the sobs coming in spurts that felt like seizures.

"Are you okay?"

Sonia looked up. A girl more or less her age was standing in front of her, a cup of coffee in one hand, car keys in the other. Sonia stepped away from the car and nodded but couldn't contain her sobs. The girl extended a napkin, and Sonia took it, wiping at her nose. "Sorry," she said.

"What happened?"

"It's complicated," Sonia said, wondering if she and Jeremiah were still together. The thought made her cry harder. She tried to calm herself down by taking deep breaths, focusing on little details: a crack in the sidewalk, the fly buzzing against the convenience store's window.

"Anything I can do?" the girl asked. "Want some coffee?"

Sonia shook her head. "Thanks."

Crumpling the used napkin in her hand, Sonia blurted out, "Actually, could you drive me somewhere? Anywhere will do. I just need to get away."

The girl with the black hair nodded, her brow furrowed in concern. "Sure. Hop in."

2

SONIA LOOKED AT her reflection in the bathroom mirror. Her cheeks were puffy from crying, her hair knotted, her eyes red. Jeremiah's jacket hung loosely on her, her arms disappearing in its sleeves. She'd fastened all three buttons, but it didn't cover up the fact she was wearing only a bra beneath.

She rolled the sleeves back and splashed some water onto her face, then grabbed some lip gloss out of her purse and applied it halfheartedly. Her phone buzzed again, rattling on the dirty rest-stop bathroom counter. Jeremiah's name took up the screen. She couldn't imagine answering the phone without breaking down in tears again. Even if he was calling to tell her to come back to his room, she still wouldn't be able to tell him whether or not she was over Sam.

Sonia silenced the phone and shoved it into the tuxedo pocket. Then she splashed some more water onto her face and walked out of the bathroom. The girl—Sonia had learned about thirty minutes into their drive that her name was Leila—was sitting in the driver's seat with her feet out of the car, gazing at the landscape of tree-lined mountains made visible only by the full moon.

"I'm sorry for making you drive this far. You don't really have to drive me all the way back home," she said, even though they'd already crossed the border back into the US and were about halfway to Tacoma. She plopped herself into the passenger seat, and Leila started the car back up, merging onto the freeway.

Leila shrugged. "I don't mind. Are you feeling better?"

"Not really." Her phone rang again, and she pressed the button on the side to make the buzzing stop.

"What were you doing in Canada?" Leila asked, checking her side-view mirrors as a semi rumbled past them.

"Family wedding," Sonia answered, to simplify. "You?"

"Just passing through, I guess."

Not even a minute had passed before the buzzing started again. "I'm sorry," Sonia said. "I'm gonna get this. He's never going to stop."

She answered the call, though she didn't say anything at first.

"Sonia?"

"Yeah," she said, her voice already starting to quaver. Just the way he'd said her name had felt off, the hurt dripping from his voice.

"My jacket. I need it back."

Sonia hesitated, looking over at Leila, who was focused on driving. "I left town." She couldn't actually hear anything coming from his end, just the dullest hum of static or wind or the air conditioner working in his hotel room. He was quiet for so long that she checked the phone to make sure the call was still connected.

"The weddings rings are in the jacket, Sonia."

Another semitrailer roared past them, blinking red lights all around it, like those atop a building warding off planes. It made everything around rumble, even the air.

"What?" As soon as she said it, though, she could feel the excessive weight of the tuxedo jacket, and she became aware of a bulkiness pressing against her chest.

"Wherever you are, you have to come back."

She patted at the inside breast pocket, feeling the box. She raised her hand up to her hair, tugging at the matted mess. She couldn't believe that she'd left the hotel wearing the jacket, that she hadn't felt the weight of the rings at any point on the drive. She knew she had to go back, but she didn't know if she could face that broken look in Jeremiah's eyes again. "Are we okay?" she said, almost in a whimper.

"We can talk about that later. But you need to bring those rings back." Jeremiah had never been so short with her.

Sonia nodded to herself, looking over at Leila, who had been listening to Sonia's conversation with a concerned look on her face. "Okay," she said, then hung up the phone, unable to bear the lack of sweetness in his tone.

"Do you want to talk about it?" Leila asked after a few moments.

Sonia crossed her arms and just shook her head. She didn't blame Leila for asking, but talking about it couldn't help. Talking was exactly what had made everything blow up so quickly in the first place. She couldn't even bring herself to ask Leila to turn the car around.

"Hey, look, we've all been there," Leila said. "If I know anything, it's that keeping your problems to yourself only makes them harder to deal with."

"Yeah? You go around telling your problems to everyone around?" Sonia said, immediately regretting her tone.

Leila lowered her head. "No, I don't. Not enough. That's why I know."

"Sorry, I didn't mean that. You've been nothing but kind to me, I shouldn't be snapping at you." Sonia looked out at the darkness of the highway. She'd gone up and down this highway plenty of times on road trips to Sam's family's cabin, but she couldn't recognize exactly which rest stop they'd stopped at, how far away from home she was.

"That's okay. You're upset," Leila said. "You know that awful feeling you get in your stomach whenever you think about whatever's making you cry?"

Immediately, Sonia thought of the car ride to the hospital after Sam collapsed. She thought of the first time she'd kissed Jeremiah. Of how she hadn't been able to write a single word in months, the pages of her notebook painfully blank, as if there was nothing at all on her mind. She thought about Martha, who still talked to Sonia about Sam as if she expected him to come out of his room at any moment. Yes, she was quite familiar with that feeling. She'd been in its grips for a year, and the only person who could make it go away was now adding to it. "Yeah," she managed to say.

"Well, right now it's feeling worse because the same thoughts are repeating themselves, bouncing around in there. You're like a teakettle begging to let out some steam. You need to let someone pull you off the stove and pour you into a cup."

"You're saying you want to turn me into tea?"

"The metaphor's a little jumbled, maybe," Leila said. "But I think you get what I'm saying. I just want to help."

Sonia looked at a car passing by, trying to get a glimpse of the people inside but seeing just a blur of metal.

"Why? Why are you being so nice to a perfect stranger?"

"I don't know. Maybe I just really like tea."

Surprising herself, Sonia managed to smile. She looked at Leila, for a second forgetting Sam and Jeremiah, wondering who, exactly, this girl was.

Leila shifted, bringing her left leg up onto the seat and tucking it beneath her.

Sonia pulled her phone out of her pocket, checking the time and subtracting the hours until the wedding. When the screen came to life, it showed the picture of her and Sam sitting on top of the troll statue in Seattle. Sonia had wondered if it bothered Jeremiah, seeing that picture, if she should change it. Even that was a betrayal she wasn't ready to commit.

Sonia was usually better at dealing with her emotions with paper and pen, but then, she'd apparently lost that ability. Maybe Leila was trustworthy, the way she talked about sadness as if she was familiar with it. Or maybe there's just a limit to how long we can hold something in before it comes spilling out involuntarily.

"About seven months ago," Sonia began, "my boyfriend of two years, Sam, collapsed in the middle of a basketball game. They rushed him to the hospital, but he died within two hours. A heart abnormality. Something myocardia? I don't know. I can never remember the exact name.

"I know most teenagers think their first love is the one and only love of their lives, but we were special." She paused to wipe at her eyes and, noticing that her phone was still lit up with Sam's picture, put it back in her pocket, knowing she couldn't handle talking about him and looking at him at the same time. "When he died, I felt that was it for me. That no one would ever come close to what we had. I didn't *want* anyone to come close. My soul mate was gone, and I was going to spend the rest of my life without him."

A tear scurried down Sonia's cheek quickly, as if it were being sucked in by a drain. She shook her head at herself and wiped the trail the tear had left behind. "God, that's just the beginning. Are you sure you want to hear all this?"

"The tea's not ready. Keep pouring."

"That metaphor is not working at all." Sonia chuckled.

"Whatever! You're not done telling your story."

Sonia rubbed her eyes, then ran a hand through her hair, gathering her thoughts. "His family was always great to me," she continued. "And after he died, that didn't change at all. If anything, they got even better. They'd call to check how I was doing, they'd take me out to dinner, invite me to the movies. Hell, they treat me better than my own family does. I'd never really had that feeling of belonging until I met Sam.

"So anyway, I was over at their house a bunch, for family dinners and barbecues and all that. And that's where I met Jeremiah. His brother is marrying Sam's sister tomorrow," she said, pulling her cell phone out of her pocket and motioning to show that this was who'd been calling her. She took a slow breath, feeling as if she were on a tightrope, and moving too quickly would send her plummeting down to another weeping session.

"At first I didn't even get that it was a crush. One day he offered me a ride home, and before I realized it, we were kissing. I felt sick to my stomach for days afterward. I mean, the last batch of flowers I'd put on Sam's grave hadn't even wilted yet, and I was jumping into someone else's arms."

Leila opened her mouth to say something, then changed her mind and waited for Sonia to continue. They drove onto a bridge, a little brown sign letting them know they were passing over the Stillaguamish River.

"We've been secretly seeing each other for a couple of months now, and despite how happy he makes me, when we're not together, I feel even more miserable than I usually do. I can't stop feeling like I'm cheating on Sam, like being with Jeremiah means I never even loved him at all, and he died wrongly believing he'd found his soul mate.

"And now Jeremiah wants to go public, or he wants to break up—I don't even know which. But I can't have Sam's family knowing that I'm seeing someone else. I can barely even think about it myself, so how could I face telling them? What if they don't want anything to do with me after they find out? I can't risk losing them."

They must have been going fairly slowly, because every now and then someone would pass them, headlights filling up Leila's car. Leila remained quiet, patient for Sonia to work through her story, as if she really expected to soak up Sonia's sadness by just listening.

Sonia's knee knocked against the plastic bag that hung off the gearshift. A half-full bottle of water sat in a cup holder, which Leila offered as soon as she saw Sonia eyeing it.

"When I ran into you," Sonia said, "Jeremiah and I had just gotten into a fight, and I needed to get away from there. But I'm an idiot and left wearing his jacket, which has the wedding rings in it." She looked over at Leila, whose serene face had taken on little hints of worry: a furrow in her brow, the slightest droop to her lips. "Do you think we could go back? I really need to bring him the rings. It'll ruin the wedding if I don't."

Leila immediately turned her blinker on and pulled over onto the shoulder, the car rumbling as they passed over the divots in the road that warned drivers they were too close to the edge. "Why didn't you say so earlier?" Leila asked, angling the car for a U-turn.

"You didn't even think twice about it," Sonia said, in awe.

"I think the last thing you need right now is to feel like no one is on your side. If all it takes is a little gas and time for me to help someone feel not alone, I'm more than happy to do it." She glided onto the empty two-lane highway, going back the way they'd come.

"So, is the awful feeling gone?" Leila asked, smiling.

"Not really." Sonia took another drink of water, her mind racing with gratitude. "But it helped. Thank you."

"My pleasure." Leila smiled.

For a second, it did seem that the awful feeling had gone away, or at least was less awful than before. But something was nagging at Sonia, a vague fear that there was something she'd forgotten. She checked the breast pocket of the jacket and found that the box with the rings was still there. Just to make sure, she pulled it out and saw the two upright rings, little silver soldiers standing at attention. Her phone was tucked safely against the waistband of her shorts.

To make sure she still had her wallet and passport, she reached down to the floor to grab her purse. As soon as her fingers felt the fibers of the mat at her feet, Sonia's hands scurried about the floor, searching for the touch of leather. She leaned over and slipped her hand as far below the seat as it could go.

"What's wrong?"

"Shit," Sonia said, picturing clearly her purse sitting on a dirty bathroom counter. "I think I left my purse at the rest stop." She unbuckled her seat belt and crawled down to get a look, her shoulder pressed hard against the faux-suede fabric of the car seat. But she knew it wasn't there.

"That's okay," Leila said calmly. "We'll stop by on our way back."

It only took them a couple of minutes to get there. There were no other cars in the lot, which Sonia took as a good sign that the purse would be untouched. She rushed out of the car and into the bathroom.

And yet the bathroom counter was completely bare, nothing on it except for puddles and the dried crust of soap that had leaked out from the dispenser. She sprinted from the door to the counter, as if she was just too far away to see the purse. But it was gone, and with it all its contents: her lip gloss; a picture of her and Sam taken at arm's length; her wallet, which contained an emergency credit card, a few Canadian bills, and her Washington State driver's license; her hotel room key; her notebook, the last few entries full of words scratched out almost as soon as they'd been written; and her US passport, the ink from her latest entry stamp not yet dry.

The weight of the rings somehow increased in her pocket, as if somehow aware that they were now an impossible world away from where they should have been.

3

SONIA AND LEILA sat in a twenty-four-hour McDonald's in a duty-free shopping center near the border. Sonia was gently knocking her head against the window, looking out at the highway, begging for a solution to suddenly occur to her. Leila was resting her chin in her hand, her elbow propped up on the table, a bag of fries cooling between them. The McDonald's employees chatted casually to pass the time, awaiting the next late-night traveler. Every now and then they'd cast strange looks at Sonia in her tuxedo jacket, shorts, and somewhat exposed bra.

"I'll drive the rings back myself," Leila said after a while, already rising from her chair. "I still have my passport."

"You don't have to. We can think of another way."

"No reason to think of another way when we already have a solution. You sit tight here, and I'll give you a call when I'm on the way back," Leila said, handing her phone over for Sonia to program her number in.

"You are a bottomless well of kindness, Leila. Thank you."

"I'll be back soon," Leila said with a smile, speed-walking out of the restaurant with the rings in hand.

Although Sonia would have preferred to avoid giving herself any more reasons to feel guilty, she lied to Jeremiah, sending him a text message saying that she was on her way.

okay, he texted back, the lack of capitalization somehow feeling unique to him.

She typed out responses and then deleted them, locked her phone and then immediately brought the screen back to life, only to turn it off again.

Sonia buried her face in her hands, pressing her palms into her eyes until she saw those little explosions of light in the darkness. She ruffled her hair, then caught a glimpse of her reflection on her phone. The auburn mass above her head barely resembled hair, so she raked her fingers through the knots. When she was done, she picked up her phone again. **I don't know about anything else, but I love you**, she typed out, staring at the words for nearly a full minute before deleting them.

Right when she started doing the math on how long it would take Leila to make it there and back—a couple of hours, at least—the door of the McDonald's swung open with a creak, and Leila sheepishly entered.

"What happened?" For a brief moment, Sonia imagined that everything had somehow magically been resolved, that the rings had been tele-transported into Jeremiah's possession.

"Border patrol wouldn't let me through," Leila said, biting her lip, her eyebrows drawn together in a near-caricature of sadness. "They found it suspicious that I just went through and I'm trying to get back in."

"Into Canada? Since when are Canadians fussy about letting people in?"

Leila looked down at the floor, shrugging. "I don't know, but they searched my car, went through all my stuff. Maybe they thought I was smuggling drugs or something, I don't know. The guy said I was lucky they weren't detaining me, but that customs agents can deny entry to anyone as they see fit."

Sonia slumped down in the hard plastic bench. She pictured Jeremiah having to tell Liz and Roger that he didn't have the rings, the truth coming out, even if Jeremiah tried to hide the details. She wondered who would be more heartbroken in that scenario: Liz, for her ruined wedding; Martha, for Sonia's betrayal; Jeremiah, for Sonia's indecision; Sonia herself, for creating such a mess of everyone's life.

"Don't worry. We'll think of something," Leila said, although her voice lacked conviction. She looked around the empty McDonald's. "Maybe someone will come in who's going in that direction and wouldn't mind dropping off the rings?"

"I wouldn't trust anyone with them," Sonia said, suddenly realizing how easily she'd trusted that Leila would indeed take the rings to Canada and come back to pick her up. She wondered if this was due to Leila's kindness, or whether it had been unloading her sorrows that did it. Perhaps it was simply because Leila seemed to care.

"What if we wait until the shift change at the border? Maybe I'll get someone who's nicer and won't give me any trouble."

Sonia gave it some thought, feeling skeptical. "If they flagged your passport, which they probably did, no one will let you through." She grabbed the jewelry box with the rings inside and spun it on the table, trying to resist the urge to throw it right across the McDonald's. Outside, in the shopping center, bright yellow signs announced special discounts on chocolates and liquor.

Leila pulled out her cell phone from her purse, as if suddenly remembering she had one.

"You know," Leila said, swiping her finger across the screen of her phone. "I'm looking at it on the map, and . . . I mean, I always knew Canada was big and that the Canadian border was long. But it's really freakin' long." She handed Sonia her phone. "You think there's any possible way that they have enough manpower to keep an eye on all of it all the time? Every single bit of it? There's no fence or anything, right?"

The map showed a few major entry points along highways. Little bubbles popped up suggesting duty-free stops like the one they were in. Between those highway entries were miles and miles of greenery. The only thing to be found between those checkpoints was an imaginary line that someone long ago had decided would separate the two countries.

"Am I crazy," Leila said, "or could we just simply walk across? I mean, if people get through the Mexican border, which is much more guarded, it shouldn't be that hard to sneak across here."

Sonia sniggered, studying the map a little closer. "That'd be a hell of a story if we did."

"I don't see why not," Leila said, excitement in her voice.

"What about your car?"

"We'll leave it parked somewhere near the highway. Somewhere like a motel parking lot that won't look too suspicious. We'll walk into the woods and head north. I have a compass on my phone, and this thing that tells you how long you've been walking in case the GPS doesn't get a signal. Then all we have to do is get to the highway and hitch a ride back to Hope. There should be enough truckers coming through that it won't be a problem. I have a friend who spent months hitchhiking across the country, and she said you'd be surprised at how easy it can be on the right highway."

"Are we on the right highway?"

"I have no idea. But it's worth a shot, right?"

Sonia zoomed in on the map on Leila's phone. "I wonder whether you could see border patrol agents if you zoomed in far enough." She handed the phone back to Leila. "How would we get back to your car?"

"We'll just do the same thing coming back. No big deal."

"No big deal," Sonia repeated, trying to connect the words to the act of sneaking across an international border. She thought about the scribbled-out beginnings of sentences in her notebook. She wondered if her writer's block might be undone by a night like this. "Okay," she said, grabbing another fry and tearing it in two, the mushy insides oozing out as if she'd just squished a bug. "Let's do this."

o o o

According to the feature on Leila's phone, they'd walked half a mile west into the woods. Sonia could barely see in front of her, so she and Leila trod carefully, thankful for the full moon shining through the spaces between trees and the light from Leila's phone saving them from complete blindness.

Sonia was nervous but giddy, her heart lighter than it had been in hours. "We are actually walking into Canada," she said, not knowing whether it was necessary to whisper. Every step they took, Sonia kept expecting someone to pop out from the darkness. Each crackle in the forest sounded like the white noise of walkie-talkies; every branch her arm brushed against felt like someone ready to apply handcuffs.

"What if we run into a SWAT team?"

"I don't think there'll be SWAT teams. Maybe Mounties or something."

"That'd be worse," Sonia said, reaching out to put a hand on Leila's shoulder, not wanting to lose her in the dark. "I'm terrified of horses."

"Horses? Why?"

"As a rule, I don't like things that could kick my head off."

"What was that?" Leila said, stopping suddenly, causing Sonia to bump into her.

"What?"

"You didn't hear that?"

Sonia stood perfectly still, waiting for the sounds of sirens or a helicopter approaching. There was the barest rustling of leaves as an overhead wind blew through the treetops. She could hear herself breathing, far-off crickets, but nothing else.

"You didn't hear that neighing?" Leila said.

"You are a bully." Sonia smacked her arm as they resumed walking, trying not to give away how afraid she'd been that they'd been discovered. Her heart was racing, and though she was terrified, she couldn't wait to make it through, to tell Jeremiah about this little adventure. If he still wanted to talk to her.

"Okay, I think that's far enough," Leila said. "We can turn north now. It should be about a mile to the border; we'll walk two to be safe, then rejoin the highway." Her face was lit up by the glow of the screen, and Sonia once again caught a flash of something melancholy in her expression. "The highway stays straight for a bit after the border, so it shouldn't be hard to find."

"Let's do it." Sonia motioned for Leila to lead the way. Her phone buzzed inside the tuxedo pocket as they continued their way through the woods. Cupping her hand over the screen to contain the light, Sonia brought the phone out.

where are you?

Sonia shut off her phone, not quite sure how to respond at the moment.

"Is that the boy again?"

"Yeah," Sonia said. "Just checking in."

Something crunched under Sonia's feet as she stepped past a branch. The sounds they made walking through the woods seemed like the only sounds for miles, and the thought was both a comfort and deeply frightening. "Do you . . ." Sonia started, feeling silly asking. "Do you have a boyfriend?"

Leila continued to lead them north through the trees. Her steps were short, cautious, her arms out in front of her in the dark. "Nope," she said after a moment. "There was this guy. I thought maybe something could happen with him. But that doesn't look likely anymore."

"Why not?"

"Ow!" Leila cried out. "Watch out for those bushes. They're thorny." Leila held them aside with her sleeve so Sonia could pass. "We had a big fight."

"Do you still talk to him?"

"I send him postcards," Leila said. "But I haven't heard from him in a while. Since I last saw him, actually."

"How long ago was that?"

"For as long as I've been traveling. Almost two months now." They walked for a few more measured steps, trying to avoid tripping on a branch or stepping into bear crap.

Leila stopped again suddenly. She held up a hand, motioning for Sonia to be still. Sonia looked around, trying to determine what had made Leila stop but seeing only the rich blackness of the forest.

"Leila, if you say something's neighing again, I swear—"

"All right, ladies," a deep voice bellowed, making them both jump. "You've had your fun. Time to turn around now."

Sonia couldn't see him right away. In fact, until Leila pulled out her phone and pointed the screen in the agent's direction, Sonia hadn't really grasped who had spoken or from where. The officer wore a baseball cap and was leaning against a tree. He seemed bulky, and when he clicked on his flashlight, Sonia realized it was on the bulletproof vest he was wearing, with all the little contraptions attached to it. He shone the light on their faces, and for a moment he disappeared behind the glare as Sonia's pupils adjusted to the light. Sonia waited for a team of officers to cuff her, her stomach tying itself into a knot. Any minute now, someone would start yelling the Miranda rights at her.

"You're Americans?"

"Yes," they both answered.

The border agent had barely shifted from his relaxed stance against the tree. It almost looked like he was on a smoke break.

"Okay, good. Thank you for attempting to visit Canada. Please have a safe trip back home. In the future, please come through an approved entry point, where border patrol services can properly document your visit."

Leila turned to look over her shoulder at Sonia. She looked just as confused as Sonia felt. "Sir, we're really sorry, we just—"

He stepped away from the tree, and Sonia was shocked to see that he was smiling. "I think my wife is getting tired of my 'you'll never believe what they told me' stories." He put his hands on his hips. "Did you really think you were just going to walk across the border?"

Neither of them offered up an answer.

"Unfortunately, you guys decided to walk right past my bathroom," he said, pointing at a tree and chuckling to himself.

"So, you're letting us go?" Sonia squeaked out.

"Have you ever filed paperwork this late at night? It's awful.

Whatever your reason for trying to walk across the border, I don't want to hear it. You look like nice girls." He paused, seeming to recall something. He pointed the flashlight back at Sonia's attire, raising an eyebrow. "Maybe a little strange, but nice. Just go back home to your parents."

He didn't have to tell Sonia twice. She grabbed Leila's arm and turned them around, speed-walking back the way they'd come, thankful that they weren't in handcuffs.

"I can't tell if I'm more relieved that we're not in jail, or pissed that we didn't make it through," Leila said.

"Let's go with relieved," Sonia said, although, with the rings pressing against her chest through the breast pocket of Jeremiah's jacket, she wasn't so sure. At first, they rushed through the woods, using their cell-phone screens to light the way back. But little by little, their pace slowed, maybe as they simultaneously realized that they would reach Leila's car in the motel parking lot with the same unsolved problem. With every step Sonia took, the rings grew heavier in her pocket.

Sonia knew there was only one other thing she could do, but the thought of it was so unappealing that she imagined all sorts of wild contingencies—how long would it take to get a fake passport? How easy would it be to skydive near the border and accidentally drift into Canada?—before allowing herself to admit it. She would have to go back home and beg her family for help.

4

WHEN THEY PULLED up to Sonia's house in Tacoma, the sun was shining between a spattering of grayish clouds. Mount Rainier loomed large over the city, its peak still white with snow, like some enormous sentinel standing guard over the city. Sonia felt a sense of panic, realizing that the wedding would start in only a few hours.

Both her parents' cars were in the driveway. They hadn't been washed in weeks, dust clinging to the windows in the shape of raindrops. Even if they were both home, the chances were that they had to go to work, and "Thou Shalt Go to Work" was commandment number one in Sonia's household. She didn't hold out much hope that they'd be able to help, even if they were willing. It was times like these that she ached for parents like Sam's, who'd drop anything for the sake of their children.

Since her house keys had also been in her purse, Sonia rang the doorbell. The sound of arguing came from inside, and she could hear her dad stomping over, muttering to himself. He answered with an angry expression on his face, as if he'd already started an argument in his head with whoever had rung his doorbell so early in the morning. He was in his baggage-handler uniform, a cup of coffee in his hand.

When he saw that it was Sonia, he said, "Oh. Hi. Everything okay? " he said, already turning back inside, leaving the door open for them.

"Yeah. You guys have work?" Sonia said, leading Leila into the house.

"Sure do," her dad replied, making his way back to the living room.

Sonia sighed. Mitch was her only chance, then.

All the curtains in the house were shut, which was no surprise. The light inside the house was permanently bleak, almost like Tacoma itself. Her parents were both seated in the living room, drinking coffee and eating microwavable egg burritos. Her dad plopped himself down on his chair, filling out his crossword puzzle. Her mom was on the couch, watching her favorite morning talk show.

Sonia's mom took another bite of her burrito and chewed with that faint smacking sound that drove Sonia crazy. The whole house smelled of beans and fake cheddar cheese. After her bite, she finally noticed Sonia and Leila standing by the couch. "Morning. I thought you had somewhere to be today. Work?"

"I took the weekend off," she said, wondering if her mom even remembered the wedding.

"I'm gonna need you to get the oil changed on my car, then, since I gave you a ride on Wednesday."

Sonia ignored the comment. She glanced at Leila, embarrassed that her parents hadn't even noticed her standing there. "Is Mitch home?"

Her mom snorted. "Where else would he be?"

Sonia motioned for Leila to follow her. They crossed the living room toward the staircase, drawing a muffled protest as they blocked the TV. A thin film of dust covered the handrail, and Sonia felt herself blush with shame. She'd never really talked about her family with anyone, not even Sam or Jeremiah, choosing instead to deal with them in her writing. She didn't understand her parents, how they'd fallen into the loop of work and irritability that seemed to define their lives. Or why they'd even chosen to become parents, since they had never once shown affection toward Sonia or her brother. In her writing, she could at least fake a familiarity with her parents' backstories, their motivations for living life as if it were a curse handed down to them.

Avoiding the basket of dirty laundry at the top of the stairs, Sonia and Leila moved down the hall. Sonia's cell phone buzzed again.

i'm starting to get a little worried. where are you?

She put the phone away and knocked on Mitch's door. "I haven't been in his room in a while, but if nothing's changed, get ready for an unpleasant smell," she warned Leila. Then she knocked again and pushed open the door.

The smell was practically tangible. It was a stink bomb of traditional-teen-boy smells—socks, sweat, the general muskiness of a body immune to its own offensive odor—mixed in with who knows what else: spilled beverages soaking deep into the fibers of the carpet, forgotten snacks rotting on his computer desk, the combined exhalations of weeks' worth of morning breath marinating in the stagnant air.

Sonia immediately started breathing through her mouth, while behind her Leila gagged. Mitch was snoring lightly, one foot hanging off the side of his bed. In the gray light coming through the blinds, Sonia could make out a white thread clinging to his neck-beard.

"Mitch," she whispered. He didn't stir. "Mitch," she said again, a little louder. He groaned and reached for a pillow, throwing it in her direction but missing. "Mitch, I need a favor."

He turned away from them. "Go away."

Sonia took a step forward, avoiding something she couldn't identify on the ground. "You know I wouldn't be here if it wasn't an emergency. I really need your help."

Mitch groaned and scooted farther away, pressing his face against the wall. "Sleep," he said, slurring a few more words afterward that Sonia couldn't make out.

Leila brought her T-shirt over her nose. "Mitch," she said, almost a yell. "Your sister needs your help. Wake up."

Intrigued by the unfamiliar voice, Mitch turned back and opened his eyes. He squinted as if the light inside the room was overwhelming. "Who the hell are you?"

"I'm Leila. Now listen to your sister."

Mitch scratched at his beard, the thread that had been hanging there coming loose onto his pillow, probably to be reacquired by his facial hair at a later time. "All right, I'm listening." From beneath the sheets she could hear the sound of him scratching.

Sonia fought the urge to tell him how disgusting he was. "I need a favor. It's going to sound a little strange, but you know I wouldn't be asking you if I wasn't desperate."

"Just say it already."

"I need you to drive to Canada for me."

"Get the hell out of here," he said, turning back toward the wall.

"Mitch, I'm serious. It's a long story, but I have Liz's wedding rings, and the wedding is today. I have no way to get there."

Mitch groaned again. "Fill up my gas tank and give me fifty bucks, and I'll let you take my car."

"You're not listening. I can't get into Canada. I lost my passport. I just need you to drive there and drop off the rings. I'll pay for the gas."

"You want me to drive to Canada?"

"It's just three hours each way."

Mitch laughed. "Have you been stealing from my stash? There's no way I'm going to drive six hours for you."

Sonia felt herself tear up. "Mitch, please. You're the only person I can ask. If you don't go, the wedding will be ruined."

"Yeah, well, that's not my problem, now, is it?"

"I'm going to hit him," Leila said, still speaking through her shirt. She didn't make any move toward him, though, and Sonia was too distraught to think of what else to do. She was used to apathy from her family, but deep down she'd thought that if she really needed them, they would put their petty selfishness aside. It wasn't pleasant to be proven wrong.

Not knowing what else to do, Sonia stood right where she was. She wished Leila would actually hit Mitch.

"Go talk to Stoner Timmy," Mitch mumbled.

"What?"

"Stoner Timmy. You can find him at the Tim Hortons in Bellingham. He runs some sort of business into Canada. He's not exactly the most law-abiding guy around, so I wouldn't be surprised if it involves the smuggling of something or other. He might know how to get you across."

Okay, so it wasn't the biggest favor, but Sonia wanted to hug Mitch for at least being a little bit helpful. But the smell made her hesitate, and then he yelled at her and Leila to get out of his room.

She knew it was a long shot, but Sonia was willing to accept any tiny amount of hope. Any lead, no matter how unlikely, was a chance that she wasn't going to ruin the wedding. They stopped by Sonia's room so she could change into more normal clothes, then rushed back down the stairs and across the living room, eliciting some complaints from her parents for making a ruckus in the morning. Then they climbed into Leila's car and headed to Bellingham to meet Stoner Timmy.

5

AS SOON AS Sonia and Leila entered the Tim Hortons, they spotted Stoner Timmy. "That's gotta be him, right?" Leila said, pointing out a guy in his late twenties sitting at a table by the window. He had dirty-blond hair that looked almost silky up front but was dreadlocked in the back. He wore plaid shorts, cracked leather sandals, argyle socks, and, despite the heat, a tie-dyed hoodie. About half a dozen cardboard cups littered his table, and he was using one as an ashtray. How he was getting away with smoking inside a rather small coffee shop wasn't clear, but it didn't seem as if anyone minded. He was scribbling fervently into a notebook, occasionally grinning to himself.

"My God," Sonia sighed, and she got into the two-person-long line for the counter. "I get the feeling I'm gonna need a cup of coffee just to get through this conversation."

"Good call," Leila said. "How are we doing on time?"

Sonia clicked her phone on. "The ceremony starts at three, so we have about six hours left for that guy to smuggle us into Canada. No big deal." Sonia looked up at the familiar menu. There weren't any Tim Hortons as far south as Tacoma, but Sam's family was Canadian and insisted on stopping at one on every road trip. She decided to order

Sam's favorite drink and doughnut, then turned to Leila, who was still studying the overhead menu.

"I don't think you've told me," Sonia said after Leila placed her order. "Why are you on this trip? Why do you want to see the Northern Lights?"

"I've always kind of been obsessed with astronomy. It's probably what I'll study when I go to school." Leila took her change, and they stepped out of line, lingering by the counter to wait for their drinks. They both unconsciously turned to Stoner Timmy, who had lit a fresh cigarette and was now doodling on one of the coffee cups. "But more than that, I think I was destined to meet Stoner Timmy. Screw the Lights. This is it."

Sonia laughed, but her curiosity had been piqued. Then their order was called, and Sonia, hungrier than she had realized, immediately bit into her doughnut, effectively changing the subject.

The maple-glazed doughnut tasted like Sam. Or, rather, not Sam himself, but the two years she'd been with him. She took another bite. The choice of doughnut had been at once a mistake and a deep comfort.

"Shall we?" Leila said, motioning toward the smoky table.

Slipping her hand into the jacket folded over her forearm to make sure the rings were still in the breast pocket, Sonia nodded and took the lead. Stoner Timmy—presumably anyway—was popping open the lids of all the cups on his table and examining the contents. When she got close enough, Sonia could see that each cup was half-full, the liquids inside too varied in color to be just coffee-based. "Stoner Timmy?"

Stoner Timmy looked up from his experiment with the cups. He narrowed his eyes in a way that seemed theatric and took a puff from his cigarette. He looked from Sonia to Leila and then back at Sonia. He was not clean-shaven, but his facial hair could hardly be called a beard. He fixed his eyes on Sonia. "I dig your eyebrows, man. Very avant-garde."

"Um," Sonia said, not sure at all how to take the comment. "Thanks. Hi. You are Stoner Timmy?"

"I've been known to respond to that name, sure. Whether I have any rights to the name is up to the gods. Or nature. Or, you know, the social security office. The man," he said, stretching out the vowel and wiggling his fingers in front of his face like a puppeteer.

"Jesus Christ." Leila chuckled behind Sonia. "This is going to be interesting."

Stoner Timmy took another puff of his half-smoked cigarette. Then, without any clear reason, he tossed the cigarette into one of the cups and immediately lit another one. "You seek my assistance?" he said, motioning at the two chairs across from him.

Sonia sat down warily, a little flabbergasted by the thought that this guy could help her solve even the smallest of problems, much less manage to smuggle her into Canada. Leila, on the other hand, sat down in a rush, composing herself quickly, though her eyes still beamed with excitement. "Yes," Sonia started, trying to figure out how to phrase it. "We heard that you can get people across the border."

Stoner Timmy looked out the window and nodded solemnly. Sonia suspected this was done purely for appearance's sake. "I know the way into the Great White North, it's true." He stroked his chin as if a long white beard flowed from it, instead of the odd tuft of hair that actually sprung from his face.

"So you *can* get us through?" Sonia said, dubious. "How?"

"Whoa, whoa, whoa." Stoner Timmy held up his hands. "What's with all the questions?"

A snicker escaped Leila. Stoner Timmy seemed not to have noticed.

"It's just really important that I get across, and I want to make sure I'm not wasting my time here. If you can get us through, tell us what we need to do."

"Rest assured, She with the Interesting Eyebrows. I make several trips a day. My livelihood depends on it," he said, making a sweeping motion over the table, as if the coffee cups bespoke great wealth. "But before I explain the how, I've got some questions of my own."

"We cannot wait to answer them," Leila said, pulling her chair closer.

Timmy ashed his cigarette. "Good." He squinted at Leila, either out of his sense of theatrics or because smoke had gotten into his eyes. "I like your moxie. You don't meet many people with moxie these days."

Sonia took another bite of Sam's favorite doughnut. Stoner Timmy was staring off into the space between the two girls.

"Stoner Timmy, the question?"

"Right," he said, snapping out of his daze. As far as he ever would, anyway. "First question. Who sent you here?"

"My brother, Mitch."

"And he works for which government agency?"

"What? He doesn't work for any government agency. He doesn't work at all. He sits around and gets high all day. When he's feeling productive, he bathes."

"Far out," Stoner Timmy said, smiling with approval. "What business have you with our neighbors to the north?"

"Why do you need to know?" Leila chimed in, clearly amused by mimicking his dramatically suspicious tone. "That hardly seems pertinent."

"The success of my business depends on the consequences of my actions in Canada. If I bring in harmless people and keep a low profile, my business thrives. If, on the other hand, I bring in undesirables, my profile is raised, and my business is in jeopardy." Sonia raised her eyebrows, impressed by Stoner Timmy's sudden eloquence. "And shit," he added as an afterthought, immediately cheapening what he'd said before. "So, if you're going over there to kill someone or cast a spell that'll cause all the forests to die, or whatever, people are gonna look to me. You see what I'm saying?"

Sonia looked around the restaurant to see if anyone was hearing this lunatic's words. But no one was looking their way at all.

"We're going to a wedding," Sonia said, pulling the jewelry box out of Jeremiah's jacket. "It's in a few hours, and I have the rings."

Stoner Timmy tucked his cigarette into the corner of his mouth and picked up the box, studying it with the wonder of someone examining a solved Rubik's cube. Sonia's phone buzzed in her pocket, and she silenced it without pulling it out of her pocket, panicking at the thought of time running out. "Please, Tim, can you help us?"

After a few quiet moments Stoner Timmy casually opened the jewelry box, only briefly taking note of the rings inside before putting it back down on the table. "So your quest involves love and jewelry," he said, ignoring Sonia's plea.

"That is exactly what our quest involves," Leila said. "One might even say that, without love and jewelry, we would have no quest."

"Like so many others." Stoner Timmy picked up one of the cups, peeked inside to make sure it hadn't been used as an ashtray, then took a sip from whatever the liquid inside was. A little bit dribbled onto his chin; it was red, like Leila's car. He wiped at it with the sleeve of his hoodie, where the stain disappeared into the swirls of color seamlessly. "You seem pure of heart and worthy of entry into the north, Interesting Eyebrows." He nodded at Sonia, then at Leila, adding, "Full of Moxie. One last thing before I tell you the way into Canada. I just need to know . . ." He paused. Sonia found herself leaning across the table almost as much as Leila was, who by now could no longer contain her smile and was grinning as if the exchange was the funniest thing that had ever happened to her. "A) Are either of you wearing a wire? and B) Are either of you Time Lords?"

Leila gave Sonia an ebullient look, her eyes wide, biting her lip to keep the giggles from spilling out.

"Are we Time Lords?" Sonia asked, incredulous. What the hell was a Time Lord, and why would Stoner Timmy suspect either of the teenage girls in front of him of being one? But asking for an explanation from Stoner Timmy would likely unleash a whole new incomprehensible bout of rambling.

"No, I'm not a Time Lord. I'm not wearing a wire," Sonia said.

Leila raised a hand. "I promise that I am not, I have never been, and will never be a Time Lord."

Stoner Timmy plucked the cigarette from his mouth and exhaled slowly, his eyes fixed on Leila. "You sure? You're not lost in time?"

"Not to my knowledge," Leila said. She was trying to suppress a smile, but a few moments went by with Stoner Timmy studying her intently, and the glimmer in her eyes slowly faded. Suddenly, it felt as if something was being communicated between them that Sonia wasn't privy to.

"You're definitely lost in something," Stoner Timmy said, taking another slow, long pull from his cigarette. "Canada may be her destination, but it's not yours," he said, his eyes still locked on Leila's.

Then he leaned closer to them, bringing with him a surprisingly pleasant smell, coconut-scented sunscreen and freshly laundered cotton. He looked over his shoulder conspiratorially and waved them in closer. "The answer to your problem lies in the doughnuts. Bavarian crème, if possible."

Sonia waited for more, but Stoner Timmy leaned back in his chair, looking intensely pleased with himself.

"Wait, what? That cannot possibly be all the information you've got for us."

Blowing smoke out the side of his mouth (and directly at a neighboring table, whose patrons, shockingly, remained oblivious), Stoner Timmy frowned and scratched at a reddened patch of skin on his jaw that might have been a rash or just the result of too much scratching. "I've already said too much." His gaze went around the room, as if scanning for a spy. Then he set his sights on the last bite of Sonia's maple doughnut. "You gonna finish that?"

Her mind already scampering to find some other solution, Sonia shook her head and pushed the doughnut across the table.

"Remember," he said, lifting it off the napkin, "the answer is in the doughnuts."

He paused for a moment, as if allowing for some added meaning to sink in. But Sonia had no idea how doughnuts could possibly get her into Canada. She turned to read Leila's response, but Leila looked just as perplexed.

When he finished chewing Sonia's doughnut, Stoner Timmy waved at a kid who had just entered the Tim Hortons. The kid approached, and Stoner Timmy asked Sonia and Leila to excuse him so he could conduct some "business stuff."

They stepped out into the early-morning sun, squinting as much at the gray-tinged Washington light as at the conversation they'd just been a part of.

"Well, that was interesting," Leila said. She was smiling a little but seemed to pick up on the fact that Stoner Timmy's bizarre advice put them basically right back where they'd started.

"The answer is in the doughnuts? How the hell does one enter a country with doughnuts?"

The question hung in the air, a small question compared to all the other ones Sonia left unasked. How would Liz ever forgive her for ruining the wedding? How would Martha feel about Sonia fleeing in the middle of the night? How disappointed would Jeremiah be with her?

Just as Sonia felt her frustrations growing into tears, Leila tapped her arm and pointed at a Tim Hortons delivery truck in the parking lot, its engine idling. The driver was unloading a stack of goods, ready to cart them inside. The store manager was nearby, checking things off on a clipboard.

"Last one," the driver said, the words carrying across the parking lot as if on cue. The manager nodded, and the two of them walked side by side past Sonia.

"Look at the license plates," Leila said. British Columbia. "That must have been what Stoner Timmy meant. The answer is in the doughnuts!"

Sonia looked back into the café, where the truck driver and the manager were unloading the cart. At this point, Sonia was willing to try anything. They speed-walked across the parking lot and peered into the back of the truck. There were cardboard boxes all around, stacked up high enough to reasonably hide behind, at least until the next delivery at the next Tim Hortons, which, Sonia knew from past road trips, was definitely on the other side of the border.

Sonia, wanting to waste no time, hoisted herself up. Then she helped Leila climb in as stealthily as she could, which was not stealthy at all. Sonia banged her knee against the bumper, and Leila almost kicked a neighboring car. Hoping no one had noticed their clumsy climb, they rushed to hide behind a column of boxes near the back. They stood together, the two of them holding their breath and trying to resist the temptation to peek around the boxes to see what was happening in the outside world. When the driver came back, he closed the door without bothering to check if anything was amiss, shutting them in darkness as he shifted into drive and pulled out onto the highway.

6

THE SMELL OF doughnuts was strong in the air, sweet just below the point of cloying. The boxes were stacked high enough to feel like a fort, and they swayed with the movement of the truck.

"Hey, Sonia," Leila whispered, using her cell phone to light up the area and finding a place to sit.

"Yeah?"

"Truth or dare."

"You're serious?"

"Do I seem like the kind of person who would joke about truth or dare?"

"Okay, dare."

"I dare you to eat a dozen doughnuts before we get across the border."

"Don't be a jerk. I'll get diabetes."

"Okay, one doughnut. Bavarian crème, if possible," Leila said stifling a giggle.

Sonia groaned softly and looked in the nearby boxes. "I can't tell what any of these are," she said, finding an easy carton to open without knocking anything over. She grabbed the first doughnut she put her hand on and took a bite. "Ugh, coconut."

"You don't like coconut?"

"You do?"

"Friendship over," Leila said.

For all the strange circumstances surrounding the ride in the truck, Sonia couldn't help but feel like she and Leila were two girls at a slumber party, up too late and trying hard not to giggle and wake the adults.

"Is it strange that I think this is kind of fun?" Leila whispered.

Sonia shook her head. "I was just thinking that." She pulled out her cell phone, the screen illuminating the inside of the truck faintly, just enough to reveal their faces to each other. "We might actually get there on time." She stretched her legs out in front of her. "Your turn. Truth or dare?"

"Truth," Leila answered quickly.

"Tell me more about that guy."

"Actually," Leila started, "I think I may have forgotten all about him. Stoner Timmy is my new dream guy."

Sonia snorted while trying to stifle a laugh. "I have to hand it to him. I did not think he'd be able to do anything helpful for me."

"O ye of little faith. Never underestimate the helpfulness of a stranger. Even if he seems borderline insane."

"Just borderline?"

"I didn't say what side of the border," Leila said with a smile.

They sat silently for a while longer, feeling the truck rumbling on down the highway, the massive tires spinning beneath them. Sonia started to relax. She leaned her head against the boxes. She imagined that this truck took the same route every day, that, though the American customs agents might search it every morning, its return trip was likely a little more lax. Her eyelids were just starting to droop when her phone went off again.

"Hey," she said softly. "I can't talk right now."

"Look, I'm going nuts over here. Where have you been all night?"

Sonia had no idea how to summarize her night into a comprehensible phone conversation. "I'm on my way now. I should be there within an hour, maybe a little more."

Forgetting for a moment the whole anger business with Jeremiah, Sonia felt the tingly anticipation of seeing him again, of kissing him hello.

"You said that last night, and you're still not here," he said.

"I promise, I'm on my way."

That pause again, the one over the phone where she could perfectly picture Jeremiah and what he was doing. Half-naked, she guessed, boxers and socks (maybe even just one), ready to jump into the shower. Even if she was wrong, it was a joy to think that she knew him well enough to guess at his actions.

"Is everything okay?" he said, finally.

"Don't worry about me, Jer," Sonia said. Through the dark she could see Leila turn her head toward the front of the truck. Sonia cupped her hand over the mouthpiece. "Are we slowing down?"

"Definitely," Leila said. "You think we're at the border already?"

"Could be." She brought the phone back to her ear and said good-bye to Jeremiah, feeling optimistic for the first time in hours.

A few seconds later, the transmission hissed as the driver downshifted into park. Sonia brought a finger to her lips, pantomiming silence. Through the metallic walls, Sonia could hear the whoosh of cars on the highway, although it was hard to tell which way the sounds were coming from. She thought she heard a door slam, but it really could have been anything.

Then came the instantly recognizable sound of keys jingling. Sonia felt all the blood rush out of her head. *Not again*, she thought to herself. *If we get caught again, it's over. I'm going to jail, I'm ruining the wedding, and no one will want anything to do with me.*

Daylight streamed in through the suddenly open door, and Sonia hopped up to her feet, even though there was nowhere to go. She pressed herself into the space between the columns of boxes as if she could camouflage herself with her surroundings. When the door had been propped fully open, there was a bit of grunting. Through a crack between two boxes, Sonia could see the silhouette of the driver climbing up into the truck.

"Come out, or I'm calling the cops."

Sonia shot a glance at Leila, who'd remained seated, her knees pulled up close to her chest. *What do we do?* she mouthed. Leila shrugged, either because she hadn't understood or because that was the only thing left to do.

"Pulling my cell phone out now," the driver called out.

"Okay, okay," Sonia said, stepping out, her hands instinctively raised in surrender. She wondered what she'd done to make the universe so set against her. Of course, as soon as that thought came, thoughts of Sam followed, and Sonia felt that she was getting what she deserved.

"What are you two doing in here?" the driver asked, one hand on his hip, the other holding up a finger at them in a caricature of an admonishing adult. "Stealing?"

"We're not stealing," Sonia snapped. "We just need to get across the border."

"And you thought this would work?"

Sonia shrugged, her eyes set on the highway behind the driver. Leila started to say something, but the driver cut her off. "I don't have time for this. Just get off my truck."

He stepped aside and waited for them to hop off, then he slowly stepped down, wincing as his feet touched the pavement, the aches of what was probably nearly an entire lifetime of climbing up and down the raised platforms of semitrailers. "You might have actually managed to get away with it if you hadn't been chatting away." He motioned at the phone still in Sonia's hand. Without a second glance back at them, he shut the door, climbed into the cab of the truck, and took off down the road, leaving Sonia and Leila beneath a cloud of dark exhaust.

o   o   o

It took Sonia and Leila about half an hour to get back to the Tim Hortons. Sonia couldn't stop checking the time on her phone. Leila offered words of encouragement as they paced down the side of the highway, but Sonia didn't think there was a chance she'd be able to deliver the rings in time. What kind of desperate last resort was there beyond Stoner Timmy?

The sun seemed to advance across the sky much faster than it should have, cutting behind gray clouds that would likely bring an afternoon shower. Cars sped by in high-pitched blurs as if mocking Sonia.

Back in Bellingham, Sonia stomped her way across the Tim Hortons and plopped herself down in front of Stoner Timmy. "The answer was not in the doughnuts."

He was sitting in the same table, smoking another cigarette, doodling on the back of his hand with a Sharpie, though there was a notebook in his lap. He looked at Sonia as if she'd never gotten up. "That's a bummer, man."

Just as Sonia was about to snap at him, she felt Leila's hand on her shoulder. "We need another way across," Leila said, her voice soft. "The delivery truck didn't work."

Stoner Timmy frowned, tucking the Sharpie into the matted nest of dreadlocks on the back half of his head. "Your quest didn't call for a delivery truck."

If Leila hadn't offered a consoling squeeze, Sonia might have exploded at Timmy. Instead, Sonia sat back into the barely comfortable plastic chair and let Leila take control of the conversation.

"Clearly, our quest did call for a delivery truck," Leila argued. "Otherwise, we wouldn't have gotten into it. We couldn't have possibly gone against our fate, now, could we?"

Stoner Timmy took a long drag from his cigarette. "Go on."

"What if our fate was to fail at first so we could meet with you again and have you show us the way? If this isn't exactly what was supposed to happen, how could it be happening right now?" This time, Leila seemed serious, no tongue-in-cheek.

Flicking the cigarette quickly in order to drop the ashes into a coffee cup, Stoner Timmy cracked a smile. "Full of Moxie, are you sure you're not a Time Lord?"

Without missing a beat, Leila responded, "Maybe I will be someday."

Stoner Timmy smacked his palm down on the table, making the cups jump and people in the restaurant turn in their direction for the first time. "Very well! I will lead you myself. This will require a dozen Bavarian crème donuts and a car!"

"Very well!" Leila exclaimed, taking her turn smacking the table, then rising to buy the doughnuts. When she returned, box in hand, the three of them walked out of the Tim Hortons. Stoner Timmy left all his coffee cups on the table, and Sonia had the distinct impression that, whenever he returned, they'd still be there.

"Should I drive?" Leila asked as they approached her car.

"No," Stoner Timmy said, snatching the keys out of Leila's hand with an unnecessary flourish. "In fact, I need the two of you to climb into the trunk."

"You're joking." Sonia tried to guess at the roominess of the trunk from the outside.

"Do I look like a joking man?"

"I'd better not answer that," Sonia said, mostly to herself.

Stoner Timmy popped the trunk and motioned for them to get in, a little too enthusiastically for Sonia's liking. But at this point she was willing to forgo rational behavior if it would get her where she needed to go.

Fortunately, Leila hadn't entirely given up, and she made Stoner Timmy give his word that they would have a safe journey across the border. "You should know," Leila added, one foot already in the trunk, "I tried crossing late last night, and they may have flagged this car as suspicious."

Stoner Timmy put a hand on the open trunk. "Full of Moxie, the answer is in the doughnuts."

With that, the girls climbed inside, curled up against each other head-to-toe, their knees bent to avoid kicking each other in the face. "Hey, Leila?" Sonia said into the eerie, enclosed darkness. "You said you'd had plenty of adventures on your trip. Anything that matches this?"

Leila laughed, a sweet laugh that, oddly, made Sonia wish they were actual friends, not just acquaintances brought together by bizarre circumstances. "This is my first ride in a trunk during all my travels. I've seen and done plenty—passionate making out on an island, jail, vomit—but I hadn't yet been smuggled across an international border by a man who sees himself as a cross between The Dude and Gandalf. So, thank you for that."

"You're quite welcome."

Sonia closed her eyes, falling quiet to avoid giving her presence away yet again.

Since Sam died, Sonia hadn't been able to deal with total darkness. It felt textured, like the dirt piled onto a coffin. She needed the gentle glow of a screen, or at least the sound of music to fill in the air around her. Even with Jeremiah sleeping next to her, she'd leave her computer playing TV shows all night, a sort of lullaby to keep her from thinking about wherever Sam was, the nothingness he was experiencing.

She could yell an apology to him as loudly as she could, yell how sorry she was that she'd found someone to love who wasn't him. She could yell the words over a megaphone, scribble them into a book for the whole world to read, and still Sam would not hear them.

Sonia wiped at the tears slipping down the bridge of her nose. The car slowed, and soon there came the sounds of muffled voices. Sonia held her breath and heard Leila do the same. The moment seemed to hang in the air, like that split second when a swing reaches its highest point right before pulling you back down. Then came footsteps, and before it happened, Sonia could see it happening, another heartbreaking setback in her efforts to not ruin Liz's wedding.

The lock on the trunk clicked, and in a flash of daylight, Stoner Timmy and a Canadian customs agent looked down into the trunk, twin blank expressions on their faces. No one said anything, and for a second Sonia almost laughed, imagining the agent's point of view: two girls curled up in a trunk, hoping to sneak across the border, a madman at the wheel holding a dozen doughnuts. Then the agent shut the trunk, and the sounds played themselves in reverse: the locking mechanism clicking, footsteps, muffled voices, and the engine roaring into first gear.

Ten minutes later, the car stopped, and the trunk popped open. Stoner Timmy's face was the only one that greeted them. He reached in, offering a hand to help them out of the trunk.

"Welcome to Canada, ladies."

He'd pulled over at a gas station where the prices listed were per liter, not gallon. Next to the gas station was another Tim Hortons, almost identical to the one in Bellingham.

"What the hell? How did that work?"

Stoner Timmy showed his empty hands. "Like I said, the answer was in the doughnuts. Don't be surprised by the effectiveness of bribes. Especially when Tim Hortons is involved."

"That's all we had to do? Bribe the guy with doughnuts?"

"Admittedly, my presence helped. The business I run has certain stockholders. Agent McGee may or may not be one of them."

Leila, taming her trunk-matted hair into a ponytail, looked curiously at Timmy. "If a bribe was all it took, couldn't we have just ridden in the car?"

Stoner Timmy smiled, pulling a cigarette pack from his hoodie pouch. "Truth be told, Full of Moxie, that part *could* have been avoided. I just thought it was funny."

Leila laughed and gave Timmy a good-natured punch to the shoulder. Meanwhile, Sonia pulled her quickly dying cell phone out of her pocket. "Holy shit. Leila, if we go right now, we can just make it before the wedding starts." She turned to Timmy. "Do you need a ride somewhere?"

Timmy pulled on his cigarette, the smoke lingering around him almost as if it were just another part of him. He turned his profile toward the Tim Hortons adjacent to the gas station, holding the pose as if to make sure everyone knew he was deep in thought. "No. I'll be fine right here."

"You're sure?" Sonia said. Leila had already given Timmy a quick hug and was moving toward the driver's seat.

"Go," he said, still holding the pose. "You've got a quest to fulfill."

WHEN LEILA TURNED into the hotel parking lot, Sonia checked herself in the visor mirror. She could see all the signs of her strange night. Her eyes were swollen from crying, her clothes wrinkled from the ride in the trunk, and a couple of tiny green leaves clung to her matted hair from the ill-fated walk through the forest. Throughout the drive, her relief at making it to the wedding on time had given way to a growing anxiousness over Jeremiah.

Sonia snapped the visor shut and looked out at the hotel. It was vaguely castle-like, with a few lakeside cabins spread around the premises to fit in with the surrounding woods. It was a beautiful hotel in a beautiful town, and when Liz had announced it as the site for her wedding reception, Sonia hadn't been able to imagine a more fitting location. The lake was a shock of metallic blue every time she saw it, the roads so calm that they almost seemed like extensions of the lake.

"Think we're on time?"

"Should be, yeah." Sonia opened her door. "I have to go look for Jeremiah." She hesitated. It felt like the time for a good-bye, but Sonia didn't want one yet. Especially not while she was rushing out the door.

"Yeah, you do that. I can meet up with you in your room," Leila suggested.

Sonia smiled and told Leila her room number and the name it was under, so that she could get a key from the front desk. Then Sonia climbed out of the car, grabbing the tuxedo jacket from the backseat. She crossed the lobby hurriedly, keeping her head down so no one would spot her and ask where she'd been. She reached the elevator and pressed the button more times than was necessary. A *ding* sounded, and then the golden doors slid open, revealing Martha, wearing a turquoise dress and a matching shawl draped around her shoulders, her hair and makeup done elegantly.

Sonia braced herself.

"There you are! I've been looking everywhere for you," Martha said, stepping out of the elevator, holding her arm across the doors to keep them from closing. "You should go get ready! You know Liz will hold it over your head forever if you're even a little bit late. Trust me, don't give her that power."

"Um," Sonia said.

Martha laughed. "Did you have trouble sleeping last night too? I was so excited, I tossed and turned all night and in the end just gave up and read a book in the tub." She put a hand on Sonia's shoulder, guiding her into the elevator. "Now go get dressed! We'll do your makeup in the car. I'll wait down here for you. Hurry!" With that, she pulled her arm back and gave a little wave, disappearing behind the closing elevator doors.

Faced with a distorted reflection of herself in the golden doors, Sonia staggered back against the wall and exhaled. At least Jeremiah hadn't told anyone. Realizing the elevator hadn't moved, she pressed the button for the third floor, the ball of tension in her stomach easing just a little, only to tighten back up when the elevator stopped, and she approached Jeremiah's door.

He answered her timid knocks in his tux (minus the jacket), his bow tie still undone, draped around his collar lifelessly. He looked surprised to see her, and relieved. But not necessarily pleased.

Sonia bit her lip, waiting for him to say something. She longed for that lopsided grin to appear, a hint that he was about to attempt a joke. It felt as if she hadn't kissed him in a very long time, like the whole ordeal of making it back was not to deliver a jewelry box and a tuxedo jacket but to stand in his arms and kiss him.

"You made it," he said drily, still his phone voice from the night before.

"Yeah." She handed him the jacket and rings, her stomach flipping as their fingers brushed against each other. She lingered by the door, silently cursing fingers for always doing that, as if something couldn't be handed off without incidental contact.

Jeremiah pocketed the rings and then slipped on his tuxedo jacket, taking a few steps into his room and taking a seat on a corner of the bed. It was still unmade, the sheets strewn about, one pillow on the floor. He looked up at her, those eyes never failing to stir something within her, especially when they shyly glanced away.

It became clear that he wasn't going to speak first. He wasn't going to offer a reconciliation, but at least he wasn't continuing the fight.

"I should probably go get changed," Sonia said, her eyes fixed on his face, begging it to slacken into its usual soft expressions.

"Yeah," he said, leaning his forearms onto his knees, studying the carpet. "You cut it pretty close."

"I know."

She wasn't sure if his silence was a sort of ultimatum—tell them, or we're through—or if he was simply hurt. She wasn't sure what her own inability to broach the subject meant, whether her reluctance to let go of Sam was a willingness to let go of Jeremiah. "I guess I'll see you at the ceremony?"

"Yeah," he said, looking up at her for a second. He gave one of those mouth shrugs that might pass for a smile with a stranger but, coming from a loved one, only showed how unlike a smile it really was.

Sonia sighed, feeling on the verge of tears yet again. "Okay," she said, then made her way back down the hall, in a daze.

She knocked on the door to her room, hoping Leila had succeeded in procuring a key.

"Did you find him?" Leila asked as she opened the door. "How'd it go?"

Sonia entered the room, shrugging. "I don't know. He didn't tell anyone. So there's that."

"Did you guys talk things out?"

"Not really," Sonia said. "I had to come get changed."

She rummaged through her suitcase, pulling out her case of bathroom products. Sonia felt sluggish, as if suddenly the slightest movement was too much to endure. She left the bathroom door cracked as she waited for the water to heat, a habit left over from showering at Sam's family's house, since they all communally hated foggy mirrors.

Sonia tested the water and climbed in, standing for probably a full minute under the hot spray, just staring at the single speck of black on the white shower curtain and trying to build up the energy to move. She cleaned the forest off her skin, and the smell of doughnuts, the hours of crying.

She rinsed her hair halfheartedly, going through the motions of bathing as if it were a Monday morning she did not want to be awake for. She shut the water off and grabbed two towels, wrapping her hair with one, wrapping herself up in the other. The air outside the shower was cold, and Sonia sat down on the toilet lid, absentmindedly chewing on the towel that hung down from her hair. For some reason, this was when story ideas would always come to her. They used to, anyway, opening lines that would spawn whole worlds, a single character popping into her head and begging to come to life.

"Leila?" Sonia called out.

"Yeah?"

Sonia pulled a thread out from the towel with her teeth, barely aware she was doing it. "Nothing. Just checking to see if you were awake."

She tried to shake the emptiness she was feeling and started blow-drying her hair. Picturing herself at the wedding, standing on the bride's side, while Jeremiah stood out of reach on the groom's side, Sonia knew she'd be stealing glances at him throughout the ceremony, trying not to get caught by Martha. The guilt came on so fiercely that it felt like a cramp, forcing her to drop the blow-drier and leave the bathroom.

Leila was standing at the window, gazing out at the parking lot, or maybe at the woods beyond. Sonia knelt over her suitcase, trying to push everything out of her mind.

"You okay?" Leila said from behind her.

Sonia sprang to her feet. "Yup." She smiled, turning back to the bathroom to start getting dressed. The shower had reestablished her normal look, the puffiness gone from around her eyes, her hair back to falling in non-crazed waves past her shoulders. She still looked tired, but a little makeup and Martha's assumption about not getting any sleep out of excitement would account for that.

A knock came from the bathroom door as she was just finishing putting her underwear on. She opened it and smiled at Leila, who was leaning casually against the wall in front of the door. "You seem a bit ..." She gestured vaguely with her hands before dropping them down to her sides. "I don't know. Off."

Sonia opened the closet and unwrapped her bridesmaid's dress from the plastic bag it had been delivered in the day before. She laid the peach-colored dress on the bed, shrugging exaggeratedly, like tearful children sometimes do when asked what's wrong.

"Pretty," Leila said, balling up the clear plastic and tossing it into the wicker wastebasket in a corner. She took a seat near the foot of the bed, careful to avoid wrinkling the dress. "What's on your mind? Need to make more tea?"

Sonia shrugged again, scrunching up her mouth. Sam used to call the expression her "Blues Face," and he'd swear that she only made it the second she realized why she was upset about something. She picked up her dress halfheartedly, unzipping it slowly, as if the act was an arduous one. "It's going to sound really dumb," she said softly.

"Sonia, I spent my night helping a stranger enter Canada illegally. I let a man named Stoner Timmy put me in the trunk of my own car and handed him the keys. On this trip, I've received three speeding tickets, four parking citations, and driven on the wrong side of the road twice, all because I was crying. I spent days—seriously, days—thinking about a boy I haven't heard from in two months.

"I sincerely doubt that whatever is on your mind is actually dumb, but even if it is, dumb is a natural part of the human condition. Especially when it comes to emotions."

Sonia wanted to sit down, but in the back of her mind she knew that Martha was waiting for her. She glanced at the bedside clock, the kind with the green fluorescent display that all hotels liked to stock.

"Okay," Leila said, "I think I know what's on your mind anyway." She combed a tress of black hair behind one ear, licked her lips, and took a breath.

"I know you thought Sam was the love of your life," Leila said, bringing her legs up onto the bed and curling them beneath her. She looked up at Sonia, who held the dress against her chest.

"Love's rare, absolutely. But it's not necessarily a once-in-a-lifetime thing. No matter how many people you're with for the rest of your life, how many people you love, there's no changing the fact that you loved Sam. But I'll tell you this. It's not gonna be that many," Leila said, pausing for a beat.

"You've been lucky to fall in love twice in your life already. The timing of it may be a little confusing, but don't think for a second that it cheapens either of those relationships." Leila stood up, reaching for the tissues by the bed and handing one to Sonia. "If losing Sam's family is the price you have to pay to be with Jeremiah, I say, pay it gladly."

Sonia walked over to the window, looking down to see if she could spot Martha waiting for her. There was nothing to be seen but the parking lot, though, the cars gleaming in the sun, like a crayon box crowded with repeats. She thought about not having to lie to Sam's family anymore, being able to kiss Jeremiah whenever she wanted to, to slip her fingers in his. A wave of giddiness tingled up her spine, making her smile.

"What if they hate me for it?" Sonia thought about what it would feel like to not be invited back to their house, to go back to the family life she'd had before Sam and his family stepped in. Then she caught a glimpse of herself in the reflection of the window and was reminded of Stoner Timmy holding his poses, trying to meaningfully stare out into the distance. She couldn't help but crack another smile, realizing how clichéd it was to stand near a window and make a dramatic statement.

"Then that's the way it'll be."

Sonia leaned her forehead against the glass, a knot of worry returning to her stomach, though the giddiness didn't go away. She turned away from the window and picked up the dress again, stepping into it. "Help me zip this up?"

Leila stood up to help, then accompanied Sonia to the bathroom as she piled her hair up into a bun.

"Shit, I'm keeping Martha waiting," she said, once she was done. She grabbed her makeup bag off the counter and strapped her feet into the heels that she and Liz had picked out together. Then she grabbed the peach-colored clutch that matched the dress and shoved in her phone and the hotel key that Leila had acquired from the front desk, as well as a couple of tissues pulled out from the box in the bathroom.

Sonia led the way to the elevators. Before she pushed the call button, Sonia faced Leila, trying to figure out what to say. "What you did for me, I'm not sure anyone else will ever match." She shook her head at the floor, maybe realizing herself for the first time how much Leila had done for her. "I feel like I owe you so much more than just this rushed good-bye."

"Don't be silly," Leila said. "You don't owe me anything. Our adventures introduced me to the man of my dreams. Right after we're done here, I'm heading straight back to Tim Hortons."

Sonia laughed, then reluctantly called the elevator. "Seriously, you have my number. If you ever need anything, just let me know."

The elevator announced its arrival with a *ding*. When they stepped inside, Leila pulled Sonia in for an unexpected hug. "Thanks," Sonia said, hugging back. "I don't know where the hell you came from, but I'm glad you did. I'd have been lost without you."

"Me, too," Leila said.

They stepped apart, and Sonia was surprised to see a tear scurrying down Leila's cheek. Then the doors opened, and Sonia spotted Martha sitting on a leather couch in the lobby, her purse on her lap. She was looking straight at the elevators, and when they made eye contact, Martha waved and started gathering her things.

"Bye," Sonia said, the word feeling small as it left her mouth. Then she smiled at Leila and hurried out the elevator, her heels clomping loudly on the marble floor.

8

IT WAS A pretty drive from the hotel to the church. Everything was green, the sky suddenly bereft of clouds. The road took them along the lake, and even though it was early August, everything seemed to be in bloom. Purple, white, and pink blossoms dotted the landscape. Bright yellow flowers grew right along the asphalt, leaning into the street, as if asking someone to take them away.

Sam's dad, Bill, was quiet as he drove, focused on the road. He hated speed and usually begged Martha to drive on their road trips. But Martha was in the back helping Sonia with her makeup. Sonia could see sweat forming on Bill's hairline in the rearview mirror.

"Other eye," Martha said, turning Sonia's head toward her to apply the eyeliner.

"What'd you do all morning?" Martha asked. "You didn't go with everyone else to breakfast?"

"Nope," Sonia said. "Just kind of stayed in bed, trying to catch up on sleep." She kept her gaze out the window, enjoying the drive, going over in her head exactly what she wanted to say. "Liz picked a good date," she said, admiring the prettiness of the day.

"It's funny, I could have sworn there were clouds earlier," Martha said, tilting her head to look past the tops of the trees they were driving past. "Even if there were clouds, I wouldn't put it past Liz to find a way to get rid of them. That girl knows how to get her way."

"Nothing like her mother," Bill said, checking the rearview mirror to see if Sonia would laugh at his joke. She smiled at him and turned away, his eyes a little too much like Sam's for her to hold his gaze for very long.

When they arrived at the church, the ushers were not yet herding people toward the door. Wedding guests loitered around the entrance, seeking shade, posing for pictures with their arms around each other. The collective murmuring of the crowd was the only audible sound, and Sonia knew exactly what she would hear if she closed her eyes and listened for words. And because she felt as if she owed it to him, she did. She shut her eyes and felt the breeze on her skin and listened carefully until in the chorus of voices she could pick out Sam's name being spoken.

Opening her eyes, Sonia looked at the church, which was large and made of stone, with a tall, vaulted ceiling and stained-glass windows. Sonia spotted Jeremiah standing next to Roger at the curved entrance of the church. He was trying not to look at her. She waited until he gave in and motioned for him to come closer, then looked around the rest of the courtyard and the grassy surroundings for Liz's white dress. For a moment, she worried that Liz was hidden away somewhere, far from the prying, if unlucky, pre-wedding eyes of the groom. Then she remembered how Liz had professed a hatred for that particular tradition. "I'm not some prize waiting to be revealed behind the curtain," she'd said. "It's dehumanizing. No, I get to mingle with my friends and family before the wedding, too. And if Roger isn't blown away by having me stand at the altar with him just because he saw me fifteen minutes earlier, then we're off to a bad start."

Roger was coming along with Jeremiah, headed in Sonia's direction, presumably to say hi to Martha and Bill. When they got there, Sonia asked Roger to find Liz and bring her over, trying to make it sound natural, trying not to think that this would ruin the wedding, exactly what she had spent all night trying to *avoid* doing.

Meanwhile, Jeremiah greeted Sam's parents, shaking Bill's hand and kissing Martha on the cheek. He navigated through the parental small talk with ease, as if he weren't a college freshman but someone much older, someone who knew exactly his place in the world. It was one of the things she loved about him: his ability to be so well-spoken when she knew him to be such a goofball at heart.

Liz arrived beaming, whatever worries she might have about the wedding temporarily put aside to cheerfully greet her parents. After a round of hugs to everyone around, her hand went back to Roger's, her fingers finding the spaces between his as if that was exactly where they belonged. Sonia resisted the urge to do the same with Jeremiah.

"Martha, Bill, Liz, I have something I need to tell you." Everyone turned to look at her, and she almost lost her resolve. She met Jeremiah's eyes, and he gave her a knowing smile, a slight nod.

"I know this is absolutely terrible timing. But I don't want to hide anything from you anymore. You guys have always treated me so well, like I'm actually part of the family." She stopped, feeling her voice start to quaver. "Jeremiah and I are seeing each other."

She tried to read the expressions on their faces, but after registering their surprise, she tore herself away, choosing instead to look at the grass and the six pairs of shoes gathered in a semicircle, their tips all pointed at her. She felt a tickle by her temple and realized only after wiping at the spot that she'd started to cry. "I'm so sorry that I didn't tell you sooner. I just didn't want it to seem like I'm forgetting about Sam. I'm not. I promise, I'm not."

Sonia unclasped her purse and pulled out one of the tissues she'd shoved inside, using it to wipe at her nose. A woman in an olive-green dress called out to Liz and started walking toward the group. Liz waved and then held up a finger, telling the woman to give her a minute.

Sonia went on. "It's too soon, I know." She pressed the tissue against her nose again and sniffed. No cute sniffles here; this was a thick, dutiful sniff, aiming to keep back the snot in her nose so that she could finish her damn apology to this wonderful family.

"It's too soon. But here it is anyway." She turned to Jeremiah, whose expression didn't give enough away. "I'm in love with you," she said. "I'll always love Sam, but I'm in love with you now, and I'm sorry that I didn't have the guts to admit it before." She turned back to Sam's family.

"And I'm sorry I didn't tell you guys sooner and that I'm telling you right now. But I had to tell you. And, Liz, I'd understand if you don't want me to be in the ceremony anymore, or"—she turned to Martha and Bill—"if you guys want me to go altogether. I'm only a part of this family because of Sam, and I'm just so sorry that I couldn't love him even more while he was here."

She could tell that people were starting to glance in her direction. She turned her head back to the grass, the expressionless shoes on the ground. She felt a hand on her shoulder and assumed it was Jeremiah's, and she might have felt strange about taking it if she didn't need it so much. But when she reached for it, she felt rings, unfamiliarity.

"Darling, look at me." Martha was smiling at her, not even an arm's length away. "It is okay to move on." Over Martha's shoulder, Sonia could see Liz dabbing at the corner of one eye with the hand that still held Roger's. She, too, was smiling. "You joined this family because of Sam, yes. But you are always going to be a part of this family. And, like any member of this family, I want you to be happy."

Around them, wedding guests started moving toward the entrance of the church. When Sonia tasted the saltiness of tears, she realized she was smiling. The sobs were under control, but the tears still flowed.

"It's a strange time for all of us, but I'm happy you told us," Martha went on. "I might have the urge to try to keep Sam alive through you, but if I do that, please stop me. You are not just Sam's girlfriend to us. Or Sam's ex, or Sam's anything. You are Sonia. Our Sonia, as far as we're concerned."

"And," Liz interjected, "if you think for a second this is going to get you out of being my bridesmaid, you are dead wrong. No incredibly-in-poor-taste pun intended." She wiped at her eyes again and hugged Sonia, Roger's arm dragged into the hug, since Liz refused to let go of him. "And you." She turned to Jeremiah, sticking a menacing finger in his face. "Break her heart, and I'll chop off your—"

"Liz!" Martha and Bill both yelled, so on cue that Sonia could imagine Liz making the threat enough times before that her parents had learned exactly when to interrupt her.

"I mean it: You hurt her, and I will hurt you back," Liz said, her finger still in Jeremiah's face.

"Y-yes," Jeremiah stammered quickly. "Agreed. If I hurt her, I would *want* you to hurt me back."

"Good," Liz said, "holstering" her finger back to her side and turning over her shoulder to look at the crowd funneling its way into the church. "Now, would anyone mind if we get on with my wedding, please?"

"Don't be a brat," Martha said. "We're having a moment here."

"It's my wedding. I can brat if I want to," Liz said, sticking out her tongue.

A breeze, by no means a perfect one—a little too warm and pollinated—blew past them. It made Sonia think of Leila, for some reason. When she felt the air rushing past her, cooling the tears on her cheeks, brushing past her skin, she got a clear image of Leila in her red car, with its red interior, with her hair flying in the breeze of an open window.

"Come on," Martha said, holding her shawl close to her shoulders. "Let's go before my daughter threatens to cut off any more body parts."

o o o

The dance floor was just starting to fill up. A little drunk off the four-course meal and the wine and the relief, Sonia grabbed Jeremiah's hand and pulled him from his chair.

"Are you ready to be amazed by my dancing moves?" he said, smirking but still looking somewhat nervous.

"I expect to be blown away."

"If at any point that's not the case, I have a backup plan to distract you by making you laugh and/or making out with you."

"I like that plan."

She was only a little self-conscious leading him by the hand in a room full of people. The most public place they'd held hands in before this was the 7/11 down the road from his apartment. On the dance floor, she turned to face him, not letting go of his one hand, putting her other up on his shoulder. His free hand slipped to just above her waist, and they began to waltz, a little off rhythm from the song that was actually playing. Jeremiah didn't know at all what he was doing, but he didn't let that stop him. Sonia pulled herself closer, waiting for the squeeze of his fingers against her hip.

"Sorry I disappeared last night," she said, looking up at him. She would have loved to see his eyes looking back at her, but they were focused intently on his feet.

"Can I get the story now?"

Sonia considered, then rested her head against his chest, his chin fitting in snugly to one side of her bun. "I don't know if *I* believe the story quite yet. It can wait until the morning."

"Okay," he said.

She pressed him closer, then felt him suddenly stumble. Liz and Roger, dancing a little more proficiently, had purposely bumped into them.

"Stop being cute together!" Liz cried out over the music. "That's our job."

Sonia laughed and then, feeling at once weird and thankful about it, kissed Jeremiah on the dance floor, in plain view of everyone. It was the kind of kiss that can propel a couple into a relationship, and it was not the only one of the kind she'd received from Jeremiah. He kept his eyes closed for an almost comical amount of time after the kiss was over, as if needing to recover from it. She put her head back against his chest, against the tuxedo jacket she'd spent all the previous night in.

A thought occurred to her, of her lost passport sitting in her stolen purse, and out of simple joy and tiredness, she mumbled it against his chest: "I have absolutely no idea how I'm going to get back home."

Treasure #17

There's a town in the mountains of Yukon that's run
entirely by children. When I parked my car, looking for
a convenience store, everyone was under eighteen and on
skateboards. I stayed there for about twenty minutes,
seized by a surreal sense that I'd unknowingly stepped
into some strange world. I haven't had that feeling since the
oxbow, when I had to keep touching your arm to make sure
everything was real. I didn't take note of the town name,
because now no one can ever prove to me that adults live
there. I should make it to Fairbanks tomorrow. Although a
part of me is convinced you're not even getting these, I'm
still going to allow myself to daydream throughout
the drive that you've been writing me back all this
time and sending them to the campsite and that
maybe you'll be waiting there for me.
Just in case: Fairlights Camp and RV Park
10245 S Airport Way / Fairbanks, AK 99709

Hudson
27 Polar Shrimp Rd.
Vicksburg, MS 39180

Leila

LEILA

1

LEILA GRABBED A nearby log and tossed it into the fire. The hidden moisture within the bark made it crackle and smoke. It was dusk. Since yesterday's arrival at the campsite outside Fairbanks, Alaska, it had been dusk more often than she'd ever seen before, as if the world were spinning just fast enough to keep the sun right below the horizon at all times. In an hour or so, it would finally get dark. Sometime after that, in the stillness of the night, the Northern Lights would maybe, hopefully, streak across the sky.

Leila turned her head away from the plume of smoke stinging her eyes, covering her nose and mouth with a sleeve of her sweater. The smell of the campfire would be in her hair and on her clothes the rest of the night, she knew, and she did not yet know whether or not she liked that.

"Hi," a little voice called to Leila. She looked up to see a tiny blonde approaching the campfire, waving. The preteen girl's smile was missing three teeth. Her parents walked behind her, the woman in a long, patterned skirt and her hair in braids, the man wearing linen pants and hemp bracelets and sporting a beard that reached his chest. "Do you want to have dinner with us?" the girl asked, not really waiting for an answer before taking a seat next to Leila.

"Dee here noticed you putting your tent up on your own," the woman said, introducing herself as Harriet and her husband as Brendan. "She made us promise that we wouldn't let you eat alone."

"Veggies on a stick okay?" Brendan asked, starting to skewer some cherry tomatoes on a twig that he'd brushed mostly clean.

Leila coughed some smoke away and then smiled at the sudden company. "I'd love to have dinner with you guys," she said to Dee. "Thank you."

"Tea sound good?" the woman asked, placing a kettle down near the fire and sitting cross-legged on the ground.

"It sounds wonderful."

Brendan squatted, burying skewers a few inches away from the fire so the vegetables would roast. "How long are you camping for?"

"I booked a spot for a week. But I'm here to see the Northern Lights, so I'll stay longer if I have to."

"First time?" Brendan clapped his hands together to brush the dirt off.

"Yup." Leila turned to Dee. "Do you know the truth behind the Northern Lights?"

Little Dee shook her head no, her blond curls bouncing like springs.

Leila knew her father had told her the story, and she could remember how he would tell it out loud, the pauses and gestures he would make. But that memory stood alone. She had no other memories to accompany the story: how old she was the first time she'd heard it, how often it would be repeated back to her, how it had made her feel before.

"Throughout time, people have had different guesses. Some believed that the Northern Lights were great big fires in the sky, or that they were birds frozen in the air. Most people today think they're just the sun's light doing funny things it doesn't do anywhere else. But all of those are wrong."

Dee was already leaning forward, rapt. Leila wondered if she'd reacted the same way the first time she'd heard the tale. It must have been when she was Dee's age or younger, for the story to stick in her memory when nothing else had.

"The real story about the Northern Lights is this," Leila said, rubbing her hands together over the fire. "Thousands and thousands of years ago, they didn't exist at all. This was back when people all over the world lived really similar lives. They hunted for food, formed families and tribes. They woke up with the sun, went to bed when it set.

"Then came a girl," Leila said, "who saw that the world was starting to get bigger, more complicated. Boats were built that could follow rivers to new places. People started painting, writing, making music.

"This girl, she saw that her life might follow a few different paths, and she worried that she'd be sent off down the wrong one. What if she wanted to become an adventurer? What if she was supposed to be a painter, but no one ever gave her a brush? All day, she thought about these other lives she might be living."

Leila paused for effect, the way she did even when she was retelling the story to herself, letting her mind linger on that last line. Dusk persisted, the sky an orange-hued purple, a few stars coming out of hiding. Leila knew it was too early, but she scanned the sky anyway, hoping she might catch the Lights trying to eavesdrop on her story. Dee seemed enthralled, too wrapped up to notice that her mom had started running her fingers through her blond curls.

"All the possibilities started filling up the girl, spreading through her insides. Her feet got so heavy, she could barely walk. She couldn't lift her arms up to feed herself. The possibilities started pressing down against her lungs, making it hard to breathe.

"Worried, her parents called the tribe's doctor. But he couldn't tell what was wrong with her. Everyone came to see her, but no one could figure out what was making her so heavy. The more people came to visit, the worse she got.

"The problem was that she could see it in everyone else, too. All the lives people weren't living. The teacher with the heart of a warrior. The farmer with the imagination of a writer. Time went by. With every visitor who came to see the girl, she just got worse. She wanted to tell them what was happening, but her tongue was too heavy to speak. Then one day, it was finally too much. There were too many lives for the girl to keep inside any longer."

"What happened?" Dee asked, leaning forward on her mom's lap.

"There was a flash," Leila said, opening her palm the way she knew her dad had done when telling the story. "The brightest flash that Earth has ever seen, and it took this girl and all the lives she'd been carrying inside her to the sky. That's what the Northern Lights are. All the lives that we're not living. Not just the girl's, but everyone's.

"According to the legend, the first time you see the Lights, your true path is revealed to you."

Dee giggled and clapped, and her parents joined in on the applause. Brendan nodded and smiled in approval. Something in the fire popped, and Leila stared at the flames as if waiting for something to emerge. This was the first time she'd spoken the story out loud. She was exhilarated by sharing it with someone else but terrified that speaking it might make it leave her memory, the way confessions unburdened a sinner of his crimes.

Still allowing herself to be lazily combed, Dee, in that way that children have of bringing questions out of thin air, asked Leila, "Where's your family?"

Leila hesitated, grabbing a twig near her feet and picking at the bark. She looked at Dee, who'd asked so damn innocently that Leila couldn't even feel her usual urge to deflect the question.

"Actually, Dee, I don't really have a family anymore. About a year ago, I was in a bad car accident," she said, waving away the smoke from her face. She could see the parents' expressions soften, eyebrows angled in sorrow. Harriet stopped combing Dee's hair.

"They're dead?" Dee asked, not stepping around the word.

"Yup. I have an aunt and an uncle who took care of me after the accident, but my parents and my sister all died."

"That's sad." Dee picked up a nearby twig, poking it into the dirt and not making eye contact.

Leila thought she saw a flash of color in the sky and turned to spot it, but there was nothing there. "Kind of. But, the truth is, I can't remember them at all." Her hand unconsciously touched the scar that ran from just above her nape to the top of her ear. It still gave her chills to touch it, even through the hair that had grown over it. Each time she felt the scar tissue, she'd imagine the piece of glass that they'd removed. She pictured tons and tons of blood, even though she couldn't remember a single drop of it. "I couldn't recognize them in the pictures or remember the days that those pictures were taken on. It's all gone," she said, trying to sound dismissive, not wanting to traumatize Dee.

"Amnesia?" Harriet breathed, holding Dee closer to her. "That actually happens, huh?" She twisted at the silver ring in her nose, adjusting it for comfort.

"The doctors said they can't tell how much of it is physical trauma and how much is caused by post-traumatic stress. Only time will tell how much of my memories I'll get back, or if they'll come back at all. The only thing I remember from before the accident is that story about the Northern Lights."

"You don't remember anything?" Dee asked, scrunching her eyes, trying to imagine such a thing.

"Nope." Leila shrugged.

"What about your birthday parties? I always remember birthday parties. Last year, I had a cake with strawberries inside, and Mommy and Daddy let me draw on the cake with the frosting, so I could put as much as I wanted, which was a lot. Then we went swimming, and I got three books." Her eyes shimmered with the memory. "And that wasn't even my best one! Seven was a really good one. You can't remember your seventh birthday?"

"I can't remember any of them," Leila said, "but I bet seven was a really good one for me, too."

"What else can't you remember?"

"Honey," Brendan said, putting a hand on top of Dee's head, "maybe Leila doesn't want to talk about all this."

"No, it's okay. It feels good to get this off my chest." She thought about Sonia, Elliot, and Bree, how she'd pushed them to unload their troubles, and she couldn't help but smile. She made a mental note to check the campsite office for mail before heading out again. It was possible the letter from Hudson she'd been hoping for would be waiting for her.

"Since the accident, I've had no idea who I really am. There were bits and pieces: my old diary, the contact list on my phone, pictures. Friends came by the hospital in tears, hugging me, but I had no idea who any of them were. I went back to school after a couple of months, but it was just too weird. Like I'd been inserted into someone else's life. I couldn't even recognize myself in the mirror. It was bizarre to have strangers know who I was more than I did. And still, nothing came back. Just the story about the Lights.

"I can't remember any of my birthday parties," Leila repeated, trying to make it sound just like another item on a list. "I don't remember when I learned to ride a bike, or if I even know how to. Although

I do know that I once learned how to swim and that my body still remembers how to do it." A pleasant shiver went down her spine as she thought about her swim in the Mississippi. She could feel the goose bumps forming on her arms.

"I can't even imagine what that would be like," Harriet said softly, Dee's hair still laced around her fingers. "How do you go back to living your old life after something like that?"

"I don't know," Leila said. "I didn't. I moved from my home in Austin to Louisiana, where my aunt and uncle live. But that didn't help at all. It just made things feel more foreign. When the insurance money came in from the accident, I decided there was nothing keeping me there. There was only one thing I wanted to do, one thing that I thought could actually help bring back my memories." She looked up at the sky again, for the moment thinking not of the Northern Lights but of Hudson, the way the sky had looked that night, full of stars.

They fell quiet, even Dee, the crackling fire and a nearby creek the only sounds in the air. It was just now getting noticeably darker, the sky a deeper shade of purple, more stars revealing themselves. There were no clouds around to block out the sky. Leila felt a rush of adrenaline flow through her.

"I'm hoping things will change tonight," Leila said. "There's got to be a reason why the only thing that stayed with me was that story about the Lights. That's why I'm on this trip." She looked at Brendan and Harriet. They met Leila's eyes, compassion coming through in their expressions. Then they both looked down at Dee at the same time. "I'm hoping that seeing the Northern Lights in person will jog my memory, that it'll bring back some of the details of my life, maybe even bring them all back.

"I'm going to stay up for as long as it's dark and wait for them to show."

Dee, who had been entertaining herself by tossing nearby things—leaves, twigs, pebbles—into the fire, rose to her feet and crossed to where Leila was sitting on a log. Without hesitating, Dee threw her arms around Leila's shoulders and hugged her tightly. "I hope you remember your birthday parties. Especially your seventh."

o   o   o

Leila had been listening to the song on repeat for nearly an hour now. It was that one line that got to her, the relevance of it so striking, she could hardly believe it every time the singer sang it. "Chasing the only meaningful memory you thought you had left," the singer of Neutral Milk Hotel nasally but beautifully whined through Leila's earphones. She'd discovered the song on the drive into Alaska, and though the rest of the lyrics had nothing to do with her, she'd flashed forward to the exact moment she was having now, lying on a blanket on the grass, looking up at the northern sky, waiting for the Lights to come up. It would have been a lot more satisfying if the Lights had actually shown up. But it'd been hours, and nothing. The sky was going to lighten up soon, and it made Leila feel helpless. She wanted to reach up to the night and dig her fingers into it, beg it to stay just a little bit longer.

The adrenaline was wearing off, sleepiness starting to set in. She couldn't decide which was more disappointing, this or the mailbox at the campsite office being completely empty. Somehow, it felt like different versions of the same thing: the Lights' refusal to make an appearance, Hudson's failure to respond. Clearly, Hudson wanted nothing to do with her.

It all felt so anticlimactic. At that very moment, her whole trip seemed useless. When she'd left her aunt and uncle in their little town outside of New Orleans, she'd felt like a nobody. Less than that, if such a thing was possible. A nonentity, negative space. Now what was she? A nonentity who had driven a few thousand miles and had a handful of good nights mixed in among all the lonely ones. The friends she'd made, if she could call them friends, barely knew anything about her, because there was nothing to know, nothing to tell them. Even that story she had told Hudson about the ants in her hometown: that wasn't her memory at all, just something that she'd read in her diary and repeated, pretending or hoping that, in saying the words out loud, they would feel like her own.

Her heart skipped a beat as a shooting star swept across the sky, its brilliant streak lingering in the dark like a ghost. She stayed right where she was, a small, uncomfortable pillow she'd bought at a camping-goods store in Fairbanks tucked under her head. She sang along with "Oh Comely" again, making sure that every line passed through her lips, even if there was only one that she really understood. She wanted the lyrics to stick to her memory, the melodies to nestle into the folds of her brain.

When the sky started to show signs of the oncoming sunrise, Leila tried to fight the disappointment in the Lights' absence by remembering the sunrises she'd shared with new friends during her travels. She tried to tell herself that her trip had been worthwhile, if only for those shared experiences. But that was a consolation, at best, and it meant close to nothing if she still didn't have a clue who she was.

She ended up staying for the whole sunrise, until the sun was no longer a watchable ball of red-orange on the horizon but its usual, blindingly yellow self. Then she gathered up her blanket and her pillow and shuffled her way back to her tent. There'd be more nights, she told herself. Sooner or later, the Lights would show up for her.

Outside her tent, she found Dee wandering about in pajamas, her hair in a ponytail. When she saw Leila, her eyes lit up, and she ran to her. "Did it work? Do you remember?"

Leila willed herself to smile as she shook her head no.

Dee pouted. "Not even one day?"

"Nope," Leila said with a shrug. "But maybe it's because I didn't see the Lights. I'll try again tomorrow." She waved a sad little good-bye and climbed into her tent to catch up on sleep. She'd been up for over thirty hours, but sleep didn't come quickly. She lay still for what felt like hours, just waiting, tallying up the disappointments of her day.

2

LEILA WAS SITTING with her feet up on Hudson's lap, his strong fingers gently wrapped around her ankles. He had this way of touching her skin, as if he drew energy from it. The air was perfect, pleasant to the point that it could just barely be felt, like a morning caress. A glass of lemonade with mint in it sat on the table, sweating, the droplets running down and forming a slight puddle that made Leila wish for a pool. She watched Hudson smiling with his eyes closed, his head tilted back, lit up by the sun. She had the urge to trace her finger over his lips.

"Happy birthday!" a tiny voice shouted, jolting Leila from her sleep.

Dee's face filled up the partially unzipped tent flap, a conical party hat resting atop her mess of blond curls. She blew a noisemaker that unrolled like a long reptilian tongue. "Happy birthday!" Dee called again, unzipping the flap so it was completely open. The air that came in was cool and lovely, like it'd been in her dream, and Leila found herself searching the tent for Hudson.

"Come on," Dee said, beckoning her out of her sleepy daze and out of her tent. "We have a surprise for you."

Leila had fallen asleep in yesterday's clothes, jeans and a sky-blue sweatshirt, both of which were grass-stained and smelled of smoke (she liked it). She pulled off the sweatshirt and tossed it into a corner, then ran her hands through her hair, patting down the cowlicks that had sprung up as she slept. Behind Dee she could see Harriet's skirt, Brendan's linen pants, other pairs of legs she couldn't recognize.

"What's going on?" Leila asked.

"Come out and see!" Dee said, waving as she stepped away from the tent. She blew the noisemaker again, and a chorus of noisemakers outside responded in kind.

From the feel of the air, it was sometime in the afternoon. Leila stretched out a little and cracked her back, then obliged, crawling out of the tent.

"What is this?" Leila asked, smiling at Dee, casting puzzled looks at the scene outside the tent.

"It's your birthday party!" Dee said, gesturing at the gathering of people as if Leila might have missed them. "I know it's not really your birthday, but it didn't seem fair that I can remember most of my birthday parties and you can't remember any of yours, even though you've had more. So at least now you'll have one to remember."

Harriet and Brendan were wearing party hats that matched Dee's and holding a cake, waving away flies that tried to land on the plain white icing. Liza, the campsite manager, was there, too, holding one of the unraveling noisemakers. A few other people Leila had never seen before were standing around, presumably other campers that Dee had summoned with her adorableness. There was a couple in their twenties, a group of guys who looked as if they enjoyed hunting and trading tips on how not to trim their beards. A scattering of families stood around the picnic tables, the children looking everywhere on the scale of happiness from thrilled to be partaking in a stranger's birthday party to flabbergasted that their supposedly loving parents had dragged them to the middle of the woods and away from civilization.

Leila felt her smile get big beyond control. The dream about Hudson finally left her, replaced by a flutter of giddiness in her stomach. She looked to Brendan and Harriet, raising her eyebrows.

"All her," Brendan said, shaking his head in astonishment and pride.

Dee took Leila by the hand and led her to the cake. "Mom says that most birthday cakes are chocolate, and so we got you a chocolate cake, in case eating it will remind you of some other chocolate cake you had once."

The cake's frosting was completely white, a blank canvas. On cue, Harriet raised a number of plastic bags full of different-colored goo. "Dee enjoyed drawing on her cake last year, and she thought you might want to choose how to decorate yours."

"And make sure you smell the cake," Dee said, still holding Leila's hand. "Daddy says smell is how people best remember things."

"That's what I've heard," Brendan said sheepishly. He smiled, then tugged at the end of his beard. "I hope it's good. It's the only cake we could find on short notice."

Leila looked around at the other campers, everyone's attention on her. She still couldn't control her smile. "I don't know what to say. This is wonderful."

"We have a piñata," Liza blurted out, pressing her hands together and clapping.

"Have you ever had a piñata?" Dee asked, hopeful. Leila shook her head.

"This is going to be fun!" Dee said. "I've never been to someone's first birthday party. We'll hit the piñata, and we bought water balloons. It's not that cold today, and my mom said that if we dry off right after, we won't get sick. Then we can play hide-and-seek, and sardines, which is like hide-and-seek but backwards. One person hides, and everyone else has to look for them, and when you find the person who's hiding, you hide with them, until there's only one person left looking." Her eyes widened in excitement.

They followed the path that led into the woods, away from the campsite office. The rest of the group tagged along behind, chatting. Harriet was wondering aloud about the proper grammar surrounding piñatas. "Do you *have* piñatas? Use them? Play with them? Just hit them?"

In a hushed tone Leila could hear Brendan filling someone in on her situation. One of the kids, a boy pretty close to Dee's age, complained about the fact that they were walking too far, and his dad, without any anger in his voice, told him to stop whining and enjoy the day.

Soon they were walking alongside the creek in the clearing where Leila had spent the night looking at the sky. If she took just a few steps away from the path, she'd be able to find the exact spot that had been pictured online. The one of this particular clearing had been subtitled with the words: *One of the many great spots for viewing the Northern Lights!*

They reached a fork in the path that Leila had not yet had time to explore, and Dee took them left, arriving shortly after at a gathering of picnic tables arranged with decorative paper tablecloths. There were bowls full of potato chips, trays of vegetable sticks with various dips, two-liter bottles of soda. Stacks of paper napkins with *Happy Birthday!* and *Birthday Girl!* written all over them were held down by rocks. Two or three pizza boxes were spread about on each table, the smell wafting to Leila as she approached. A group of three middle-aged men had stayed behind to keep wildlife away from the feast. They were stubbly, sipping calmly on bottles of beer. One of them waved with his free hand; the other two stood from the benches and smiled.

"It's your party, so you get to choose how we start," Dee said. "We can do the cake first, or the pizza, or the piñata, or the games." She swiveled her head around the picnic area a few times, her hair bouncing even more than would correspond to the amount of her movements. "Mom! Where's the ice cream?"

"We put it in the creek," one of the stubbly beer drinkers said. "The water will keep it from melting."

"Oh," Dee said. She let go of Leila's hand and walked around, inspecting the rest of the party supplies. Then, content, she looked back at Leila. "So, what do you want to do first?"

Leila bent down and picked Dee up in a bear hug, and the little girl squealed in delight. "Thank you." She held Dee for a second, then lowered her back down and repeated the thank-you to Brendan and Harriet and the rest of the campers who were gathered around.

She found herself starting to get a little choked up, hardly believing the kindness of these people. Dee's sweet-hearted impulse to throw her a birthday party, her parents' willingness to follow through on it. If anything could shake her memories out of hiding, why not kindness?

"Let's start with the pizza," Leila said, putting her fingers around Dee's shoulder and leading them to the nearest picnic table.

The birthday party was rich in everything Leila loved about her trip. She wondered if everyone got the same thrill she did from meeting new people, or if it was uniquely enjoyable for her.

The three stubbly beer drinkers, for example, were Ron, Geoff, and Karl, three cousins on a fishing trip. They were born a year apart and barely had to nod at each other to know exactly what the other was saying. The young couple was newly engaged after surviving a four-year long-distance relationship. One of the kids, a reserved twelve-year-old, claimed he was a poet and that a dog had once eaten 250 pages' worth of his work, leading him to quit writing for a couple of years.

Leila wished she could hear every conversation happening simultaneously, but instead she settled for letting her focus drift in and out, so that what she got was a medley of people digging into each others' lives.

An intimacy, however fleeting, formed in the air, and Leila tried not to simply sit back and observe it all happen but to throw herself into the scene. She'd discovered that much about herself: her simultaneous desires to observe others from a distance and integrate herself in their lives.

After pizza, conversation, and creek-cooled ice cream, Leila decided that their next activity would be hide-and-seek. She hid in terrible hiding spots so she could have the pleasure of seeking others. She loved pretending not to see the kids hiding, their stifled giggles as she paused right in front of the bushes they were crouched behind.

When the grown-ups tired of hide-and-seek and retreated to the beer coolers, Leila decorated the cake, then announced that it was time for the piñata. Dee clapped her hands and handed Leila the broom handle that served as the hitting stick.

"I don't want to go first," Leila said. "I'm really strong. No one else will get a turn."

Dee shook her head. "Nope, the birthday girl has to go first."

"I'm serious. It could explode all over the place. I'm that strong."

Baring that gap-toothed smile, Dee crossed her arms, refusing to take the broom handle back. "You have to go first."

"Well, if you insist. But you can't blame me when there's no candy left because it all exploded," she said, containing her smile.

She stepped up to the piñata, allowed Harriet to blindfold her, and after being spun around a few times, made a vaudevillian display out of falling down on her first swing. "Did I get it?" she called out from the ground, the audience of children delighted by the performance. Then she got up and passed the broom handle to Dee, the rest of the children taking twenty-second turns swinging at the piñata, a wide circle spread around them to avoid inadvertent hits. During the twelve-year-old poet's turn, the piñata gave way with a crack that sounded just like a home run, and everyone rushed to collect the candy that rained down.

After the piñata, a tired lull settled into the party. Dee waved Leila over to one of the picnic tables to cut the cake. A single candle stood in the middle of the cake, lit and buried almost halfway in green frosting meant to look like the Northern Lights. The campers crowded around Leila and sang "Happy Birthday," Dee the loudest of them all. When they were done, Dee said, "Now you blow out the candle and make a wish, and if you wish really hard and don't say it out loud, it'll come true." She was kneeling on the picnic bench next to Leila, leaning back from the table as if trying to resist the urge to blow out the candle herself. Her cheeks were red from the sun and the running around, and she was wrapped up in a post-water-balloon-fight towel, shivering slightly.

Leila paused, wondering what to wish for. The little flame flickered, wavering in the brisk air. How funny it would be if wishing on a store-bought candle would bring back her memories. She imagined blowing out the candle and the mailman immediately coming up the path, looking for Liza to deliver a handful of envelopes. Among them, a letter from Hudson, or a postcard—anything that would break the silence. She imagined Hudson himself walking up the path. What about wishing for a normal life, one that didn't revolve entirely around what was gone?

With Dee's eyes expectantly studying her face, Leila took a deep breath, remembered that this was just a candle on a cake, not a miracle, then pursed her lips and wished only to see the Northern Lights. The flame disappeared in a wisp of smoke.

Dee leaned into Leila, whispering, "Did it work? Do you remember?"

Leila could only smile. "Thank you, Dee. I'll always remember this party."

"Who wants a slice?" Liza said, taking over the duties of cutting the cake into manageable squares. Several people responded with yeses, nos, and requests for just a tiny little sliver.

Dee lowered her head. Leila could see tears welling up in her eyes. "Hey, what's wrong?"

Dee sniffled, tightening her mouth. Her bottom lip was still quivering from the cold. "It was supposed to work," she said. "You were supposed to remember by now." Then she jumped off the bench and ran toward the path, that curly ponytail bouncing as she disappeared around the bend.

Leila called out after her, but Harriet was already getting up from her seat. "Don't worry," Harriet said. "She'll be okay. She tends to overreact when things don't go exactly how she wants them to. You enjoy your party."

Leila tried to do just that, accepting a slice of cake, making conversation with the rest of the partygoers. If Dee was still upset when she came back, Leila would give her a little white lie to appease her. She kept turning to look over her shoulder, wanting to see Harriet carrying Dee back to the party. After about twenty minutes, just as Leila was starting to worry that Dee had taken things a little too hard, Harriet appeared up the path, frantic and in tears.

"I can't find her anywhere!" she cried out. "Dee's gone!"

3

LEILA SEARCHED THE woods alongside Dee's parents, trying to be a calming presence. She was thankful, this time, for night's slow approach.

They'd been scouring the campsite for a couple of hours, everyone spread out into groups of two or three to cover as much ground as possible. Every few seconds, calls of "Dee!" sounded through the trees, making whatever birds remained in the area start and flutter away. The sound of their wings filled Leila with a sense of dread. But she didn't dare lose her composure in front of Brendan and Harriet. She looked uselessly at the surrounding forest, trying to spot anything in between the trees other than darkness or more trees.

Brendan had an arm around Harriet's shoulders, but he looked just as grim and torn up as she did. When they said their daughter's name, their voices sounded thin, as if hanging on by a thread. A park ranger named Rick walked along with them, shining a flashlight into bushes, looking up at branches that were way too high for Dee to have reached. Sloppily overweight, with bored eyes, Rick looked more suited to be a mall security guard than anyone who spent time outdoors, much less a park ranger.

"Kids that age," the ranger started to say, "they tire out pretty quickly. Sometimes their instincts are a little off, and they keep wandering, getting more lost. But a girl who's been camping before, like you say, she'd know staying put is the best thing to do. If she ran away after an argument, my guess is that she'll be found when she wants to be found."

"It wasn't an argument," Leila muttered. She should have come up with something, some meaningless little detail that would have made Dee feel happy for her.

"Either way, I wouldn't worry," the park ranger insisted.

"Yeah, well, I'm worrying," Harriet said.

It killed Leila that there was nothing more active they could do but look. It made her feel useless to call out for Dee, to arrive at a clearing and stare across the plains with her hands on her hips, not knowing what else to do.

The air was getting colder. It wasn't about to freeze over or anything, but Leila pictured how tiny Dee was, how she'd left wrapped up in a damp towel, and she was struck by panic. The world suddenly felt full of threats. Hungry animals, hidden cliffs, poisonous plants that could inflict harm after just a touch. Cancer, unforeseen heart conditions, car accidents.

Leila took a deep breath. "Maybe she made it back to the campsite by now."

"Don't think so," the park ranger answered, all too quickly. "They would have radioed me." He kept staring up into the trees, oblivious of the looks Leila and Brendan were shooting at him.

"Any sensitivity training in your line of work, Rick?"

"Nope," Rick responded. "Why do you ask?"

Harriet flashed a secret smile at Leila, rolling her eyes. Her heart wasn't in the gesture, but that was understandable.

"Just wondering if that charm is natural." Leila leaned down to pick up a twig so that she could have something to occupy her hands with. The twig was swarming with tiny black ants, though, and she tossed it back to the ground. She zipped her jacket up as high as it would go and hid her nose behind the fabric.

"I hope she didn't make it out this far," Rick went on, not even bothering to show any real concern on his face, his voice monotone. "Another mile and we'll be in pretty heavy bear territory."

"Really, Rick? That's the commentary you're going with at this particular moment?"

Rick adjusted his belt and continued leading the way down the path. "I'm not sure what you mean. Bears and other wildlife are a serious concern to recreational campers in the area."

Harriet cringed, her fists tightening at her sides. Brendan, at odds with his usual relaxed demeanor, looked like he was getting very close to punching the ranger.

"Rick, how about you and I keep going this way and we let these two backtrack? In case we missed anything, or Dee returned to the campsite," Leila suggested.

"Not a bad idea," Rick said. "But I've been instructed to stay with Mr. and Mrs. Maclin."

"How about I stay with them, and you just go away?"

"Still no," Rick responded, oblivious. "What happens if you come across a pack of wolves and don't have my dart gun to protect you? What then?" He patted the holstered weapon by his side as if it were a loyal dog.

Leila shook her head in disbelief. She looked at Harriet and shrugged. "I tried."

"I know," Harriet said. "You go ahead and turn back. I think the more spread out we are, the better."

"You sure?" Leila didn't want to leave them alone to deal with the obtuse ranger, although a part of her was thrilled to get away from him.

"Yeah. Just, you know, watch out for violent animals. And give us a call if you find her," she said, pulling out her cell phone to exchange numbers.

"Cell phone signal isn't great out here."

"Goddamnit, Rick," Leila said.

"Go. Save yourself." Harriet offered a smile, which seemed like a particularly brave thing to do. She was sure the last thing Harriet felt like doing was smiling. If given the choice between smiling and, say, curling up on the forest floor and bawling until her daughter came back to her, she'd probably choose the latter. But she was smiling anyway, marching on, not losing it.

Leila turned on her heels and went back the way they'd come. The path they were on was a hiking trail, a long but not especially difficult one, which ranger Rick had theorized would be the most likely for a nine-year-old to take.

She surveyed her surroundings as she walked, but after hours of doing just that, it was hard to be hopeful. But somehow, still, it was downright enthralling to watch leaves shudder in the wind, to watch whole treefuls of them shake and flutter like a mass of people interacting in a room. The beauty of the place was almost reassuring, as if no harm could come to Dee as long as she was lost here.

A branch cracked somewhere nearby. Then came the pitter-patter of footsteps, very light ones. Leila stood still, making no noise of her own to be sure she wasn't imagining things. There they were again, feet making their way across the ground. "Dee?" Leila said. Immediately the footsteps picked up their pace. They were somewhere nearby, in the trees just beyond the trail. If it were still daytime, or even the earlier stages of dusk, Leila could probably have seen her.

"Dee, it's Leila!" she called out, breaking away from the path toward the sounds of sneakers coming down on leaves, faster and faster. Before she knew it, Leila was running through the woods, avoiding bushes, hopping over obstacles, shielding herself from low-hanging branches, pine needles that stung her face as she increased her speed. "Dee! Don't run."

She was out of breath already. In her past life, she'd enjoyed going out for runs. She knew this from the well-worn running shoes in her closet and Murakami's *What I Talk About When I Talk About Running* sitting on her bookshelf. But this was the first time she'd run since playing Drunkball, since fleeing from the cops on the island, Hudson's hand in hers.

"Dee! Slow down."

It was hard to imagine Dee's short legs moving as fast as they were. Leila prayed the girl didn't trip on something on the ground and hurt herself. The image of blood flashed through her head, and she sped up until her legs were burning, chasing the footsteps, which, improbably, were getting farther and farther away. The sound of rushing water was getting louder, almost enough to drown out the footsteps. Leila prayed for one of those clearings near the creek, for a glimpse of Dee.

Sweat ran from her hair down to her back, cold by the time it clung to the fabric of her sweatshirt. *She's going to get sick*, Leila thought to herself. *She's going to get hurt, she's going to remain lost, and it's all because I can't remember a damn birthday party*. Tears started running down her face as she thought of the pothole that had blown out two tires of her family's car, making her dad lose control. That pothole that had made the car wrap itself around a streetlight post, rendering seat belts helpless in the face of physics. One stupid hole in the ground had taken everything away from Leila, and it was *still* taking things away.

"Dee!" Leila cried out, no longer sure that Dee could even hear her.

Without enough warning, it was night. Between strides, it seemed, darkness had taken over. It was hard to tell how long she'd been running. Only a moment, it seemed, but Leila's lungs ached for air to breathe, and her legs were no longer able to push her forward at the same pace. She demanded more of them, begging them to take her just a little farther. And they did, for a moment. They kept her going, just enough for her to see a break in the line of trees, the creek running serenely in the distance.

Leila reached the clearing, nearly wheezing, her hair damp and sticking to her forehead and her neck. She avoided the urge to double over so that she could look across the field and see . . . a deer. A poor, frightened deer, sprinting for her life through the grass, headed for the shelter of another batch of trees. It was barely a silhouette in the dark, almost no color to it except for the streak of white down its back. But it was clearly a deer, and within a second or two it disappeared into the woods again, leaving Leila alone in the field to catch her breath.

She put her hands on her knees and leaned over, shutting her eyes against the disappointment, sweat and tears trickling down her chin and dropping onto the grass. A headache appeared, throbbing right along the scar on her nape, beating in time with her heart.

When she'd recovered somewhat, Leila walked over to the creek and splashed some water on her face, wiping it dry with her sleeve. Her face stung with the cold. It took her a while to realize that this was that same clearing pictured on the website. She must have taken a shortcut through the woods, or else she'd been running longer than she realized.

Her legs were shaking, weak. Her mouth was drier than she'd ever felt it before. She knelt down to the creek again, cupping her hands together and drinking from the nearly freezing water. When she tried to stand back up, her legs refused. Instead, she dropped down onto the grass, stretching her legs out in front of her.

That's when she saw a figure standing about a hundred yards down, right around the spot where Leila had laid herself down the night before. Small, upright, ponytailed.

Leila rushed to her feet, and, despite the tired complaints of her legs, she ran across the field. Dee was whole, unharmed, smiling, even. As soon as she reached Dee, Leila wrapped her up in her arms, unable to contain the tears of joy. A flurry of parental thoughts went through her head: *I was so worried, don't ever do that to me again, where were you, I'm just glad you're okay.* But she was too happy to say any of them, just kept on hugging the girl.

"Leila, look," Dee said.

Leila pulled back and noticed that Dee was looking up at the sky, one arm raised and pointed at the heavens.

The Northern Lights were in full bloom. Waves of green light streaked across the sky, tinged with gold and purple. And they moved, like living, breathing things. No sky Leila had seen before could compare to the beauty she was seeing above her. It didn't feel like some accident of nature but rather something that was purposefully unleashed on the world. She understood now, why there were so many myths surrounding the Lights, why ancient peoples thought they were proof of some benevolent god wanting to remind them of his love. They were majestic, like nothing she'd ever seen before. As breathtaking as her run through the woods.

She recalled her favorite part of the story, the bit about the warrior. She waited for her dad's voice to continue the story, waited for the details surrounding the story's telling to start to fill in. But that line was repeating itself through her head in the same unclear voice in which she'd been recalling the story ever since she woke up in the hospital.

The Lights were as beautiful as she'd been hoping for, and she refused to blink as she stared up at them, scouring her empty mind for even the dregs of her past life, even the ashes of it, one single spattering of dust left over from her life before the accident. But no catharsis stirred within her, no epiphany bubbled up to the surface, not a single memory presented itself at the sight she was beholding.

Leila tried shutting her eyes and clenching her jaw, as if her memories were just hiding in some dormant muscle. The only images that flashed through her mind were those of photographs she'd been shown at the hospital, her sister's school pictures and her parents' wedding album. She remembered the picture of the four of them at the beach, how surreal it had felt to be staring down at herself without knowing when or where the picture had been taken. She shut her eyes so tightly, they hurt, and when she opened them again, little white spots appeared.

The Northern Lights were absolutely breathtaking and absolutely meaningless. She might as well have been staring at an exceptional sunset or sunrise. She might as well have been looking up at the starry Mississippi sky alongside Hudson. Truth be told, the latter would probably carry more weight. Her entire trip had been for naught, a pleasant, deluded distraction from the reality she had to face: Her previous life was lost to her, perhaps entirely.

Leila looked down from the sky and put her hand on Dee's back, happy to see that Dee was wearing a sweatshirt that looked to be warmer than hers. She wiped her face dry, then said, "I'm glad you're okay."

Dee gave her a confused smile before turning back to the lights. "I'm glad you're okay, too. Aren't they pretty?"

Exhausted, Leila dropped down to the cool grass. "They definitely are."

Dee joined her on the ground, laying her head on her shoulder. The Lights continued their display as if aware of their audience and purposely putting on a show. Slight changes caught Leila off guard, spurring involuntary noises of delight, which were gone just as easily as they came, as if carried off by the wind.

o   o   o

Brendan and Harriet ran to where the girls were sitting by the creek. Ranger Rick lagged behind, speaking into his radio and nodding as if he'd known all along. The couple was in tears and smothered their daughter in a flurry of hugs and kisses.

"I'm just glad Leila found you," Harriet said, Dee in her arms. She smiled at Leila and mouthed a thank-you.

Other campers from the birthday party were showing up, keeping a respectful distance to let the family have their reunion. Leila stared on, happy that the night had not, after all, ended in tragedy.

She tried to keep the disappointment over her lack of memories away for now. There was a time for that grief, and that time was when she was on her own.

Dee giggled, delighted by the attention showered down upon her. "I didn't know I was lost. I was just sad and wanted to be alone for a little while."

Brendan put his forehead against his daughter's and smiled, hugging his wife at the same time. "Next time you're sad, please be sad somewhere a little less big and scary." He kissed the two most important women in his life and closed his eyes, thankful, no doubt, for the ability to hold them both at the same time.

Watching the family, Leila realized that a happy, tearful reunion was what she'd been hoping for all along, maybe even expecting, despite reality. *I'll never have that*, Leila thought. *No one's going to scoop me up into their arms like that, make me feel that I belong nowhere else. I will never have that reunion, and it's time I understood that.*

Her thoughts went to her aunt and uncle in Louisiana, the only family she had left. They were young and didn't have any children of their own yet. They'd opened up their home and their hearts to her, and they'd even wished her luck on this misguided trip she'd been so intent on having. They'd helped her buy the car, helped her learn how to drive it. Leila didn't remember a thing about them before the accident, but they were the only family she had left.

It was time, she realized. It was time to stop chasing after all that she'd lost. She had gone on this trip because she needed to be away from an unfamiliar life, and somewhere along the way she'd become lost herself. She'd come to believe that a few lights parading gorgeously across the sky could change something within her, something that had very likely been damaged beyond repair. It was time to let go of the mad desire to remember. It was time to start living whatever life would come. In the present, not the past. It was time to go home.

4

LEILA WOKE UP slowly, allowing herself to nod off a few times until it was clear that sleep had left her. She sat up and took a drink of filtered creek water from her thermos. Then she unzipped the flap of the tent, tossed her packed duffel bag onto the grass, and climbed out into the late-morning sun.

The air was quiet around the campsite. The smell of breakfasts cooked over open fires lingered, sausage and bacon and instant coffee's second-rate aroma. Through the trees she could spot the colorful fabric of other people's tents but no movement. Everyone was probably out on their morning excursions, hiking, fishing, bird-watching. Leila grabbed her phone and plugged in her earphones. Before she unlocked her screen, she tried to clear her expectations that a notification would be there, but she was still disappointed when the phone had nothing new to tell her. She disabled the repeat-song option and clicked away from Neutral Milk Hotel's "Oh Comely," swiping her finger up and down the screen to select a random song.

As music filled in the world around her, Leila began dismantling the tent poles. She worked languidly, in no rush to be gone. For some reason, music sounded particularly good at that moment. Each note sounded crisper, each lyric's meaning clear and poignant. It wasn't even a new song; she remembered listening to this one in the car with Bree.

When she finished with the tent, she carried it and her bag over to the campsite office, leaving them by the door as she went inside to check the mail.

"You sure you don't want to stay a few more days?" Liza said, once Leila told her she was leaving. A batch of mail had arrived, and Liza was working her well-manicured fingernails through the stack painfully slowly, sorting envelopes and junk mail into different piles. "What made you decide to go?"

"It's just time," Leila said, trying to read the envelopes over Liza's shoulder. One earphone dangled between them while the other kept piping in background music just for her. "Do you know where Dee and her parents are? I wanted to say bye before I go."

"They went into town to buy some supplies," Liza said. She reached the last envelope and placed it on one of the small piles on her desk. "They should be back soon."

"Nothing?" Leila gestured at the stacks of mail.

"Sorry."

"That's okay," Leila said. She thought about leaving a forwarding address, but maybe it was time to let go of Hudson, too. If he'd wanted anything to do with her, he would have made it known by now. She was going to have to content herself with the memory of that night. Ironically, maybe she had to learn how to forget.

Leila went back outside, carrying her things to her car. She placed them in the trunk, then walked around and plugged her phone into the car's jack. Lowering the windows and turning up the volume, Leila took a seat on the hood of her car and waited for Dee and her family to come back. When certain songs played, Leila could remember exactly where she'd been driving when she'd first heard them: an endless straight stretch of cornfields somewhere in Kentucky; stuck in traffic between Indiana and Illinois; in a lonely hotel breakfast room, the cord from her earphones dangling and dipping into her maple syrup as she watched a girl's junior-high soccer team line up for the Continental breakfast, chattering nonstop.

She closed her eyes against the sun, wondering for some reason how Elliot's meeting with Maribel had gone. Within a few minutes Harriet, Brendan, and Dee pulled up in an olive-green Prius, parking in the spot next to Leila. Harriet was driving, her hair up in a ponytail for a change, exposing a long, elegant neck. As soon as the car stopped, Dee unbuckled her seat belt and scampered out the door to greet Leila.

Leila slid off her hood and was immediately wrapped up in Dee's hug. Even though Leila was short herself, Dee's arms barely reached Leila's waist.

"Good morning," Harriet said, popping the trunk and bringing out a couple of reusable grocery bags stocked with vegetables and handing one to Brendan.

"Morning," Leila said.

"Mom and Dad bought me some watercolors today," Dee said,

unwrapping herself from Leila's side. "They came with a bunch of brushes, so if you want to paint with me, you can. Are you busy?"

"I don't think I can," Leila said, leaning over to be at eye level with Dee. "I have to go back home." She'd done it quickly so as to not stretch out the good-bye, but now that the words were out, they seemed brusque. She worried how Dee might react.

"Oh." Dee looked down at her feet. "It's not because of me, right? Because I was lost but not really lost?"

"No, of course not. I did what I came here to do. I saw the Lights."

"That's true." Dee offered a smile. Leila studied her eyes, which didn't seem to be wetting. "It's okay that you can't remember. I know it's not your fault, or my fault, or anybody's fault. I was sad about it, but I'm okay now."

Leila laughed and ruffled Dee's blond locks. "Good. I'm okay, too."

"You're not . . ." She trailed off. "You're not going to forget about me, right?"

Leila's breath caught in her throat, tears threatening to come. She pulled Dee in for another hug. "No way."

o   o   o

Without the spontaneous detours or the ambling curiosity that had defined her trip north, Leila made it back to Louisiana in a little over a week. Pulling into town, she found it strange to be somewhere that felt even a little bit familiar.

Leila still needed her phone's navigation system to guide the way back to her aunt and uncle's house, but the area looked familiar. It was strange to have memories attached to the places that passed by the window, to look at this particular arrangement of fast-food chains and stores and remember. All she could remember was leaving, and the occasional trip with her aunt up the highway to a nearby mall or movie theater, but it was still more than she was used to.

The lights were on in her aunt and uncle's house when she pulled into the driveway. She engaged the emergency brake, shut off the engine, and sat there for a few seconds. She patted the dashboard, congratulating the car for its efforts. Hudson must have done wonders to keep an old car like this running fairly smoothly for over 10,000 miles.

"Stop thinking about him," she said out loud. Languidly, she pushed open the door and made her way up to the house.

She could hear clamoring in the kitchen, something sizzling in a pan, a knife coming down repeatedly onto a chopping board. "Hey, guys!" Leila called out. Immediately her aunt Cathy emerged from the kitchen, wiping her hands dry on a towel that was draped over her shoulder.

"Leila! God, it's good to see you again. We missed you." They embraced briefly. "Come to the kitchen. Tom and I are making your favorite."

Leila followed along. "My favorite?"

"Yeah! We figured you'd be hungry by the time you got here. How was the drive back, by the way?"

"It was fine," Leila said. "Long."

"I'd say! You've driven more at the age of seventeen than many people will their entire lives." Her aunt laughed, entering the kitchen and going straight to the cutting board to continue chopping vegetables.

Tom, busy sautéing onions, celery, and bell peppers in a large pot, laid the wooden spoon down and gave Leila a quick hug. "Good to have you back."

"What are you guys making? It smells delicious." She examined the kitchen, unsure what to make of all the ingredients. Sausage, a pot of rice, shrimp, chicken, canned tomatoes, bell peppers. There was a spicy aroma she couldn't quite identify.

A look passed between Tom and Cathy, one that Leila had caught plenty of times on the faces of classmates in Texas. The look that said, "She doesn't remember." Before, seeing that look had embarrassed her, as if she were to blame for not remembering. Now she was resigned to the fact that she would have to get used to it, that unless she cut everyone completely out of her life, it was a look she'd always encounter.

"Jambalaya," Cathy said. "This was your mom's recipe. Our mom, your grandma, used to make the absolute worst jambalaya, and your mom swore she'd never feed her kids bad jambalaya." She grabbed a handful of chopped okra, holding the pieces against the flat side of the knife to help her transfer them into the pot of rice. Wordlessly, Tom put a hand on his wife's waist and kissed her cheek, holding his face against hers for a moment before returning his attention to the pot of softening veggies.

Leila resolved right then and there to not get too involved in herself, to not allow her own sorrows to make her forget others. Her aunt was still grieving the loss of her sister, and Leila could not remember the last time she'd asked her how she was coping.

"Can I help with anything?" Leila asked.

"You must be exhausted. Why don't you sit down? We weren't sure exactly when you'd arrive. This might still take another thirty minutes or so."

"I'd rather stand, actually. It feels good to stretch my legs. I can set the table, if you want. I'm experienced now. I've seen the world. On my travels, I even met an expert table-setter. I think I learned a thing or two."

Tossing the cutting board and knife into the sink, Aunt Cathy took out a skillet and placed it on the stove with a drizzle of olive oil. Then she turned to look at Leila, her hands on her hips, a smile spreading across her face. "We would be honored to have the services of someone who's witnessed an expert table-setter. I only hope our place settings are not too plain for someone so revered. Please use our finest china."

Leila, always happy to engage in banter, was about to respond, but something stopped her before she could get a word out. That smile.

God, it wasn't even a clear image, but she remembered that smile.

Her mom used to smile like that. That exact angle, the deep dimples, the perfectly straight if not entirely white teeth. It wasn't from a picture or a video, either. This was a memory. Fuzzy and barely felt, like a word that she knew the meaning of but couldn't quite define. But a memory nonetheless. Leila's aunt had her mom's smile.

Almost immediately after the joy of this realization—and it was a split-second realization; her aunt was still looking at her expectantly, waiting for the repartee to continue—Leila felt, maybe for the first time, the ache that her family was truly gone. She'd done plenty of feeling sorry for herself since the accident, but she hadn't had anything real to miss about her family until now. And now it hit her that anything she gained of them, any sliver of a memory that managed to break through the fog in her brain, would carry with it a feeling of loss. For the rest of her life, any thought about her family, regardless of how happy she'd be to have it, would be tinged with grief.

"If you hear the sound of breaking glass, it means your china is not up to my standards," Leila said finally, meaning to leave the kitchen to go set the table but not being able to bring herself to do it until her aunt's smile had faded.

5

LEILA GLANCED AWAY from the book for a second, keeping her finger on the spot where she stopped so she could easily find her place again. The song that had come on the speakers was a great one, and under normal circumstances she wouldn't dare to change it. But the book she was reading was enrapturing, too, and the song's lyrics were so good, it'd be like trying to read two things at once. She hit the skip button until she found an instrumental piece that would serve as good background reading music and then went back to the book.

At the foot of the couch was a book she'd finished earlier that day. A glass of sweet tea was sweating a ring onto the coaster-less wood of a nearby end table. The window behind the couch was open to the green backyard, a breeze coming through that could never be matched by a fan. Aunt Cathy and Tom had gone into the city for the day, leaving Leila with hours full of music, books, and leftover jambalaya to look forward to.

Since coming back, Leila had discovered the following: 10:30 a.m. was the perfect time to wake up; it struck the just-right balance between sleeping in and not wasting your day. Jambalaya was the greatest food on earth, especially how her aunt (and her mom) made it. A scar on her elbow, barely noticeable, had come from a fight with her sister when they were little. Exactly what they'd fought over, Leila couldn't remember, but the image of Olive scratching her and then tearfully apologizing when she saw the blood had come to Leila only instants after she'd discovered the scar while showering.

Rather than attempt to remember everything, Leila was going to focus on discoveries. Whether she was rediscovering something from her past or unearthing something completely new, she realized, didn't matter.

That's what she'd done with the music on her phone during the trip. It's what she would do with everything else. Starting with the books in her room. Aunt Cathy had managed to enroll Leila in the local high school on time so that she could retake her senior year. The first day of classes was two weeks away, and Leila planned to go through as many books as she could until then, discovering.

Leila took a sip of her sweet tea, then turned the page, the moisture from the glass sticking to the book. She read on, sinking farther into the couch and further into the book, thoroughly pleased. The world around her was comprised only of details: the cool, leather couch beneath her, the air tickling the back of her neck, the taste of the tea on her tongue. Everything else was forgotten, taken over by the book.

She didn't know how long the knocking had been going on when she finally noticed it. If she hadn't finished a chapter almost exactly between songs, she might have just dived right into the next chapter and not heard it at all. Using a blank postcard from Alaska as a bookmark, Leila paused the stereo and listened for where the knocking was coming from, if it was still there.

A moment or two passed by silently. Leila was about to put the music back on when she heard it again, coming from the front door. She left the book on the couch and ambled over to answer the door and sign for whatever package was being delivered. Already, she wanted to return to the book. Barely paying attention to her surroundings, Leila opened the door.

It was only when she saw his face that she realized how often she'd been dreaming of him showing up just like this, though there was a little more stubble on his chin than she remembered, and bags under his eyes, as if he'd been driving all night. His T-shirt was wrinkled, his jeans loose, as if he'd recently lost weight. He'd gotten some sun over the summer, which had lightened his hair and darkened his skin and made his eyes seem as if they were under spotlights.

His name had been on her tongue for so long, it practically leapt out of her mouth of its own will. "Hudson," she said.

"You were right." He had his hands together and was cracking his fingers. She found herself studying them, expecting to see them grease-stained, as if he'd just left the garage. "It took me way too long to realize that you were right." He bit his bottom lip and looked at the ground but then forced himself to meet her eyes again.

Leila was too stunned to say much of anything. She just kept looking from his hands to his face.

"That night on the oxbow, I knew exactly what I was doing. It wasn't even that far in the back of my mind, the consequences of missing the interview. I wanted to stay in Vicksburg, I wanted to stay in the garage, I wanted to keep my life." He ran a hand through his hair and then grabbed a hold of the back of his neck as if it was hurting. "You were right. I was afraid of change, even if it was for the better. And I should have realized it when you told me. But I was stupid, and instead of listening, I freaked out on you, and I've spent the last couple of months trying to figure out a way to tell you that." Hudson shook his head, a smirk on his face. "I can't believe you gave me the best night of my life and I never asked for your phone number. I couldn't call you, couldn't write. And so I went to Texas. I went to the town you told me you grew up in. With the anthills. I was in Fredericksburg for the last two weeks, trying to figure out where I could find you, hoping you'd be back home soon."

Leila furrowed her brow, about to ask about her postcards, if he'd even gotten them. She'd been looking at his mouth, practically zooming in on his lips, the memory of them on hers giving her goose bumps. Then what he was saying clicked. "You went to Fredericksburg? I only lived there until I was eleven."

He laughed and shook his head, rubbing the back of his neck with his hand again. "Yeah, I figured that out eventually. And then I remembered your Louisiana car registration. I just knew that I needed to find you, that I needed to apologize."

"Hudson," Leila said, stepping out of the doorway. She couldn't believe that it had taken her that long to move toward him. She didn't know whether to throw her arms around him in a hug or a kiss or what. After all this time of thinking he wanted nothing to do with her, here he was, standing right in front of her, wanting her back in his life.

"I'm sorry I yelled at you back then. I'm sorry I let you go." He took a step forward so that only an arm's length separated them. It was probably just the memory, but she thought she could smell the Mississippi River on him. "I know it's crazy after just one night and after two months of nothing, but, Leila, you're the surest thing in my life."

The words moved something inside her, sending a smile to her face. In a blur, the distance between them disappeared, and they were in each other's arms. His kiss was just like she remembered it, soft and strong at the same time, his lips feeling like they belonged on hers. Happiness swept through her. Not relief, or peacefulness, but pure joy, maybe for the first time.

She was home.

ACKNOWLEDGEMENTS

FIRST AND FOREMOST, thank you for picking up this book. Maybe you haven't even read it and just flipped through to the back, but at least you picked it up off its shelf, or your friend's coffee table, or from a big, heaping pile of other books that you could have chosen instead. People like you, people who pick up books, you're the reason I get to do what I do. So, thanks.

I also get to do what I do thanks to my editors, Annie Stone at MIRA Ink and Emilia Rhodes at Alloy. They helped this story reach all the places it needed to go. Writers bring stories to life, but editors nurse them to health so that they can one day grow up and be not just stories, but books, with shiny covers and potential readers and rambling acknowledgements sections.

Thanks, also, to Josh Bank and Sara Shandler at Alloy for their help and to the entire MIRA Ink team for all their support and excitement over my book. Thanks to Dawn Ryan for her role in making it all possible. To Leah Kreitz for her hospitality in New York and everyone else who's hosted me on my travels throughout the years. Thanks to RuffaloCODY, the NBA and any other job I applied for out of college that didn't hire me and, in a way, directed me toward the life I now have.

To my parents and siblings, whose love, support, teasing, encouragement and managerial skills were crucial in the years leading up to this. Thanks to Chris Russell, David Isern and Maggie Vazquez for being almost as proud of me as my mom is and for giving me a reason to travel to go visit them.

I'm extremely thankful to be where I am, doing what I get to do. I wish I could acknowledge everyone that deserves to be acknowledged—from those closest to me who've provided constant support, to passing acquaintances who were unknowing muses, and right down to all the authors, musicians and filmmakers whose wonderful work inspired me to create some of my own—but my memory is too flawed and this page is too small.

Q&A with ADI ALSAID

What inspires you to write?

Everything. The urge to write has been with me since I was a kid and it can be triggered by anything, big or small. I've written stories inspired by heartbreak and stories inspired by sweet potato fries. What does it most often, though, is people, the spaces between them and how those spaces are bridged or gapped.

The role of travel and self-discovery plays a large part in *Let's Get Lost*. Is that something that is personally important to you?

Definitely. My first big trip on my own was to Israel when I was eighteen, and I consciously made it about self-discovery. 'Now's the time to figure out what I like,' I told myself, maybe thinking it might lead to deeper realisations, maybe just curious about what, exactly, people saw in coffee (and finding out). I came back from that trip more confident, less shy, funnier (I like to think) and convinced of travel's ability to make you a little more yourself. I feel Leila might be able to relate.

Tell us a little more about yourself. Where did you grow up? Where else have you travelled?

I was born and raised in Mexico City, where I currently live after a few stops in Israel and the US. I coach high-school and elementary basketball at the American School Foundation, which I attended while growing up. Ever since that first trip to Tel Aviv, I've travelled every chance I could get. I've taken two cross-country trips across the US, visiting over twenty-five states. Beyond the States, though, I feel I'm just getting started.

What five words would you use to describe *Let's Get Lost*?

Mississippi, adventure, movies, Tim Hortons.

Are any of the characters in *Let's Get Lost* based on you or people that you know?

I think most characters I've written have a little piece of myself in them, and most have little details stolen from real people. Leila putting her feet up on the dashboard and marking her toes on the windshield, for example, is something an ex-girlfriend used to do. The character I most relate to—or at least would have in high school—is Elliot. My two specialties back then were unfinished short stories and unrequited love.

If *Let's Get Lost* became a movie, who would be in your fantasy cast?

It's a good thing casting directors exist, because if I was ever put in charge, I'd probably cast Jennifer Lawrence to play every role, male and female alike. If I had to choose? Shailene Woodley seems to have a stronghold on YA adaptation roles and I have no complaints about that because she's wonderful. I could see her being a good Sonia. Liam James from *The Way, Way Back* would fit as Elliot. Leila feels very real to me, but I can't imagine who might fit the image of her in my head.

How do you hope readers feel after finishing *Let's Get Lost*?

Is there a word for the specific feeling of peacefulness you get when you finish a good book? When it happens to me, I kind of look around seeing the world as a more literary place, amazed that the people around me don't see it, too, that the experience was contained to me. Readers will react differently to the same book and, as a debut author, I know I have to expect a wide variety of reactions. But if anyone at all gets that feeling when they're done with *Let's Get Lost*, I'd be thrilled.

What does winning really mean?

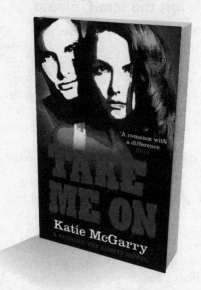

Champion kickboxer Haley swore she'd never set foot in the ring again after one tragic night. But then the guy she can't stop thinking about accepts a mixed martial arts fight in her honour. Suddenly, Haley has to train West Young. All attitude, West is everything Haley promised herself she'd stay away from. Yet he won't last five seconds in the ring without her help...

'The love story of the year'
—*Teen Now* on *Pushing the Limits*

www.miraink.co.uk

'I've left some clues for you. If you want them, turn the page. If you don't, put the book back on the shelf, please.'

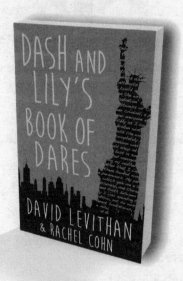

Lily has left a red notebook full of challenges on a favourite bookstore shelf, waiting for just the right guy to come along and accept its dares. But is Dash that right guy? Or are Dash and Lily only destined to trade dares, dreams, and desires in the notebook they pass back and forth at locations across New York? Could their in-person selves possibly connect as well as their notebook versions? Or will they be a comic mismatch of disastrous proportions?

www.miraink.co.uk

Read Me. Love Me. Share Me.

Tell us what you think. Did you love any of these books? Want to read other amazing teen books for free online and have your voice heard as a reviewer, trend-spotter and all-round expert?

Then join us at **facebook.com/MIRAink** and chat with authors, watch trailers, WIN books, share reviews and help us to create the kind of books that you'll want to carry on reading forever!

Romance. Horror. Paranormal. Dystopia. Fantasy.

Whatever you're in the mood for, we've got it covered.

Don't miss a single word

 twitter.com/MIRAink

let's be friends

 facebook.com/MIRAink

Scan me with your smart phone

 to go straight to our facebook page